REJECTION

By

Thomas K. Matthews

Ellie,
It's a good one!
Tom K. Matthews
2012

Otherworld Publications, LLC
4949 Old Brownsboro Rd. Suite 113
Louisville, Kentucky 40222
www.otherworldpublications.com

Interior design and typesetting by Lynn Calvert
Cover design by Thomas K. Matthews

Printed in the United States of America

Paperback ISBN: 978-1-936593-00-2
Hard Cover ISBN: 978-1-936593-01-9

REJECTION

By

Thomas K. Matthews

Writing is an adventure. To begin with, it is a toy and an amusement. Then it becomes a mistress, then it becomes a master, then it becomes a tyrant. The last phase is that just as you are about to be reconciled to your servitude, you kill the monster and fling him to the public. - *Winston Churchill*

Thank you Stacy and Ian for your unwavering faith in my literary quest.

My special thanks to Andrew McAllister for his editing skills, guidance and undying friendship. My regards to Greg McCarthy for his support and keen eye. Thanks Chris! Heartfelt appreciation for Jerry Shapiro for his constant nagging and Garrett Colbert for his daily ear and unwavering support.

The borough of Malcolm New York is fictitious, but inspired by the many coastal burgs my wife and I visited on our journeys.

Thanks Dad and Mom.

LOU DRAKE – NEW YORK CITY 2011 9:00 AM

New York was in general tumultuous calamity; all taxi cabs and urgent pedestrian migrations that clogged the streets. Long and black, chromed and whisper quiet, the limo negotiated traffic. Lou Drake felt the familiar tug of the surreal as he looked around the limousine's sumptuous interior. Deeply tinted windows muted the morning sunlight, which reflected off fine crystal glasses and gleaming leather as the driver pulled to the curb at 1290 Avenue of the Americas.

Even after several years of this celebrity treatment, Drake had never gotten used to it. Deep down he still thought of himself as a cop, a public servant who cleaned up the messes people made when they couldn't get along.

But not anymore, he thought.

The driver quickly hopped out to open Drake's door. The young man's uniform was starched straight and he wore a gloss black cap. He stood rigid as a soldier at attention while Drake hefted his girth out of the deep upholstery.

"Relax," Drake said with a smile, "it's not like you're driving the President around today."

"Yes sir," the driver said, but his face remained serious.

"What's your name, son?" Drake said.

"Josh, sir."

Drake held out his hand for a shake, which the young man returned with a satisfyingly firm grip.

"Well thanks for the drive, Josh." Drake handed the young man a twenty. "And forget the 'sir' business. Just plain old Lou will do."

"Thank you, sir— I mean... Lou."

Drake chuckled. "Thanks," he said.

"Mister Drake?" a voice called and Drake turned to see a smiling woman waiting for him on the sidewalk. She was pretty but too thin in Drake's opinion. Sharp in a pearl gray suit, her blond hair was cut short and gave her a look like an eighties pop star.

"Mr. Drake, I'm Stephanie Bowman. Welcome to Rolling Stone."

Drake's meaty hand engulfed hers as they shook.

"Pleased to meet you Stephanie," he said with a disarming smile. "And call me Lou."

"Okay," she said.

Stephanie led him through the glass doors into a large lobby.

"They're ready for you upstairs," she said. "You're in conference room three."

"Sounds great," Drake said.

"I've read all your books," Stephanie said. "The last one gave me the shivers. I couldn't sleep for a week."

"Gracious me, we can't have that."

Stephanie pressed the elevator button and they rose to the sixth floor where the doors opened with a ding.

"Can I get you something to drink?" Stephanie asked.

"Diet Coke, if you have one," Drake said.

"I do," she said. "I even have the flavored kinds if you would prefer."

"Vanilla would be nice," he said as they walked from the elevator to the conference room.

She said. "Make yourself at home and I'll be right back with your drink."

Drake surveyed the room as he took a seat. As a former Detective he had a talent for taking in a scene with a quick scan. He instinctively categorized the details and came to a judgment. This room struck him as an ominous chapel to those who had influenced the world with the written and spoken word. Artsy black-and-white photos of celebrities adorned the walls, silent reminders of statesmen, rockers and authors interviewed over the years. Brooding Mailer, pouting Capote, and the cautious King looked back at him from their frames. Drake found it strange that he might now be included in this group.

At least it was print and not television. No hour in the make up chair, enduring sweet talk from the attending personnel as they tried to make him presentable. Drake glanced at his reflection in the glass wall and saw an overweight, ruddy-cheeked man in a good suit that fit badly. No question about it, he had a face for radio.

Stephanie arrived with the soft drink and a tall glass of ice.

"Here you go," she said as she placed the drink in front of him.

"Thanks Stephanie," he said with a smile.

Her helpful manner reminded him of the flight attendants in first class. He half expected her to tell him they would be landing in an hour.

Stephanie left as the interviewer came in with an intense rush of flashing eyes, jet-black hair, and an energy drink. Thin and Asian, he wore a Free Tibet t-shirt, jeans and white athletic shoes.

"Hi Lou," he said, "I'm Robert Chang."

Chang set a small digital recorder and legal pad on the table and they shook hands.

"Glad to meet you," Drake said.

"The pleasure's all mine," Chang said as he dropped into a chair. "I was thrilled when the suits told me I drew this assignment. I'll be recording, is that okay?"

"Thanks Robert. The recorder is fine," Drake said.

"What you do is so intense," Chang said as he clicked on the recorder. "I mean, BODIES OF EVIDENCE was just wild."

"Thanks," Drake said.

"What was that like," Chang said, "interviewing someone who killed 36 people?"

Drake thought back to the many hours in a cramped cinderblock room on death row, digging for gory details while the killer chain-smoked.

"That was Gary Malden," Drake said. "He was a piece of work all right. I was with him every day for two months and he never looked me straight in the eyes once."

Chang shook his head in wonderment. "It must have been like hanging out with the devil."

"I suppose," Drake said, "but talking with a killer is really like talking to anyone. First you make small talk, try to earn their trust. Then you can push deeper into what makes them tick."

"That must be hard to hear," Chang said.

Drake nodded. “Sure, but by the time I work my way into a killer’s mind I find I’ve gotten used to who they are and the shock has gone away. At least that’s how it works for me. Then the challenge is to write it down so other people can understand. Very much like what you do, I assume.”

“That’s true,” Chang said. “Let’s back up to when you started as a writer, back when you were a cop. Okay?”

“Sure,” Drake said.

Chang glanced at the notes on his legal pad. “You were a Detective in 1990,” he said, “and then you ran into some issues.”

Drake nodded. “I was accused of mishandling evidence on a murder case.”

“As I understand it,” Chang said, “that was just the start of your troubles.”

“I’ve made no secret about it,” Drake said with a wry smile. “After they busted me back to patrol I went south pretty fast. I knew I was a scapegoat but had no idea who was behind it. My wife left and for a while I was just going through the motions.”

“And later your book HALLS OF JUSTICE exposed the real circumstances surrounding that case and not only exonerated you, but led to the resignation of some high ranking people. Am I right?”

“Yes, it was time of vindication for sure.”

“Yet the book that launched your writing career was PEN & THE SWORD, which was made possible when you solved a case that nobody else could. Wasn’t that your true vindication?”

Drake inclined his head in acknowledgment.

“I was as low as a cop can sink at the time,” he said, “burned out and about to retire in disgrace.”

“So what turned the situation around?” Chang asked.

Drake sipped his soda and gave the question some thought. Finally he said, “I thought more like a writer than a Detective.”

Chang gave him a surprised look. “You’ll have to explain that one.”

“You’re a writer, right?” Drake said.

“Sure,” Chang said.

"So before you came in here you knew what you wanted to ask, and you had some idea what I might say. You had an outline, right?"

Chang nodded toward the legal pad. "Absolutely."

"Cops don't always think like that. They look at the case and try to figure it out. I thought about the scenario as if I were writing it. That way I could use my imagination and think like a character, as though I was inventing the situation."

"So you thought like a killer," Chang said.

Drake nodded. "And it worked."

"That's wild," Chang said. "Did you ever worry that you would start to act like a killer too? Or is the average person incapable of that?"

"Trust me," Drake said with a laugh, "normal people can be driven to commit terrible acts."

"How so?" Chang asked.

"Okay," Drake said, and he leaned forward to gaze intently at Chang. "Imagine all you have slaved to achieve, all that you dreamed of, and all that defines you has been slowly taken away. Your self-image is shattered. Imagine that your life, your self esteem, your very soul has been stolen and you find yourself in a pit of raging despair. I can tell you, young man, at that low point of undeniable darkness you may find yourself capable of not just murder, but an insidious drive to punish and decimate."

Chang nodded slowly as if he were trying to process this.

"Is that what you learned from interviewing serial killers?" Chang finally said. "Or have you been in that raging pit yourself?"

Drake sat back and took another drink. He gave Chang a bemused look.

"Ever write a book?" Drake said.

"Not yet," Chang said.

"Does that mean you plan to some day?"

"I've thought about it," Chang said.

"As you should," Drake said, "but here's something not everyone knows. The first book I wrote was actually a novel."

"Was that MORTAL WHISPERS?"

"That's right," Drake said, "and that manuscript was rejected over a hundred times. I almost gave up on the whole idea of ever becoming an author."

"You're kidding," Chang said. "That book became a New York Times bestseller, and you had that much trouble getting it published?"

Drake shook his head in disgust. "Imagine pouring your soul into a creative effort and then being told over and over again that your best is not good enough. It can really sap your confidence."

"Sounds painful," Chang said.

"It's like running into a brick wall, and then having no idea how to get past it."

"But yet you kept going."

"Actually I quit writing for a while," Drake said. "Turns out I had to lose myself to find out who I really was. I had to reclaim myself as a cop before I could become a successful author."

"But obviously your novel was eventually published."

"Sure," Drake said, "but only after I caught a few breaks, solved a sensational case, and published five true crime books."

Chang looked thoughtfully at Drake.

"This seems like an emotional subject for you," Chang said.

Drake took a deep breath and rubbed his ample stomach.

"It surely is," he said. "I guess it's all wrapped up in some painful times I went through."

Chang leaned forward slightly and the intensity in his eyes brightened a notch. Drake could tell that his interviewer's instincts had gone to high alert.

"Tell me about that," Chang said.

Drake found his mind wandering back there, to that rainy night where it started, when he was at his personal bottom. This was a subject he had never discussed in public.

"There's not much to tell," he said.

But Chang was apparently not so easily discouraged. "You mentioned losing yourself," he said. "Did that have something to do with those painful events?"

Drake sighed. That had been one of the longest nights of his life.

"Something like that," he said.

"And the sensational case," Chang said. "You're talking about the first book you published, right? PEN & THE SWORD?"

Drake chewed on his lip for a moment. He couldn't see any harm in answering that one.

"That's right," he said.

"I read that book again to prepare for this interview," Chang said, "and I made some notes." He tapped his legal pad. "And when I went back through my notes, I realized something."

"What's that?" Drake said.

"In the book you tell the killer's story and how you broke the case, but you don't say much about what the experience was like for you. You don't talk about thinking like a writer, or what it felt like to gain the killer's trust."

Drake rubbed his cheek and didn't reply right away. Chang just looked at him with an inquisitive gaze and let the silence stretch out.

The secret had burned away in Drake's gut for so long. How many times had he felt like telling the whole story? He looked at Chang with his confident air and his digital recorder and something clicked inside Drake. Why not now? Some people found salvation in church; maybe Drake could find it in the hallowed halls of the greatest rock and roll magazine in the world.

"All right Robert," he said. "Hold onto your butt because I'm going to tell you something I've never told anyone but my wife, my agent, and my publisher."

Chang grinned. "All right," he said enthusiastically. "Let's tell the world how Lou Drake faced the evil and came out a celebrated true crime writer."

"How much time do we have?"

"Man, we can take all night," Chang assured him.

"Just a second," Drake said. He pulled out his cell phone and called down to the limo. "Josh, it's Lou. I may be a while."

"No problem," Josh said. "I just broke the spine on MORTAL WHISPERS. It's all good."

Drake snapped the phone shut and leaned back in his chair.

"I had just been assigned a new partner," he said. "It was raining and we got a call about a foul odor in a studio apartment in the village."

"Go on," Chang urged.

"Well, I screwed up real bad and all hell broke loose."

Drake drained the last of the Diet Coke as he thought about how to tell the story. An ironic smile came over his face.

"It was a dark and stormy night," Lou said.

CHAPTER ONE

Fall arrived with a cooling wind that invited clouds and light rain to the dusty streets of Malcolm, New York. All summer the lanes and curbs had baked in the humid heat, now the sprinkle made slurry of the sidewalks. There was a promise of distant winter and the city drew a collective sigh.

Malcolm tucked itself in a coastal hollow just south of the pageantry of Greenwich Village, harboring its own charm and its own artsy atmosphere. Many called it the poor man's Greenwich, until they visited and found Malcolm to be quaint and quiet, devoid of the lunatic fringe to the north.

An NYPD patrol car slowly crawled down University Avenue on this serene night, its tires a wet hiss on the street and the headlights turning each raindrop to a rainbow gem. Lou Drake sat in the passenger seat reading a detective novel while his partner Mitch Dodd drove with just a thumb on the wheel. In stark contrast to Drake's bulk, Dodd had a thin build and the unlined face of a rookie.

"Why do you read cop books?" Dodd asked. "Don't you get enough of that from the job?"

Drake turned a page without looking up. "'Cause the cops in these books get to work better cases than us."

"So what?"

"Kid, we're patrol. We write traffic tickets and arrest drunks, break up fights between college students and otherwise have a shit job. I know you are looking at being a Detective. Go ahead, step up the macho shit and kiss the right asses and someday make Detective. But I'm knocking on the door to moving to Florida and playing shuffleboard."

"I figure you get out of the job what you put into it," Dodd said.

"You want to wear those civilian clothes, keep your hair long and dream of one day golfing with the mayor? That's just great. But it ain't all it's cracked up to be."

"So you're just going to coast until then? Is that what you're saying?" Dodd said.

Drake snorted. "All I'm asking from the job is a pension."

"Damn, you've got a shit attitude."

Drake lowered the book and looked at his partner.

"I used to be you, kid," Drake said. "But it's not all wine and roses."

"How would you know?" Dodd asked as he stopped the cruiser at a red light.

"Trust me, I was..." Drake stopped. He couldn't be bothered to get into all that history, especially not with some snot-nosed rookie.

"You were what?" Dodd asked.

"Nothing," Drake said. "Don't listen to me. I'm just a grouchy old fart who lost his momentum a long time ago." He went back to his book.

Dodd shook his head dismissively as he continued to scan the street ahead. The windshield wipers moved with a grumble over the glass, smearing the light rain into blurry arches across his vision.

"I still say those books are a waste of time," Dodd said. "They're all made up. Those cases never existed."

Drake felt an unexpected stab of annoyance cut through his apathy. He glared across the front seat at his partner.

"You have no clue what it takes to write one of these. Writers do shit loads of research, work with cops and do a lot to make sure they write something that comes across as real, not just some made up bullshit. And there's those like Wambaugh and Tracy who were cops and became writers. Show some respect."

"Right," Dodd said with a smirk. "Like you know how much work it takes to write a book."

Drake could feel the color rise in his cheeks. "As a matter of fact I do," he said. "I wrote a novel a few years ago."

The surprise was obvious on Dodd's face, even in the dim glow of the dashboard lights.

"You're shitting me," Dodd said.

"Like I said, you got no clue what you're talking about."

"What," Dodd said, "you got it published and everything? I could walk in a bookstore and it'll say Lou Drake on one of the covers?"

"Yeah well, that's the sad part," Drake said. "Everyone who read the story says it's pretty damn good, but I sent it to half the publishing industry and nobody gave it a look."

"So you're not really a writer then," Dodd said with a chuckle.

Drake felt the muscles in his neck bunch and tighten. He had a sudden urge to throttle his partner.

"Screw you," Drake said. "I'm not the only one going through this. You have any idea how impossible it is to even get an agent right now, let alone a publisher?"

"Okay, yeah it sucks they said no, but great you actually wrote a book. Maybe you could let me take a look at it." Dodd tried to be magnanimous. Drake huffed and went back to his reading.

"Seriously, I would like to take a look at it. I would."

"Thanks," Drake gave his partner a false smile. "Maybe I'll do that."

"After all, if you can write a crime novel I can make Detective," Dodd said.

Drake took in a deep breath through his nose and tried to calm down. Why should he care what this scrawny little bastard thought? He went back to his book.

"Careful what you wish for kid."

The rain scattered the signal into embers and the streets lights illuminated the drizzle, each drop descending like dying moths touched by liquid flame. A few people walked the wet night, most making their way to the next intersection to stamp off their shoes and enter the warmth of the local bookstore coffee shop.

Drake pointed to the left as the prowler moved forward. "Pull into the bookstore, I want some coffee. You fly, I'll buy."

"Sure." Dodd parked the cruiser in a red zone and unclasped his seat belt.

"Bring me one of those toffee bars too."

"Yes sir. Anything else?" Dodd waited.

"Nope," Drake said and went back to his book.

Dodd walked past the tables of new releases to the coffee shop where a cluster of men sat with their laptops open and their coffee gone cold. They traded horror stories about writers block, workshops, those damn agents and spineless publishers. He chuckled under his breath.

Writers, they were all the same.

A tattooed, pierced and androgynous teen in a green apron took his order. Dodd waited and eavesdropped on the conversations. Ironic, Dodd thought, they would congregate in a bookstore surrounded by those who succeeded in bringing their words to the world. Drake fit right in and Dodd wondered if this is where Drake came when he was off duty, to sit and commiserate with his fellow losers, making excuses.

No matter, Drake retired in six months and Dodd would get a new partner. Then two years of exemplary duty and ace the exams, then transfer to investigative duty. After that Dodd would request a promotion to Detective and his future was set. His uncle did it in seven years, his cousin in six. Dodd's plan was to do it in five. Fit and driven, intelligent and blessed with great instincts, he knew nothing would stop his meteoric rise.

His name was called and he carried the coffee and dessert back through the display stacks, out the doors and into the drizzling night.

"Good luck," he muttered under his breath as he walked back to the cruiser.

Dodd returned and handed Lou the small cardboard carrier box.

"Thank you," Drake said as he put his drink in the cup holder. Lou ate his desert in three large bites. He coughed, took a sip of coffee and asked for his change. Dodd started the engine and returned to the rain on the windshield and the grumble of the wipers

"Car 15," the radio crackled.

"Here," Dodd said.

"Check out the apartment at135-B Delancy Street. Outside walk up. Neighbors are complaining of a foul smell coming from the second floor alley studio."

"Copy that," Dodd snapped back. "We're on it."

"Jesus," Drake said, "you gotta' be such a brown nose? Answer with a yes and be done with it."

"Just following protocol," Dodd said as he turned a corner and started scanning for the address.

"Spare me," Drake said.

Dodd stopped at the curb beneath a hulk of a tenement building. The alley was a chasm of dark, the streetlights casting a halo only a few feet into the space between the two buildings. An iron staircase rose from the alley floor to an iron mesh landing, which fronted a metal door with a mailbox wired to the railing. A zigzag of fire escape ran the height of the six-story brick tenement. Rain dripped off the corrugated aluminum overhang and chugged from a gutter pipe beneath the metal stairs.

"Looks like Freddy Kruger lives here," Drake said.

"Well, let's check it out." Dodd took off his seat belt.

"You go," Drake said and shifted his bulk.

Dodd stopped and gave him a disbelieving look. "We both have to go."

"Hey, you know so much about everything, you should be able to handle a bullshit call like this."

"Look," Dodd said, "it's standard procedure to—"

"It's gonna' turn out to be a dead dog somebody forgot to feed," Drake said, "so you don't need a hack like me to help you. I'm just the pathetic guy who can't even get a book published, remember?"

Dodd shook his head in obvious disgust. "You're an asshole, you know that?" He got out and slammed the door.

Drake smirked with satisfaction as he watched Dodd slog his way into the alley. The little prick would come back drenched. It served him right.

Dodd's flashlight twitched over wet bricks as Drake watched him climb slowly up the rusted stairs. Dodd paused at the top outside a door, and then reached for his collar. Drake's radio rasped to life with Dodd's voice.

"The door is ajar and the smell is disgusting," Dodd said. "There's got to be something dead in there."

Drake rolled his eyes. What a pussy.

"So what are you waiting for?" Drake said into his radio. "Go in and take a look."

Drake couldn't quite tell through the rain-streaked windshield, but he was pretty sure Dodd flashed him the finger before disappearing inside the apartment.

Dodd suddenly came backing out of the apartment with one hand near his face. He stood outside the door for a few seconds as if he couldn't decide what to do, then turned and started clambering down the stairs as quickly as he could go. Drake wondered what kind of weak-ass story he would come back with.

Ten feet above the sidewalk Dodd lost his footing and tumbled the rest of the way. One foot caught awkwardly on the metal railing and spun him so his head and shoulders hit the ground first. He landed with all the grace of a wet sack and didn't get up.

"Jesus Christ," Drake said as his hands fumbled at his seat belt.

Dodd was writhing in pain when Drake made it to his side.

"Where are you hurt?" Drake asked.

"My leg," Dodd said through clenched teeth.

Drake looked down and swallowed hard. Dodd's foot lay at an unnatural angle and something that could only be broken bone was pushing his trouser leg out. There was blood and it spread quickly.

Drake took a steadying breath and thumbed the button on his mobile radio.

"Dispatch," he said, "Car 51 requires immediate medical assistance at 135 Delancy. Officer down. Possible broken leg."

"Roger that," the dispatcher's voice came back.

Dodd grabbed a fistful of Drake's pant leg. "Tell them to send backup," he said, the pain obvious in his tortured voice.

Drake looked around but could see no obvious threat. "I don't see why—"

"And a detective," Dodd screamed at him. "There's a body up there. A fucking body, okay? You won't believe what it looks like."

Drake felt a wave of cold wash through his gut. He was starting to get a sense of just how badly this night was going to end for him. He finished the call with the dispatcher and knelt down beside his partner.

"Hang in there," he said. "Help is on the way."

"Fuck you," Dodd hissed. "You should have been there."

Drake knew he was right but there was nothing he could do about it now.

"What did you see in the apartment?" Drake said.

"Oh man," Dodd groaned. "That is some truly messed up shit in there."

"What?" Drake said. "What's up there?"

But Dodd only shook his head and whined, as a fresh stab of pain seemed to grab him. Drake couldn't tell if the sheen of wetness on Dodd's face was from sweat or rain. When his breathing was more under control again, Dodd groaned and laid his head back.

"Oh God," Dodd said, "that was just seriously wrong."

Drake sighed and stood as an ambulance pulled up, its siren winding down. He moved to one side and answered as few questions as possible while a small crowd arrived in more vehicles, first patrol officers and then detectives in their cliché trench coats.

Dodd had already been stretchered and hauled away in the ambulance by the time Detective Michael Collins descended the metal stairs from the apartment and cornered Drake in the alley. Drake couldn't believe it. Of all people, why did it have to be his old partner who caught this case?

"What the hell happened here?" Collins said.

"Dodd slipped on the stairs, broke his leg on the way down."

Collins pursed his lips and gave Drake a cold stare. After a few moments he said, "What do you make of the scene in the apartment?"

Drake's stomach clenched. "I haven't seen it," he said.

Collins nodded. "That's what I heard."

"I had to stay with Dodd. He was hurt and I—"

"Have I got this right?" Collins said. "You got a call for possible foul play and you let a rookie go in there alone while you sat in the car?"

Drake could feel the color rise in his face. "Yes but—"

"What were you thinking?" Collins thundered.

Drake couldn't think of anything to say.

"I can't believe you," Collins said. "You never would have left me hanging like that when we worked together. What the hell happened to you?"

"C'mon, Mike, gimme' a break here."

"I'll tell you what I'll give you, a first-class ticket up those stairs so you can see what you were too lazy to investigate the first time."

"Yeah, sure," Drake said.

He trudged over to the metal stairs with an all-too-familiar weight bearing down on him; he still felt humiliated and ashamed whenever he was faced with what his career had become. As he started climbing the slippery stairs he soon realized how easy it would be to fall, especially if you were in a hurry.

At the top of the stairs he blinked at the rain and took a quick inventory of the shabby entry. The mailbox listed to the left and was jammed full soggy correspondence sticking out the top. Before him was a metal security door with a cracked wire mesh window. The door stood wide open now and the smell wafting out was unmistakable; there was something dead inside and the death had not happened recently.

Drake moved inside so he could see the apartment's living room. For a moment his mind refused to register what he was looking at. He heard a strange sound, like a cat mewling, and then realized it was coming from his own throat. He took an involuntary half step backwards.

"Oh God," Drake said, and stumbled out the door to the landing with his hands over his mouth. He managed to hold down the vomit.

"Holy shit," he murmured to himself. "This is beyond inhuman."

Drake looked down to see Collins watching him from the street, a look of disgust on his face. As the two men stared at each other, the rain started again and slowly washed the small pool of Dodd's blood into the gutter.

CHAPTER TWO

Captain John Andrade leaned back in his wooden swivel chair and stared across his desk at Drake. The sight made the Captain shake his head in exasperation.

Drake's eyes were red with repressed emotion. He seemed to radiate sadness, shame, and anger. Sweat turned the dark blue of his uniform to near black, with spreading crescents beneath his arms and a blot below his neckline. His face was dotted with nervous perspiration.

"So what the hell am I supposed to do with you?" Andrade asked.

Drake didn't answer. He just stared into his lap and wrung his meaty hands.

"You're a twenty-year veteran," Andrade continued, "who screwed up so bad that his partner has been telling the medics, the nurses, the Detectives – anyone who will listen – how you left him hanging. You're six months from a pension and now I have to figure out what to do with you."

Drake still wouldn't meet his eyes.

"You're coasting, Drake, that's plain as day. You've pissed off your last three partners and now this. I have half a mind to send you packing early and watch you try to make it with nothing but social security. Oh, I forgot, you don't get that until you are sixty-three."

"Yes sir," Drake managed.

"That's it? *Yes sir?* Your insistence on breaking protocol is the reason you're no longer a Detective. First the Hennings Case ten years ago. I know you've been through a rough time, but this kid Dodd may limp for the rest of his life. You understand that?"

"I do, sir."

"*I do sir.* Jesus Drake, you better say something to help me see your side of this. You've got to explain your attitude or I may have to suggest suspension. Then it'd be out of my hands. An investigative review could get you canned, and then you *will* lose your pension."

"I'm sorry, sir. I know I've been a pain in the ass and you're right – I have been coasting. After the demotion and my wife left ... I guess my heart just went flat. All I ever been is a cop. I used to love the job. Now I just want it to end."

"Maybe you should talk to somebody," Andrade said.

"You mean like a shrink?"

"Whatever works, you know."

Drake snorted. "I've been to see counselors, dietitians, personal trainers, life coaches, you name it. They all say the same thing; I'm not happy. Even my girlfriend says so."

Andrade raised one eyebrow in surprise. "You met someone after your wife left?"

Drake shrugged. "It's no big deal. She works at a Dunkin' Doughnuts a few blocks from here. We're on again, off again, depending on whether I feel like answering her phone calls."

Andrade sighed. It figured; why would Drake's personal life be any less pathetic than his performance on the job. It all added up to an easy decision for Andrade.

"It must be your lucky day," Andrade said. "I'm going to give you a break."

The trepidation was clear on Drake's face.

"I'm transferring you to the cage," Andrade continued. "You'll have no street duty and hopefully you can manage to stay out of trouble. Just keep your nose clean, do your paper work and in six months you can quit this place and settle down to whatever you want to do."

The tension seemed to drain from Drake's body. He slumped down in the chair and ran his fingers through his sweat-soaked hair.

"Thank you Captain," he said. "It sounds perfect."

"What do you think you'll do after you retire? Fish? Play cards?"

Drake hesitated for a moment, but then seemed to decide to open up. "I've got a book I want to write, a crime drama. My second."

"Good idea. Write a book, get it published, make a million dollars and retire in style, right?"

"Something like that."

The Captain nodded, but somehow he didn't really believe that Drake's retirement would have anything to do with style.

Michael Collins sipped coffee from a Styrofoam cup and leaned on the wall as he waited in the hallway outside the Captain's office. He could make out none of the words coming through the door, only the rise and fall of the Captain's voice like harsh water running over stones in an angry stream. Drake was silent, or his voice was too low to puncture the veil of the heavy oak door.

The door opened and Drake emerged looking like he had just been through a fifteen-round fight. He seemed barely able to drag his fat bulk along. Collins nodded at him as he passed but received barely a flicker of acknowledgement in return.

Poor bastard, Collins thought, *but he asked for it.*

"Collins?" The Captain called.

Collins entered the office and handed a folder to his superior.

"This is the report on the body they found in the alley apartment tonight," Collins said as the two men sat on opposite sides of the Captain's desk.

Andrade nodded and flicked open the folder. "So give me the short version," he said.

"It was ugly and brutal. Looks like some sort of ritualistic killing. No forced entry, so the victim probably knew the perp. The coroner thinks the victim was probably alive when the cutting started. I don't know how somebody could live through having your guts cut out like that, but the coroner says it was most likely the case. He'll have a better opinion once the autopsy is done. We came up with no witnesses, no prints, no bloody shoe prints, no fibers, no traces of the killer at all."

Andrade looked at the crime scene photos. This was definitely sick stuff. "Who's the victim?"

"Lewis Allan Petre. Full time waiter and part time literary agent. There were query letters stacked on the desk, a couple of manuscripts sitting around. We took his computer and he had about a thousand emails on his website mail server. Looks like he had not read any of them for a month. Everything was covered with dust so I don't think Mr. Petre was doing much in the way of book sales. His last cell calls were his work, a girl in New Jersey and assorted other acquaintances. No landline. No priors, not even a parking ticket. Single and worked at the Red Kettle Café, paid his taxes and was a model citizen."

"A nobody, basically," Andrade said.

"That may be, but nobody deserves to go like this. His goddamn eyes were cut out and put in his hands. This is like Jack The Ripper or something."

"What now?"

"We'll work it and hope for the best. We've done a full collection of everything at the apartment and I have my group going through it. Maybe we'll get lucky. I called the girl in New Jersey and she says she barely knew him. She's a writer and a friend had referred her to the victim. I'll follow up and talk to other people he knew."

"Jesus, another beautiful day in paradise," Andrade said. "Can you handle this or do we need to call in the big guns from the task force?"

Collins made a face. "Nah, we can get by without those assholes. Unless we get a string of cases like this one."

"Jesus, bite your tongue. Any word on how Dodd is making out?"

"High as a kite and still complaining about Drake. The nurses are getting tired of the story."

"Well, I stuck Drake in the cage so hopefully we don't have to worry about any more screw ups."

Collins shook his head. "That Drake, damn. Hard to see him that way. I remember when he won that bet at the Christmas party by doing a hundred push-ups. That was, what, ten years ago? Now he looks like he couldn't handle a steep flight of stairs."

"Yeah, but that was also a hundred pounds ago."

Collins shrugged and dropped his voice. "Remember, we helped make him that way."

Andrade gave him a glare. “Stop. Remember our agreement, not a word. We didn’t make him eat himself to what he is today. Another man would have taken a higher road. I know I would have.”

“Okay,” Collins said, “like you said, he made his own choices. Now he’s in the cage and we won’t have any more trouble.”

“We should be so lucky,” Andrade said with a grimace. “Maybe you should go make sure he finds his way to booking without accidentally shooting someone.”

CHAPTER THREE

The village was quiet. Tuesday nights were generally dull as most people worked through the week so they could afford a drive north to Greenwich and the bohemian nightlife of the weekend. The weather cleared and the temperature dropped. Ice formed on damp steps and trees hanging on to late season foliage gave up the struggle and went to sleep overnight. Once-green leaves died with beautiful shades of orange. The Liquid Amber in front of the bookstore turned the heavy shade of fresh-spilled blood and the hand-shaped leaves waved a dead grasp to the frigid air.

By seven o'clock on Tuesday night the usual suspects had strolled into the coffee shop tucked into one corner of the Borders bookstore. Members of the group tended to arrive in ones and twos, slipping past the stacks of newly arrived books as though avoiding lepers, and taking their seats around the cluster of tables in the coffee shop area. The group was loose, with no regimented meeting schedule or order to their affair. They were a congregation of kindred spirits, each drawn by the need to commiserate with fellow souls. They gathered in the enclave of round tables and bright lights, beyond which the main bookstore was two stories and stocked well with the current offerings.

At the age of 63, Sandy Alexander was their unofficial leader. He had published a collection of short stories in 1982 and this momentous achievement gave him seniority. He even had a book signing at this very location. The critics, unfortunately, found the writing inspired but the stories cliché.

Sandy always carried a copy of his book to their gatherings, keeping it encased in a plastic cover and stored in bubble wrap. He often pulled it out and said things like, *"This is the reason"* and *"This is who we are."*

Kevin Pooter put his laptop on the table where Sandy was sitting and then went to order his coffee. African American, Kevin's skin was not just black, but so dark it seemed to swallow light. Even the overhead fluorescents did not reflect off his bald head.

"Hey man," Sandy said when Kevin returned with his drink. "Have you changed your name yet?"

Kevin just grinned and shook his head. He was used to this by now.

"I'm telling you," Sandy said, "no agent is going to take you seriously as long as you keep typing Pooter on the cover page."

Kevin spent his free time researching the trends in publishing and speculating on what would be next big thing. He was famous in the group for proclaiming that the success of the first Harry Potter book was a fluke and the market could never sustain a series based on a children's story. Most of his other predictions weren't much better. The only reason he was able to spend time writing was that his wife had a great job and he took care of the kids, the consummate househusband.

Dale Thomas stomped his feet at the door, though there was no snow or slush to remove. Dale was scarecrow thin and tall, with a shock of red hair that stuck out in all directions.

"Hi troops," he said as he pulled a third chair over to the table.

With a steady postman's salary and great pension plan, Dale always joked he could never be a starving writer.

"There's Shakespeare," Sandy announced.

Brian Shakespeare was built like a fireplug. His head barely showed over the paperback racks. He compensated by lifting weights and challenging larger men to arm-wrestle. He never lost. A trust fund brat, he carried his current manuscript with him in a weathered leather satchel, a habit he stole from Stephen King. Brian was jovial, likeable and drove a Porsche. He wrote over-developed adventure stories that lost themselves in tedious detail. An agent once signed Brian, only to drop him when he refused to streamline his manuscript.

"Are you still working on the new epic?" Sandy asked.

"Got the new bestseller right here," Brian said. He pulled out a manuscript wrapped with a rubber band

and dropped it dramatically on the table. "I'm up to eighty-thousand words."

Kevin produced a computer memory key from the breast pocket of his shirt and held it high. "I passed fifty thousand this morning on mine," he said.

Brian gave him a thumbs up. "Rock on, bro."

The core group was complete when Franny Jacobs arrived. She stood five-foot-eleven, which translated to over six feet tall if she happened to be wearing heels. Unfortunately her height was coupled with a build that resembled a left tackle. She habitually dressed all in black as she believed it to be slimming. On this night she also wore a silver chain with the female symbol, which hung between her ample breasts.

Franny seared her pages with a quill pen, putting down her feminist dogma with the fervor of a Pentecostal minister. Her work was often published in local feminist newsletters and she once had an article printed in Vogue. Her career might have taken off but she offended the opinion editor for the Post and was blacklisted as a troublemaker.

Franny had no sooner draped her black jacket over the back of a chair and sat down when Sandy leaned forward and beckoned them all to move in close.

"There he is again," Sandy murmured, pointing surreptitiously over Kevin Pooter's shoulder.

The group turned to look in that direction. An obese man sat a couple of tables away, reading a Patterson hardback. He moved only occasionally to absent-mindedly reach for his chocolate chip muffin.

"I don't even think he's reading," Sandy said. "He hardly ever turns the page."

"So what?" Kevin whispered back. "He's not bothering anyone."

"I think he's listening to us," Sandy said.

Franny chuckled. "Hey, maybe he's an editor and he's looking for new talent."

"No, he's a cop," Kevin said.

The group members all looked at Kevin in amazement.

"I heard him talking to someone in the stacks one day," Pooter said. "His name is Drake."

Sandy nodded slowly. “Well he may be a cop,” he said, “but I bet he’s also a writer.”

“Either that or he’s staking us out,” Franny said with a grin.

“Mark my words,” Sandy said. “Our heavyset friend over there wishes he were part of our little community, the village idiots of Malcolm, New York.”

CHAPTER FOUR

NYPD Precinct Ten squats on University Avenue, a brick-faced, neighborhood station with inviting front doors and a dated but functional lobby. Arrestees are brought in through the back, then taken to the booking cage where their paperwork is dutifully filled out and all personal possessions bagged. After mug shots and prints, the arrested citizens are placed in a common cell or the drunk tank. Separated by gender and seriousness of their crimes, all precautions are taken not to mix the common thief with a suspected murderer. Not that there were many of those in Malcolm; by Manhattan standards Precinct Ten was a quiet station.

In the last eighteen months the cage had processed only two murder suspects and five rapists. Despite seasonal tourist traffic, there were only 145 robberies. Of the 92 felonious assaults, most were the result of drunken brawls. The townspeople bragged about their low crime rate and loved to compare themselves to other regions of New York.

Outside the doors of Precinct Ten, University Park sprawls across the village square. On any given day the park hosts students, a few homeless people and a statue of Horatio Benedict Malcolm. He made his fortune during the revolutionary war and celebrated by starting a law university for men. In 1924 the school opened its doors to women and diversified its curriculum to include business and education majors. Though small, the university admissions requirements were as stringent as any major school and a degree from Malcolm was highly respected.

Drake was bored nearly to death after six days in the cage. Detectives and beat cops came and went past his glass walls of seclusion. Some gave him a disinterested look; most paid no attention at all. He had plenty of down time for reading his books, but even that got old in a hurry as it no longer had the guilty thrill of wasted time. Drake had taken to listening for brief snatches of conversation as the working cops went by.

Line three rang and Officer Serena Johnson answered.

"Processing," she sighed into the phone with her Puerto Rican accent. Her phone skills were legendary and some cops called in just to hear her answer.

Johnson was all hips and blue eye shadow, with heavy breasts and lips to match. Each ear displayed a spectrum of four gemstone earrings and her hair was tied back in a long ponytail. Her uniform hugged her roundness with a sensual sense of proportion. She kept Drake laughing most days as she referred to herself as *The Goddess*. "Look at all those old paintings in the museums," she often said. "Those ladies don't look like no Cameron Diaz, they look just like me."

"One moment please and I will transfer you." She handed Drake the receiver. "For you, sugar."

"Thanks," he said. "Lou Drake."

Detective Paul Kellerman's voice came through the line. "Uncle Lou, I just heard about your new assignment."

"Hey Buddy," Drake said. "How's your dad?"

"Hating retirement. I bet if he could get in a time machine and go back to when you guys were patrol partners, he would do it in a heartbeat."

"Yeah, well, like they say, those were the days. How are things at Station One?"

"Another day, another case," Kellerman said. "So what happened to land you behind a desk?"

"I messed up a bit, so now I get the easy life. What can I say?"

"That doesn't sound like you. My dad is always going on about how great it was to work with you. You're a better cop than that, uncle Lou. Is it the retirement?"

"I guess so." Drake felt the sting of embarrassment that was becoming all too familiar. "We were a good team, for sure. You can tell him I'm looking forward to joining him in about six months."

"Well, Dad felt like calling the Precinct to bust some balls when he heard what happened to you. Are you gonna' be okay?"

"Piece of cake pal. After all I've got The Goddess here to look out for me."

"Who?"

Drake laughed. "Never mind."

"Well just remember, I—"

"Yeah, I know. You became a Detective because of me."

They hung up and Lou scowled. He was not Paul's blood uncle, but a close as any relative could be. Drake's mother died when he was twelve, and the Kellerman house became his sanctuary. The home was a haven for a young boy needing more than a dad who worked odd hours as a cop. Sadie Kellerman became auntie Sadie and as Lou grew up, Paul Kellerman followed him everywhere.

With no siblings of his own Drake liked the boy looking up to him, nearly idolizing him. Then Drake's father unexpectedly died of a heart attack just after Lou joined the force. Without his father, Lou relied on the Kellerman's for his emotional support and, ironically, found himself partnered with George Kellerman.

Now young Paul was another person Drake let down with his lost soul and pathetic attitude. He promised himself he would visit George Kellerman and endure his disappointed expression and verbal beating. Drake took some solace in knowing the visit would end with too many beers and stories about the old days.

CHAPTER FIVE

Paul Orland dropped off his last fare, three intoxicated fifty-something women dressed like twenty-somethings who flirted with him from Parkside Lane to the new condo conversions on Harbor Street. The best looking of the not very attractive women luridly suggested he come with them upstairs.

"You are a nice lookin' man and we are some hot mamas looking to please," she slurred.

"Oh, I normally would," he assured her, "but I gotta' go home and rub my poor grandmother's feet. She's not doing so well and my shift is over. You have a great night, okay?"

"You don't know what you are missing," she leered and he assured her he knew exactly what he was missing.

The two in the back seat giggled like they had never heard anything so hilarious.

"Honest ladies, I have to get the cab back to the garage before my shift ends."

"Too bad," the woman said and Orland just smiled and nodded until the ladies gave up and tottered off into the darkness. He switched on his out-of-service light and steered the cab down University, past the park and into his own neighborhood.

As far as Paul was concerned, driving a cab was only a temporary source of income until his business kicked into high gear. He had dubbed it Orland & Associates Literary Agency, although his only associate was his dog Rufus. A friend designed him a website that gave the impression he was a mover and shaker in New York publishing. The email queries from hopeful authors had started dribbling in within days, and before long he started receiving a thousand email queries a month, not to mention hundreds more in the snail mail. The super in his apartment building was always complaining about his overflowing mailbox in the lobby.

With a rumble and screeching complaint, the mesh security door rose and he drove into the basement garage. As he climbed the stairs toward his apartment he found himself dreading the chore of opening his email program and wading through the evening's onslaught of book ideas. Most of the queries were poorly written and easy to dismiss. For these he had a program that replied with an automatically generated rejection message.

Unfortunately even when he did find a strong pitch, he lacked the connections with the high-dollar editors so he was unable to generate much in the way of book sales. So far the only revenue generated by Orland & Associates came from selling friend's books to small specialty presses. He hoped that a couple more such sales might give him a reputation with the mid-level publishing houses and then maybe, just maybe, he could start making some real money.

Orland turned the lock, stepped inside his small apartment, and was surprised when Rufus was not there to greet him. A whine and a jingle came from behind the closed bedroom door and Orland groaned. Had he unintentionally shut Rufus in the bedroom all day? The dog was a mixed breed, heavy as a horse and could do some serious damage if he got cabin fever. And Orland didn't want to think about the stinky mess he would have to deal with if he didn't get the dog outside in time to do his nightly business.

"Hang on Rufus," he said as he strode down the short hallway. "I'm coming."

Orland pushed open the door and flicked the switch on the wall, but the light did not come on. The jingling noise repeated itself from deep in the dark corner of the bedroom.

"Rufus?"

It was the last word he ever spoke.

The following morning dawned with dark clouds and driving rain, as though the weather gods were angered by the events in Malcolm. In the comfort of his apartment Detective Collins spread cream cheese on a toasted bagel and took a bite as his cell vibrated on the counter. He chewed and swallowed quickly as he flipped open the phone.

"Yeah?"

"Are you on your way in?" Andrade's voice sounded hard.

"Just leaving. What's up Cap?"

"We just caught another murder, and it's just as weird as the last one."

Collins hung his head and leaned his elbows on his kitchen counter. "What happened this time?"

"Animal control found a dog smeared with blood running around University Square. They ran a scan and the mutt was chipped. When the owner didn't answer a phone call a patrol car went by and the door was locked, the knob smeared with blood, so they broke in. They found the victim hanging from a chin-up bar in the bathroom doorjamb."

"Didn't look like a suicide?"

"Not unless the guy could tie his own hands behind his back, cut off his own dick and put it in his mouth."

"Give me the address," Collins said, "and I'll be right there."

Collins revved the engine of his Mustang and drove as fast as the weather would allow to the crime scene. When he arrived a uniformed officer directed him upstairs to a one-bedroom flat. The body was still hanging, while the coroner waited for permission to cut it down. Around the victim's s neck was a choke chain collar with a dog license attached. Collins could see the red, bone shaped tag with *ANSWERS TO RUFUS* etched into the surface. A length of yellow nylon rope supported the corpse, tied to the drainpipe beneath the sink in the small bathroom.

Collins judged the dead man to be six feet tall, since his toes scraped the floor. The body was obviously hauled into place after being incapacitated. He was naked and his legs covered with blood. No sign of a struggle. This time there were bloody footprints and the shoes that made them left in plain sight at the foot of the bed. Collins guessed they belonged to the deceased. He was careful to avoid stepping in them. Bloody handprints on the wall had dried to red rust brown.

"Damn," he muttered.

"My sentiments exactly," the patrol officer standing nearby said.

"Was it you that found him?" Collins asked.

The officer nodded. "No forced entry. The door was locked when we got here. He was some kind of writer. There are manuscripts."

"Okay, good job. You can wait outside."

Collins walked to the door of the room and stood looking back at the carnage, trying to get a sense of how things went down. Overall the scene was neat, unhurried, and chilling.

The forensics team arrived so Collins turned his attention to the kitchen. The table was covered with stacks of envelopes and paper bundles piled around a laptop. The envelopes were addressed to Orland & Associates Literary Agency. Most were unopened.

"He's an agent too," Collins muttered to himself as he flipped through a couple of paper-clipped bundles of paper at the top of one stack. They were sample chapters that had been sent to the victim.

A cold feeling seeped into Collins' gut as he quickly arrived at the obvious conclusion. No way could two mutilated literary agents be a coincidence; he was most likely was dealing with a serial killer. And this was no ordinary killer. Collins was up against a twisted mind capable of sick depravity.

Collins knew the press would turn this into a bright spotlight of sensationalism, the likes of which had never before been trained on the borough of Malcolm.

"Fuck," he spat as he watched the black bag containing Paul Orland wheeled out of the apartment.

CHAPTER SIX

Drake arrived at the station with a dozen doughnuts and four coffees. After two weeks he had developed a precarious camaraderie with the three policewomen he worked with. On his first day they all gave him a shoulder so cold he shivered, but with his relentless dry sense of humor he managed to eke a smile from each of the three ladies. Today he bribed them with sugar and caffeine; making friends through a common weakness. Each of them was overweight and made no bones about it. Flowers were lost on these three, but doughnuts were better than diamonds.

"Good morning ladies," he sang and placed the box on the central counter. "I have coffee. Good coffee, not that sludge they make here. I brought cream and sugar and, oh, and these." Drake opened the box with flare and carefully picked out a chocolate old fashioned, took a bite a rolled his eyes.

"Those are for us?" Regina asked and placed her small hand on her large hip. African American and tough as nails, she wore her hair in rows and was rumored to be a black belt in something. She had enough jewelry to pass for a gypsy and wore her shirt out, making her look like she had a solid torso with no delineation from bust to bottom.

"If you would like one," he said with a smile.

"What are you up to?" Selena asked, her Puerto Rican eyes flashing with good-natured suspicion. "You think you can buy us with that?"

"I am not buying anything but doughnuts," Drake said.

"Yeah, right." Edna laughed through her smokers cough. "You are going to try and tell us you brought those in just because you wanted to be generous?"

"I have no agenda," Drake said and held up three fingers in the sign of the Boy Scout's honor.

"You were never a boy scout," Edna said with a chuckle as she took a bear claw.

Drake liked Edna, who was close to retirement herself. She could have been someone's grandmother but for her filthy mouth. Drake urged them all to take a doughnut and the other two helped themselves.

"Don't forget your coffee."

A cluster of officers passed by outside the glass of the cage. One the officers looked in and snorted at the sight of Drake eating a doughnut. "Just what he needs," the guy said to his companions as they passed out of sight down the hallway.

"Don't listen to that shit," Serena said. "That Ratcliff has room to talk. He's as fat as you and then some."

Drake smiled with gratitude.

Andrade emerged from his office and came down the hall with Michael Collins. They hustled past the cage toward the Detective's office.

Detective Thibido charged up behind them. "Are you kidding me?" he called out as he approached the other three. "Who could cut off a guys dick and stick it in his mouth like that?"

"Shut up," Collins hissed and Thibido stopped abruptly.

Drake looked at Edna who gave him a sour expression.

"Sounds like we got ourselves another killing," she said softly.

"Apparently," Drake whispered and Serena nodded.

Drake's detective instincts kicked in, not to mention the curiosity of his writer side. He had seen the kind of mutilation Thibido mentioned as a message in mob killings, the sign of an informant. Was that what was going on here? Drake wished he knew more.

He stared from the confines of his work area out into the station. At that moment, the cage felt as much like a cell to him as the ones downstairs. The hall to his right reached out to the reception lobby and to the desk sergeant and to his left to the Detective's office. Straight ahead was Andrade's office, the conference and interrogation rooms. Each direction led to real police action while he sat here shuffling papers. Drake felt the familiar funk that had plagued him since he was demoted.

"Why won't you listen to me?" a voice whined as an officer brought in a middle-aged woman in handcuffs. She was well dressed but obviously intoxicated. "My father knows Rudolph Giuliani," she said. "This is going to mean your badge."

"Well Officer Mooney," Drake said. "What do we have here?"

"This is Ruby Lopresti," Mooney said. "Drunk and disorderly and resisting arrest. She has been read her rights and has, obviously, decided not to remain silent."

"Oh, a smart ass," the woman roared. "That will cost you. That will goddamn cost you!"

"Wonderful," Drake said with a sullen tone as he pulled out a booking form and looked around for a pen.

Ruby suddenly vomited and passed out. She hit the floor in her own puke. Mooney's sleeve was wet with sour bile and the stench was overpowering.

"Aw shit," Mooney said. "Now who the hell's gonna' clean this up."

"We got it," Drake said as he and the three women came around the glass to help put the unconscious woman in a wheelchair. Another officer wheeled her down to the drunk tank.

Drake retrieved a mop and bucket from the break room and cleaned the mess as Mooney went to change his shirt. *This is what I'm reduced to,* Drake thought as he slopped the mop across the floor, *cleaning up barf.*

Soon the cage was back to normal.

"You okay?" Serena asked him. "You look like you just lost your best friend."

Drake did his best to hold in the sigh. "It's those murders, I guess," he said after a moment. "There was a day when I would have been right in the middle of all that."

"I know," Serena said and cocked her head. "I looked you up. Six months to go and you're stuck in here. Seems a shame."

"You looked me up? How?"

"I'm the precinct archive manager, remember? I got access."

He gave her a thoughtful look. "Exactly how much access do you have?"

She raised one eyebrow. “Enough to show you what’s what and what’s not.”

Drake sighed. “I appreciate what I think you’re saying but I don’t want to get you into any trouble, and I’m in enough already.”

“I’m fine,” she whispered. “Nothing you can do will get me in any trouble. And you, what they going to do, fire you?”

“Yes, and take away my pension,” he said.

“Never gonna' happen, doughnut man.”

Serena crooked her finger for him to follow her to the back office where she handed him a green file folder with a dozen or so sheets of paper inside.

She spoke quietly. “I made a few copies from the case files for those two murders. Why don’t you take a break and find a quiet corner where you can look these over.”

Drake hesitated, but she seemed so earnest that he accepted the file. He glanced around to make sure no one could see and flipped quickly through the pages. At first glance, they provided a good overview of the investigation so far. The last page was a detailed list of Petre’s personal information and tore it into pieces and flushed it down the toilet. It was no his place or need to have Petre’s life in his hand. Drake folded the remaining papers and jammed them in his pocket.

Back in the cage, Drake gave Serena a quizzical look as he handed her the empty file folder back. “Why are you doing this?” he said.

Serena smiled at him and leaned in close. “Cause you’re one of us now and we gotta look out for each other.”

She turned on her heel and walked away. Drake gaped at her in amazement for a few moments, then hustled off toward the restroom. He took a stall, dropped his pants, and began to read.

CHAPTER SEVEN

Captain Andrade stared out of his office window with his hands behind his back and his brow furrowed over his blue eyes. He had eighteen years in with the NYPD, five as a captain. Now his mind reeled with the ramifications of this second killing. The ferocity of it was astounding, making the details of the first murder less a random act of brutality and more a possible pattern of violence. There had never been a serial killer in Malcolm. It was just not that kind of place. To imagine it was just out of reason, like seeing a dog ride a bicycle. It just wasn't possible.

Unlike Petre, Orland had a family in Buffalo and they were being notified as Andrade pondered the situation. The murder would bring outcry, press, and attention from the outside. It would bring tourists, darkly curious to see the small community where the killings took place. He warned his detectives not to discuss publicly a connection between the two killings, or speak to the press. He knew a rush to judgment would be irresponsible. He prayed forensics came up with something this time.

"Captain Andrade?" his secretary came over the desk speaker.

"Yes Andrea?"

"Detective Collins is here to see you."

"Send him in."

Collins appeared at his door and Andrade gestured for him to take a seat. "What do you have?" the Captain asked.

"Forensics typed all the blood and it's all the victim's," Collins said. He laid a file folder on the edge of the desk. "The shoes that made the footprints belonged to the victim, and none of the handprints on the walls have prints. Apparently, the killer wore latex gloves. The bulb in the ceiling light was unscrewed. They figure Orland walked in, was stunned with a tazer and then killed while in a stupor."

"And no witnesses?" Andrade asked.

Collins shook his head. "Some neighbors say they was a kid walking down the street, some say with a dog, but they could not say if it was that dog, what the kid was wearing or even what nationality he was. Besides, no kid could have pulled this off. This killer would have to be strong enough to overcome a six foot cab driver."

"Not just a cabby," the Captain said, "another literary agent. That's a pattern."

"Possibly," Collins said.

"You're not sure?"

"I tracked that lead myself," Collins said and pointed to the folder. "Agents are quite literally a dime a dozen. I found one web site that listed more than two thousand agents in the New York area alone. Another site listed nearly two hundred agents living around here."

"So it could just be a coincidence," Andrade said and rubbed his face.

"And the murders are so different. It could be the same killer in both cases, but we can't say he's targeting agents specifically."

"Yet," Andrade said. "How long before we have analysis on the rest of the evidence?"

"A week, maybe less."

"I have to call NYPD homicide this afternoon and make a report. We can't afford to have this become a media circus."

"I agree, sir."

The squawk box on the desk buzzed with Andrea's voice again. "Lieutenant Bradshaw from central is on the line."

"Thank you." He gave Collins a frustrated roll of his eyes. "Speak of the devil." Andrade pushed a button. "Hello Patrick, how are things downtown?"

"Fine, but I hear you guys are having some fun out there. Chief Smythe asked me to call and see if there was anything we could do to help."

"Nope," Andrade said with more confidence than he felt. "We have it under control."

"Really?" The disbelief in Bradshaw's voice was obvious. "You don't figure you've got some sort of psycho running around out there?"

"Hey, you know how it is. It's early days. We're keeping all our options open. So far it looks like the first one was some loser who went home with the wrong companion, and last night looks like a sex play gone bad. Cab driver, a late night and a bad choice."

Andrade felt like he was tap dancing.

"All right," Bradshaw said, "but keep us in the loop."

"Will do."

Andrade hung up and glared at Collins. "Find this asshole. Get me some hard evidence and make sure I wasn't just blowing sunshine up Bradshaw's ass. If this goes south, we could be very screwed. I don't need to remind you that if this is a serial it becomes federal and then we have the FBI involved. That would be unfortunate for both of us, now wouldn't it?"

Collins blew out through pursed lips. "You're telling me, but I don't think it will come to that. I'll lean on the lab and tell them we need answers yesterday. Meantime, I'll brief the squad. Make sure the patrol guys know to look for anything weird. Let's hope these are two separate psychos who have moved on."

Andrade gave him a skeptical look. "And what do you think the chances are of that?"

Collins just shook his head and shrugged.

"All right," Andrade said. "Get on it."

Collins nodded and left the office.

Andrade walked back to the window and stared out, not looking at anything in particular. He felt like the ground was slipping out from under him.

He had spent eighteen years on the force, several of them shining flashlights down dark alleys and responding to "shots fired" calls. Despite all that, he had never felt so vulnerable.

Andrade was raised in the projects, born to a Mexican father and black mother. He had been schooled in the trenches and blessed with size, intelligence and a thirst for power.

In school, he ran a small gang, then realized the true strength was in law enforcement. The word on the street from the drug dealers in his neighborhood had always been that business was only good when they paid off the cops. Best of both worlds, Andrade realized, enforcing the law and breaking it at the same time. One day a cop came to school and spoke on staying away from drugs. He drew the kids into a dialog and asked what Andrade wanted to be when he grew up.

"Mayor of New York," Andrade said, which made the other kids laugh.

"Don't laugh," the cop warned. "Work hard and stay out of trouble, and you could be just that."

"Can you be mayor if you were a cop?"

"Absolutely. You want to be a policeman?" the officer asked.

Andrade answered enthusiastically. "Yes," he said.

"Then there are some programs to help you get started."

Andrade heeded that advice well. Since graduating from the police academy, he had always looked ahead to the next tier of authority. He brandished his hard luck story and ethnic heritage as he climbed the ladder to Captain.

And then came the Hennings case and some difficult choices. At least they were difficult for Collins; Andrade found the decision easy. Deep secrets, proverbial skeletons in the closet that had lain undisturbed for ten years. Nosy feds could jiggle the handle on that closet and revive the long dead specter. The consequences would be dire, and the best way to avoid that was to crack this case and make the whole mess go away.

"Christ," he said with a sigh and returned to his desk.

He scanned down the list of literary agents left behind by Collins. Both Petre and Orland were on the list, but that told him nothing about who the next victim could be. He found himself wishing he could hand this case over to his most capable Detective, the one capable of teasing out the hidden details. Unfortunately, that person was sitting in a shame-driven stupor in the cage.

Sometimes the price for a bad decision must be paid long after the fact.

Captain Andrade closed the file, pushed it back to the edge of his desk, and barked out a sour laugh as fear rose in his heart.

CHAPTER EIGHT

The rain moved out of New York and the sky was September blue. The days were sunny but cool and the nights cold with a light wind coming in from the west. The air smelled of damp leaves and fireplaces.

Drake sat at his kitchen table on a late Saturday afternoon and tried to muster the courage to open the box sitting in front of him. The smell of a toasting English muffin filled the room as late autumn sunshine streamed through the window. Drake's portable heater droned away near his feet. Despite their size, both he and his girlfriend Robin felt the cold keenly and had a difficult time keeping warm. When they slept together, they were like Eskimos beneath piles of bearskins.

This was the first sunshine the box had seen for ten years. The contents had long resided in the bottom of a drawer, sulking in the dark, the contents yellowing with age. On late nights when sleep eluded him, Drake often thought of the box and felt the remorse of abandonment and cowardice. He wondered if this was a bit like women felt after giving up a baby for adoption.

The muffin popped up and Drake smothered it with butter. He was glad for an excuse to procrastinate, but soon the muffin was gone, the plate placed in the sink and Drake was back staring at the box.

He took a steadying breath and opened the top. Inside he saw a thick stack of rejection letters held together with a black metal clip in one corner. He picked them up and riffled through them, remembering the many times he had plucked the self-addressed stamped envelopes from his mailbox, hoping against hope that this time would be different, only to see the all-too-familiar messages. *"Our agency is not accepting new authors at this time,"* the letters said, or more succinctly, *"This book is not for me."*

Drake set aside the letters and lifted out the bulky manuscript. The title was centered on the front page: MORTAL WHISPERS. He turned the page and began to read. By the end of the second chapter, he was already forming ideas about how he would revise the manuscript if he were to re-write it today. The story still felt strong, but now with a fresh perspective he saw where improvements could be made.

"Okay," he whispered. "I can do this."

Drake returned the book to the box and went to his closet. From the top shelf, he pulled down the typewriter, placed it on the table and plugged it in. It hummed quietly and he hit a single key. The Daisy wheel leapt from its long slumber and clacked against the empty barrel. He carefully opened the seal on a fresh pack of bond paper, pulled out a single sheet and fed it into the machine. He felt a growing sense of urgency as he wound the paper into the starting position.

He had no more than placed his fingers on the keys when the phone rang.

"Hi honey," Robin's voice said. "I'm on break so I thought I'd check in, see what you're doing."

"I'm sitting down to do some writing."

"Really? Good for you."

"Yeah, well, I have a new idea and I decided I need something to do after I hang up my badge."

"Lucky you. I'll probably be a Dunkin' Doughnuts Assistant Manager for the rest of my life. That sounds sad, doesn't it?"

"Tell you what," Drake said. "Maybe this'll turn out to be a bestseller and then I can take you away from all that."

"Is that a proposal?"

"Gotta' go," he said with a laugh. "See you tomorrow."

It was a strange game she played, repeatedly steering conversations around to her bleak future and his promise to save her from her plight. Then her inevitable question.

Is that a proposal?

He often wondered why she bothered with a guy like him. He asked her once and she got angry. Hands on hips and with her face red, she unleashed a barrage of threatening pop psychology and told him never to ask that question again.

"You are good man and I love you," she said.

Drake thought of her as a hopeless optimist, waiting for the day when he would magically emerge from his downtrodden state.

He returned to the typewriter and checked that the margins were set. With his fingers placed in the proper position he awkwardly typed a mindless series of words. He felt a sense of growing elation with each snap of the eager ball and the shifting movement of the paper. The simple act of putting words on paper seemed to make him feel less empty.

"Whew," he said. He could feel a smile starting to creep into the edges of his mouth. It was an unfamiliar sensation.

And he loved it.

He opened his briefcase and pulled out the copies of the case files Serena had given him. The margins were scribbled with notes he had made while reviewing the reports, including a story outline scratched on the back of one page. He quickly scanned through the notes, then rolled a fresh sheet of paper into the typewriter. A new cover page quickly emerged.

TORN JUSTICE
BY
LEWIS HENRY DRAKE

He stared at the words for a second, then with shaking hands he pulled the cover page from the typewriter and rolled in a fresh sheet.

Take the chance, he told himself. Trust your gut. Just write, write anything as long as it feels like yours. No matter if it is brilliant or total crap, just write and let go of the results.

He thought back to what his old composition teacher told him before he graduated. Thinking and composition do not go hand in hand — true writing comes from the heart.

The typewriter seemed to respond of its own accord as his fingers flashed. The sure clack of text against clean bond paper was sweet therapy indeed. Drake felt driven as he poured out page after page about the rainy night he and Dodd got the call. Dodd's screams from the wet pavement found their way onto the page, as did the eerie light emanating from the open door up the metal stairs. He described the smell of death, the dark alley, and the desperation he felt when he crouched next to his partner. Drake wrote about shock and personal misery, his fear and the knowledge that this night could turn out to be the end of his career.

Drake's fingers cramped at one in the morning. He flipped through the pages and figured it came to about two thousand words. Drake was satisfied and spent as he neatly stacked the sheets, read through them and sighed. The writing was rough, yes, but damn he felt good.

In high school he was praised for his skill, even had a teacher suggest that he should consider writing for a living. But after graduation, he looked to law enforcement. As a child, he accompanied his father to the Bronx station house, sat at his dad's desk and made pretend phone calls. Officers tousled his hair and his dad showed him where his grandfather walked his beat before retiring. Drake had grown up with a blue legacy, complete with trips to the Blue Moon tavern, a cop's bar, to sit on a stool and sip a Roy Rogers as his dad had a beer and laughed with his colleagues after their shifts. The Drake men had always been cops and his dad and granddad both shook his hand the day he went into the academy.

But the words were always in him. They came through in his impeccable arrest reports, and later in the reports he wrote as a detective. More than once he was asked to write press releases and promotional copy for his union local.

The feeling took him back to his start as a writer, when he saw an interview where Joseph Wambaugh mentioned he would be at the San Diego State University Writer's Conference. Drake took a few days of vacation time and attended. He managed to corner Wambaugh for fifteen glorious minutes where they talked about being cops and writing.

Talking with Wambaugh awoke the sleeping author in him and he knew he could no longer keep the desire at bay.

Drake flew home and immediately bought an electric typewriter from a pawnshop. Though his wife scoffed, Drake explained it was always his dream to write a novel. She laughed and shrugged as Drake began writing for an hour a day. Six months later, he had completed a first draft. Several friends read it and liked the story, though Drake knew it needed polishing. He pulled a thousand dollars out of savings to have the manuscript professionally edited, and educated himself on how to submit a book for publication.

With that, effort came the hopes and fantasies of publication, money and notoriety. He shopped the finished manuscript around and found the publishing industry to be profoundly disinterested. After thirty rejections Drake began to lose hope. His wife made it clear she thought it was foolish and they did not have the money, or him the time, to be writing books he could not sell.

After a hundred rejections he began to believe her.

“Face it honey,” she said. “Why would anybody want to publish a book you wrote? It’s not like you’re a celebrity.”

He found himself resenting the pages. The manuscript became a taunt and a reminder that he was not good enough. Even Collins patted his shoulder and dismissed his efforts.

“C’mon Lou,” Collins said with a laugh, “it’s not like you were really going to hit it big and leave the force. You wrote the book, and that’s more than most assholes do. It’s something to brag about when you retire. You know, bore the rookies.”

Not long after that Drake stuffed the manuscript and rejection letters in a box and dropped the bundle into a drawer. Unfortunately, he couldn’t forget about it. Like a sore that would not quite heal, the box kept calling to him on those late, sleepless nights.

But not on this night. After rolling a fresh sheet into the typewriter, ready for what Sunday might bring, Drake went to bed. Sleep came easily and he dreamed of murder.

As Drake dreamed, Michael Collins was up studying the case reports, pouring over the pathology reports detailing the trauma to each body. Collins had picked up the reports earlier that day from Kathy Morey, Head of Pathology. “These are beyond human,” Kathy Morey, had said, “like Jack-the-Ripper evil. These bodies were not traumatized in a rage. This was methodical.”

“Could it have been done by a doctor?” Collins asked her. “Is it that kind of methodical, somebody with training?”

“I’d say no,” she said. “More like somebody with a careful hand and the time to make a point. Thank God these people were out of it when this done to them.”

“But one was drugged and the other stunned. You think it was the same perp?”

“Hard to say,” she said. “Could be, but the style looks different and the handling of the victims. Like, well, like... I don’t know.”

Could be. I don’t know.

Her words whispered in his head.

Collins gulped down his cold coffee and rubbed his temples with his palms. The only commonality between Petre and Orland was their sideline ambition selling books to publishers. To sell books you had to have writer clients and they were a dime a dozen. After plowing through website after website he was shocked to see how many people were now hoping to get a piece of an ever-shrinking pie of publishing opportunities. Sites for writers guiding them through how to write a book, create a query, target the market, find an agent, avoid the wrong agents and get work edited, polished, doctored and reviewed.

Alternative publishing was abundant if you had the cash to plunk down and hope for the best. He found print on demand, vanity presses, small presses, huge publishers and the list went on and on. In New York alone there had to be thousands of writers, millions in the whole country, sending their precious words to a chosen few in hopes of ending up on a bookstore shelf. It was overwhelming. Collins found a site that listed thousands of agents, affiliated with as many agencies and a small review after each name. Some were very clear – *HIGHLY NOT RECOMMENDED!*

It seemed the publishing game was filled with con men just waiting to bilk desperate and vain writers out of a few bucks.

REAL AGENTS DO NOT CHARGE FEES!

The more Collins tried to fit the two murders together the less he believed that the agent connection was viable. The glove and footprints were intentional at the cab driver's place, whereas the other scene was careful and clean. The two methods of death, while brutal in both cases, were dramatically different.

But then again, he could find no other connection, and no clues in either case that led him closer to identifying the killer.

Or killers.

Try and catch me!

"Shit," he said to the early morning and decided to let it rest.

He'd had too much coffee and his head was overly full with facts and theories. Collins took a pill and watched television until he dozed off. With a snort and a jerk, he woke and switched off the TV, then stumbled off to bed and fell asleep with his clothes on.

Night moved toward dawn with a lack of human urgency and the coming sunrise announced itself with a red glow against a purple-black sky. The relaxed arrival of morning mirrored the careful work of the killer as he finished with another victim. Careful to leave no trace, the figure backed out of the basement apartment, closed and locked the door and slipped unnoticed into the coming day.

CHAPTER NINE

October brought clouds and rain to New York. The temperature fell, the wind came up and the last of the autumn leaves fought to save themselves so the tourists would have something to look at when they arrived for the weekend. But the wind prevailed and by Saturday the orange and red leaves clogged the gutters like Mardi Gras confetti. Overnight the neighborhood windows were adorned with jack-o-lanterns cut from orange construction paper. Pumpkins sat stout and bold on front porches.

Drake arrived at the station house with doughnuts once again, but these days he was careful not to indulge. Instead he carried individually wrapped cheese sticks to munch on when he felt temped. Edna noticed and asked what was up.

"Doctor's orders," he said. "He wants me to lay off the sweets for a few weeks until my next physical."

In truth, the doctor had nothing to do with it. Drake was simply enjoying what he saw when he stepped on the bathroom scale every morning. He had seen an infomercial about the profound results people were having losing weight eating nothing but protein. It sounded too good to be true — all the meat and eggs and cheese he wanted and still drop pounds? Yet the scale did not lie. So far he was down 11 pounds.

Drake also continued his work on the new novel. He was up to five thousand words in two weeks, fleshing out a story about a cop just like him and using the two murder cases as inspiration. Much to his surprise he found he enjoyed the Internet research, learning about the climate, people and details of San Diego where the story was set. When he completed the novel he planned to return there and attend the writer's conference again. After all, he would be retired by then with all the time in the world to travel. Robin thought it was a wonderful idea and had vowed to get back into bikini shape.

"My doctor wants me to lose weight," Edna rasped. "Stop smoking too. Showed me a chart and said a woman my age and my height should weigh 115. Can you imagine, me at 115? He's nuts."

"I got that much just in my ass," Regina said and patted her rump. "But that's the way my man likes it."

"Ain't that the truth," Serena laughed and took a doughnut. "More to love."

Collins showed up in front of the cage.

"Hey Drake," he said. "You got a minute?"

"Sure, what do you need?"

"Come with me," Collins said, and set off down the hallway.

They made it as far as the door to the men's room when Collins turned abruptly and unceremoniously pushed Drake inside. They were the only ones there.

"Jesus, what's wrong?" Drake asked, feeling manhandled.

The look of disdain was clear on Collins' face. This made a spike of fear stab at Drake's gut, despite how pissed off he was about being pushed around.

"Look Drake," Collins said, pointing his finger. "I heard you have been asking about the two murder cases, poking your short-time nose into shit that doesn't concern you."

"What? No, but even I was, I was there when it started —"

"And you fucked up, remember?"

"Yeah, sure, how can I forget?"

"Drake, you have five months to go and everybody is watching you. Andrade cut you some slack because I asked him to."

"Hey guys," Thibido said as he came into the bathroom. "Don't mind me, you guys do whatever you were doing before I got here. Relax, I won't tell anybody you're queer for each other."

"Shut up, asshole," Collins said and Thibido looked away. "Drake, meet me at Molly's Saturday at 11:30."

"Sure," Drake said.

Collins ripped open the door and stalked out.

"Aw, you girls having a fight?" Thibido chided.

"Go do your mother," Drake spat and followed Collins out the door.

Back in the cage Drake fumed. It was bad enough to be stuck in the cage but he sure as hell wasn't going to take shit like that from anyone, least of all his former partner.

Drake's internal tirade was interrupted when Henry Smythe showed up at the cage. Smythe was Chief of Detectives from NYPD Station One.

"Is Captain Andrade around?" Smythe asked.

Medium height and dressed smartly, Smythe carried himself with the grace of a man you expected to have a British accent.

"He's not back from lunch, Chief," Regina said. "You want some coffee while you wait?"

"No thanks. I'm early, so I'll just hang out. Are those doughnuts for anybody?"

"Yes sir," Drake said.

"Got half an old fashioned? Thanks," he said with a smile as Drake handed it to him on a napkin. "What you reading back there?"

"Andrew McAllister," Drake said and showed the cover. "True crime."

"I know McAllister. Did you read NIGHT ANIMAL?"

"I did," Drake nodded. "I liked it, and BRUTAL FORCE was even better."

"Didn't read that one. Think I'd like it?"

"It's as good as any of the others," Drake said. "It's about dirty cops."

Smythe nodded with pursed lips. "Sounds good, Officer Drake, maybe I'll look for it."

Drake nodded, wondering how Smythe knew him.

"You're close to retirement, aren't you?" Smythe said.

How the hell did he know that? "Yes sir, in a few months."

"Is that a good or bad thing?"

"Sir?"

"I've talked to a lot of retiring cops and it seems about half can't wait and the others are scared to death. They have no idea what they'll do with themselves in the civilian world."

"Bit of both, I think," Drake said. "I'll miss some things, not others."

"Like bad cops?"

"I'm sorry?" Drake asked.

Smythe seemed to consider him for a moment, and then looked at Drake's colleagues.

"Can you ladies give us a minute?"

This caused a few raised eyebrows, but the girls nodded willingly enough, stepped into the adjoining office and closed the door.

Smythe lowered his voice. "Misuse of the power we are given is a crime against the service, and the people."

"Yes sir," Drake answered slowly. He had no idea where this was going.

"I remember you and the Hennings case. I was vice then. We all watched that go down."

Drake felt frozen, he had no idea if was about to be chastised or get sympathy.

"Can I ask a question?" Smythe said. "And I mean no disrespect."

"Of course," Drake said, his voice almost trembling.

"What happened back then?" Smythe asked. "How could a case as airtight as that go south? And we all had you pegged as a good Detective. It didn't make any sense that you'd make so many mistakes."

Drake's heart beat so fast and hard he feared it would rattle the windows. Sweat dampened his shirt beneath his arms as Smythe fixed him with a piercing stare. His tongue went dry.

"Sir, may I speak freely?"

"Of course," Smythe urged.

"I was as surprised as you, sir. When the evidence came out on Hennings I was floored about what I supposedly had done. But —"

Andrade's voice interrupted him. "Hello Chief. You're early."

"Yes," Smythe said, "but your fine officer kept me entertained while I waited."

Smythe looked Drake in the eye. "We should talk some more."

"Yes sir," Drake muttered and looked away.

Andrade shook the Chief's hand and they walked back to the Captain's office.

For the next hour Drake could do nothing but run the cryptic conversation over in his mind. He was just going through the motions as he and the girls tended to the normal daily routine.

An hour later he held his breath when Smythe showed up in front of the cage once more with Andrade at his side.

"Thank you for your time, Captain," Smythe said as the two men shook hands.

Andrade gave Drake a serious glare before heading back to his office.

"Thanks for the doughnut, Drake," Smythe said and placed his hand on the counter.

"You're welcome sir," Drake smiled and Smythe gave him a nod. When the Chief walked away Drake noticed a business card embossed with the seal of the City of New York lying on the counter. He stared at it for a second, and then quickly snatched it up and shoved it into his pocket before anyone else could see it.

Something serious had just happened, and Drake had no idea what it was.

"By the way," Smythe said as he stopped and looked back. "How is officer Dodd?"

"Uh, I heard he's doing okay. He's out of the hospital and on the mend."

"Been down to see him?" Smythe asked.

"No, but I've been meaning to."

"I suggest you do that," Chief Smythe said, then turned and walked briskly away.

"What the hell was that all about?" Serena asked in a hushed voice.

Drake shook his head, still staring into the lobby. "I don't have a clue."

"Sounded like he had somethin' more he wanted to say to you, that's what I think," Regina said.

"I suppose," Drake said as he returned to his computer. It did indeed sound like that. What else could the card be but an invitation to get back in touch with the Chief?

Drake flinched when Serena's lips spoke next to his ear, her sultry voice low and airy.

"You like to read?" she asked. "Oh yeah, that's all you do. I got something I think you would like to read."

"Oh yeah?" he asked hesitantly.

"Uh huh," she said and dropped a folded piece of paper next to his mouse pad. Drake slipped it into his pocket with the business card.

"Thanks," he whispered, his tone unsure.

"By the way," she hissed low, her eyes suddenly full of fierce seriousness. "If somebody asks you where you got this, you say you found it on the street, you understand?"

"Yes ma'am. Do I owe you a thank you?"

"Sugar you don't owe me a damn thing," she whispered and walked away.

Drake excused himself and went to the bathroom. His heart raced as he entered a stall and locked the door. He pulled the folded paper from his pocket, dropped his pants for realism and slowly opened the note. It was a photocopy of a letter from former Chief of Detectives Alvin Fitzpatrick to Andrade's predecessor Captain Peter Holloway. He read, drew an angry breath and folded the letter up again. Drake pulled up his pants, shoved the note back in his pocket and returned to the cage.

"Where did you get that?" he asked Serena.

"I told you, I got access," she said.

"Is there more?"

"Not like that," she said.

"What does it mean?" He hated the pleading tone in his voice but he couldn't seem to help it.

"I think it means you should call that handsome Chief and have a talk."

"Yeah, I think so," Drake said.

As he returned to his desk, thoughts tumbled in his head like fighting cats, all flying fur and flashing teeth. The words in the letter joined the fray and his head throbbed from the implications.

He would call Smythe.

Damn straight, he thought and without meaning to he snapped a number two pencil in half. *And introduce yourself to the writer's group!*

Yes, that is absolutely goddamn right!

Constructed in 1908, the Station 10 building originally housed only two underground brick cells accessible by a flight of steps that descended behind the old courthouse. Inmates languished in damp quarters deprived of food, water and proper facilities. Many died of malnutrition, scurvy or pneumonia. Not long after, Malcolm's first five-story structure was built behind the station to house university staff, local police, the county defender, and the court prosecutor.

By the thirties the station expanded to a full precinct with a new bank of holding cells and an execution chamber, complete with an electric chair aptly named *the last seat in the house.* Staff from the town's tubercular hospital lived behind the station and commuted to the facility by ferry each day. Over the years the town and the station grew and modernized. The electric chair and old courthouse were now displayed in the town museum, the last reminders of the small waterside village's rough past.

Serena entered the small back office of the cage where she managed the electronic archives. She pushed a series of numbers on a keypad and opened the security door at the back. This led to metal stairs, which provided access to the old cells, now used as storage for boxed hard copy files and the station's holiday decorations. No longer cold and damp, the rooms were clean and environmentally controlled. More importantly for Drake, Serena reigned here as queen.

Since Drake had been assigned to work in the cage she spent a few minutes each day looking through the old files on the Hennings case. That was where she found the letter to the old chief at the bottom of a stack of interview transcriptions.

Careful to avoid the watching eyes of camera surveillance, she snuck the letter upstairs, made a copy and returned the sheet to the box before anyone knew the difference.

Sly, that's what she was. Her mama always said so. Serena was curious about this fat cop with the bad attitude. Her computer told her where he lived and his standard life details, but the password-protected information regarding his demotion became a serious tease to her intensely curious nature. References to Hennings gave her the key to what to look for in the boxed files. From there it was a matter of digging, something Serena loved to do.

When she was a girl in Spanish Harlem, her family knew if there was a piece of pie missing from supper's dessert, a dollar out of Grammar's purse, or a boy unwilling to look his girlfriend in the eye, most likely Serena was to blame.

There's a sneaky streak in that girl as long as my arm, her aunt used to say. Many times the priest came to the house. "Just a visit," he would say, but he always made a point of sitting with her and discussing God's wish that all his children should walk a path of righteousness. Serena listened and played with her long hair, all the while wondering if the fine holy man found her desirable. She knew most men did.

After high school she wanted adventure and freedom and thought she would find both in the military. Serena joined the Air force and hated every minute of it. One of the perks of service, though, was college and her eventual focus on law enforcement. She wanted nothing to do with walking a beat and carrying a gun, so she took the opportunity to augment her military training in technical data control with a Bachelor's degree in computer science. She breezed through the academy and applied for the position of resident manager for the Malcolm station. That was two years ago.

Today her orders were to hunt through old case files to search for similarities between unsolved cases and the current murders. With cool efficiency, she removed each folder from a box, scanned it thoroughly and placed the examined folder into a new box. She performed her task under the constant watchful eye of the surveillance cameras. Ironically, the VCR banks were in the archive room with her and the monitors only linked to the sergeant's desk and the cage. The front desk monitor was broken, however, so she had full access as long as the desk was quiet and the cage was empty.

In four hours she scanned half the boxes dating back ten years. Pick and scan and close and box, again and again. All the while planning to slip into the last of the Hennings files and give them a once over. It had become an obsession, driven by the discovery of the letter and the details of the investigation. She wasn't doing it just for Drake, though she had come to enjoy his company, but also for her own desire to know the truth.

"Serena," the intercom buzzed. Andrade's voice was almost robotic over the speaker.

"Yes sir?"

"Can you please come to my office?"

"Be right there."

She stretched her back, climbed the steps and walked to Andrade's office. His door was open but she knocked lightly with her knuckles.

"Come," he said. "Please close the door." She took a seat in front of his desk. "Thanks for coming up. I know you're busy with the case reviews. Any luck?"

"None so far," she said. "I'm halfway through."

"I was looking over your record with us. Two years on the job, good reviews and targeted for promotion in a year. I see you were recommended for an operations commendation for streamlining our data system and overhauling our back-up procedures."

"Yes sir," she said

"You have a good start on a fine career with us," he said and looked back at her folder. "Single, hard worker, career-minded and sharp. It would be a shame to lose all that."

Serena's mouth went dry in an instant. Was she wrong about how much the surveillance cameras showed? Her mind raced through a quick inventory of what someone might have seen.

"What do you mean?" she asked.

"You have access to sensitive materials and special clearance. It is your responsibility to ensure that material stays safe and secure. However, a scrap of torn paper referencing the Petre murder case was found on the men's room floor"

Serena felt a stab of annoyance ... but also a measure of relief.

"And?" she said.

"We suspect this shred of paper originated from your file room. As you are the only one with access, we have to suspect you made the information public."

She sat up straighter and glared at the Captain with all the defiance she dared. "There are others with access," she said, "not to mention the detectives with access to the actual case files."

"Yes, but the detectives are not in the habit of working on their case files in the rest room, and no one would have any reason to access the archived information without authorization, especially to read it in the restroom."

"And you're saying I would have a reason to read it in the men's room?"

He gave her an exasperated look. "Of course not, but you could have given it to someone."

Serena was shaking her head before he finished speaking.

"With all due respect sir, I know very little about the Petre case and care even less. I see no grounds for you suspecting that I would supply secure information to anyone. I have no allegiance to anyone or anything but the oath I took to uphold the law. I suggest somebody who had something to lose, or something to fear from that particular case, must have helped themselves to that information."

"Well," Andrade said and sat back in his chair. "Those are strong accusations."

"Nothing compared to what you just accused me of," she snapped. "Frankly I'm surprised you would even entertain the idea without first looking into who would benefit from accessing those files. I have no reason to do so."

"Watch what you say," he said. "Of course all other possibilities have been explored and those came up empty. The final suspicion lies with you."

"Then we are at an impasse. I have explained myself and will not repeat it. If you feel there is more to explore, as you put it, I suggest we call Station One and involve a higher authority."

"No, that won't be necessary," Andrade said. "I believe you and I'm sorry to push, but I had to know you had not breached the department's trust."

"Thank you sir." She got to her feet. "If there is anything else?"

"Not at this time."

"Did you review the security tapes? If somebody was in the archives it would have been picked up on the cameras, right?"

'We did," he said. "All we saw was you."

"Then we have a mystery."

Andrade nodded. "Indeed we do."

Serena swept out of the Captain's office and walked the hallway in a controlled rage. Damn asswipe pseudo boss, with his big hair and plastic smile. A guy like Andrade would last about five minutes in the military.

She found Drake in his seat and thumped the back of his head with her knuckles as she walked by him.

"What?" he said as he rubbed his head.

She crooked a finger for him to follow her to the adjoining office. Once they were inside with the door closed she rounded on him with fury snapping in her eyes.

"Next time wait until you are out of the goddamn building before you do your bathroom reading," she said in an angry whisper. "You left evidence. Remember what I said to you about this?"

"I ... well, yes."

Drake lowered his eyes and appeared to shrink in stature.

"Thank you very much," she hissed and pushed by him.

CHAPTER TEN

On Friday night the bookstore was busy and the coffee shop was lined up. Each patron asked for their favorite drink by spouting a custom concoction of ingredients and size to the two high school students behind the counter. The two youths frantically wrote directions and names on plastic cups with markers. They moved from espresso machine to blender, from fridge to pastry case, a well-oiled machine of colored hair, pierced facial features and confusing gender. They served up the drinks with the fervor of manic short order cooks.

The members of the writers group were in fine form and the discussions ran from the ordinary complaints to the rumors of the day. Each resented the new batch of commercial fiction that arrived and a new vampire book was all the rage, filling the gap created by the delay of the new wizard boy epic. Release season coincided with the fast approaching holiday buying frenzy. The writers shook their heads, criticized the authors and secretly wished they were a part of that commercial success.

Sandy Alexander sipped a mocha, Brian Shakespeare tapped at the keys of his laptop, and Franny expounded on her latest piece written for the local free rag.

"So, I swear," Franny said, "this ludicrous battle over gay marriage is only another way the frightened white male is trying to retain control. If they lose the ability to constrain wedded bliss to opposite genders, more women will feel free to dispose of their guilt-driven desire to be taken care of. This would empower straight women as much as the homosexuals."

"Here, here," Shakespeare said and gave her an exaggerated limp-wristed salute.

More writers arrived and the crowd was lively. Kevin Pooter rushed through the stacks and dropped into an open chair next to Carl Nesbit. He was excited and his breath came in deep gasps. Sandy looked over his glasses and Pooter raised his hand in a gesture of apology, took a deep breath and coughed.

"Holy shit," Pooter huffed, "You won't believe this!"

"Calm yourself, my son," Sandy crooned. "Now what is the boggle?"

"I have a friend in NYPD traffic who helps me with my criminal stuff. Yeah, anyway, he called me last night to let me know there were two murders in the village."

"What?" Carl asked and leaned toward Pooter. "When?"

"Don't know when," he said and sat back, "but there were two killings and, get this, they were both literary agents."

"Know who?" Sandy asked with a frown.

"Lewis Petre and Paul Orland," Pooter said.

"Damn," Carl hissed. "Orland turned me down about six months ago."

"They know who did it?" Franny asked.

"They don't. But my contact said it was nasty ass shit. He said it's a closed investigation for now, but they should have a press conference in the next couple of days."

"Petre," Sandy said, "I know him. Talked with him at the university conference last year. He looked at my query package and said my stuff sounded interesting and then later he sent me a rejection form letter. Far as I know he never sold a thing. A buddy told me he was a waiter, repping part time."

"It's awful, of course, that two people died," Franny said, "but isn't it kind of understandable? I mean, given how frustrated we all are with agents."

"Know what?" Shakespeare said. "I actually thought about that once, what a cool deal it would be if somebody started killing these assholes off for being such dicks."

"Yeah, who hasn't?" Sandy added. "I even had the idea of writing a book about something like that, a disgruntled and crazy writer who decides to start offing the people who said no."

"Okay," Pooter laughed. "That would get you nothing but some nervous agents and a few restraining orders."

"But it would be original," a voice came from beyond the circle.

"That it would," Sandy answered and looked at the fat man who offered the opinion. "Make a damn good story if you could write it so it didn't come across as a veiled threat."

"It would work great," Drake said, "if the story was structured so the murders were just a symptom of the whole problem with the publishing industry in general."

"I've seen you," Pooter said. "You're always nose deep in a crime book."

"True enough." Drake stood and approached the group. "My name is Lou Drake. I'm a cop and a writer."

"Another Wambaugh," Carl said.

"No, afraid not. But I do my best. I just started a new book, inspired by the killings you were just talking about."

"Really?" Pooter asked. "That's cool. Are the police close to solving them?"

Drake took a seat with the group.

"Well, I'm almost retired," he said, "but I've heard enough to know they're not sure what they are dealing with. They haven't made a definitive connection and are still looking things over."

It was not a lie. The written reports were vague and he had not seen the coroner's reports.

"In other words, you'll tell us shit," Franny spat and sucked her iced latte through a straw. "Cops."

"No, I'm being straight. I only know what you know."

"Which is nothing," Brian said. "No matter, I got the next big seller right here!"

Sandy leaned forward, pointed his finger on the table and looked around the group with a leer that reminded Drake of a camp counselor telling a ghost story.

"The cops don't want us to know anything," Sandy continued. "They never do. It's standard procedure in cases like this. They let out just a bit of info and leave the details of the murders out. That way they know they have the killer when they find some whack job who knows the killer chopped off a particular body part or some such shit."

"But some of us find out anyway," Pooter said with a malicious grin. "Remember, it ain't what you know, but who you know. And it's nice to know cops."

"Don't believe everything you see in the movies," Drake said. "Most departments are filled with leaks and secrets are hard to keep out of the press. They pay too well. Cops make peanuts, so every dollar helps."

"Well, Officer Drake," Sandy said with a wry grin. "Welcome to the village idiots unofficial writers group. We're happy to have you,"

The other members of the group took Sandy's words as a cue and chimed in with welcomes and handshakes of their own. Drake offered to talk cop shop with anyone who needed realism in a story and he seemed to be enjoying himself. After all, Sandy thought, coffee and doughnuts, lamentation and commiseration; isn't that a writer cop's dream?

After a time the others drifted away until it was just Drake and Sandy.

"Better call it a night, store closes soon. Tell me Officer Drake, what's your new book about?" Sandy asked as they left the bookstore and stood in the cold parking lot.

"Ha, well," Drake rubbed the back of this thick neck. "Me, I guess."

"Write what you know," Sandy said with a nod.

"But it's fiction. I'm writing about a burned-out cop waiting to retire who has the opportunity to break a big case and go out a hero."

Sandy laughed. "You mean instead of a zero."

"Yeah, corny I guess."

"It's been done, but so has everything else. There is no such thing as an original idea anymore. But you said it earlier, if you handle it right, well that is another story altogether, isn't it?"

"Shakespeare's pretty confident about his new book," Drake said.

"Maybe he has really done it." Sandy shrugged. "Eventually one of them will come up with the next big thing. Maybe even you."

They shook hands and Sandy started to walk away.

"Or you," Drake said.

Sandy stopped and came back.

"Drake, listen to me. I'm a has-been of the worst kind. I got lucky and published a book. But then I was too afraid to try again because I thought the second time around would be ugly."

"Oh, I don't believe that."

"Believe it Drake." Sandy pulled the preserved paperback from his case. "I wrote this over twenty years ago. I pull it out and wave it around and make people think I made it. Bottom line, I'm a coward. These people look up to me because I have published, no matter how long ago. In the land of the blind, the one-eyed man is king. So this is my one eye. I guess I wanted to tell you this because you obviously still have hope. You truly want to end up on these shelves in here. Honestly, I haven't had that genuine desire for ten years."

"Why did you give up?" Drake asked.

"Rejection," Sandy said and rubbed his temple with his index finger. "Pure and simple, it was the rejection. Enough to jade the heart, freeze the mind and shrivel the talent. Constant and relentless rejection is like the schoolyard bully who finally breaks your spirit and makes you not want to go to school anymore."

"I can see that," Drake said. "I got a few rejection letters on my first book, well, about a hundred of them. My wife said some things and I ran into some trouble and I forgot all about wanting to be a writer for a long time."

"Murder brought it back?"

"No," Drake said, "self hatred did."

"Come again?"

"I hated myself and then realized I was sick of that. I started writing because I needed something to distract me. Now I do it to save myself from my own personal gallows."

"Very poetic," Sandy said.

"Well, you know, we writers are full of shit."

"That we are. Drake, do me a favor. Write the hell out of this book of yours so you can leave that infernal police cesspool and get published and make us all proud. Do it for us and yourself and invite me to your book release party."

"Sandy, how many rejections did you get," Drake asked.

"745," Sandy said and took a long breath, exhaling into the chilly night as though blowing smoke from his burning soul. "Funny how you remember the big numbers."

"Wow," Drake said quietly.

"It's not the number, it's the weight. If you stop and ponder the weight of the average rejection letter, a single page of bond paper? It's nothing, like a feather. Five hundred rejections is a ream of paper, about five pounds of actual heft. But the collective weight of those palpable words, even a simple *NO*, is a collective ton of *NO* laying on your psyche, pressing you down and squeezing out the dreams. Rejection crushes the soul and sucks the life out of you and whispers that working in a cubicle is a grand idea."

Drake pondered Sandy's words as he drove home to where Robin waited for him. They made small talk that led to slow and thoughtful lovemaking. Afterward they spooned and Drake breathed in the sweet smell of powdered sugar and brewed coffee from her hair.

"You going to let me read what you have written so far?" she asked as they lay together. Her voice was distant, somewhere between sleep and now.

"Absolutely," he whispered and kissed her softly. "Tomorrow."

"I have to work early," she said.

He promised she could read it whenever she had time. She snuggled closer and said she loved him.

"Me too," he said and they fell asleep in a tangle of loving limbs.

CHAPTER ELEVEN

Halloween drew closer and the weather was cloudy, cool and dry. Drake wasted the morning trying to write but it was useless. Instead he tried to prepare himself for his meeting with Collins. Should he write a few notes about what he would say if questioned about his recent behavior, just in case it got nasty and he found himself tongue tied? That thought dredged up the Hennings case and the days Drake spent in the hot seat, answering question after question. He remembered interminable days struggling with the suggestions presented to him, the allegations thrown about and the sneaky way Internal Affairs posed their questions. Yes meant no and vice versa when it came to sorting out Hennings, the murder, the case and the confusing shit storm that followed.

Joshua Fairbanks Hennings owned Malcolm, or so he often told people when he was drunk. And he was drunk a lot. Hennings liked to refer to himself as a functional alcoholic, amazing his partners by drinking four double scotches and still effectively negotiating a million-dollar deal. Those deals spread across the full spectrum of the borough's real estate, business and social sectors.

On July twenty-third, 1990, Lou Drake and Michael Collins were called to a crime scene in the harbor district. Possible homicide. They arrived at the upscale penthouse and pushed past uniformed cops to the master bedroom. Angela Hennings lay naked on the bed, her legs hanging over the footboard. She was covered in blood from eight gunshot wounds, and her face wore an expression lost between anger and surprise. Scurrying officers collected evidence like ants, dragging the tidbits to a colony of processors. They collected and filed fibers, spent shell casings and took copious photos of the scene. Angela Hennings was the still and patient focus of garish and frightening angles of blood-splattered flesh. Drake looked at the splatter patterns and decided the headshot came first, following which the gunman emptied the rest of the bullets into her torso. First the victim endured the assault of bullets, and the unflattering lens of the coroner's camera attacked her once more.

Back then analyzing a crime scene was like breathing for Drake, as if his mind took the entire event in as a series of high definition still shots. In 1998 Drake received a special certificate, voted on by the entire Detective team, as having the greatest ability to read a crime scene. No matter how much blood, disarray or noise, Drake surveyed the details and could reenact the events in his mind like a Navaho tracker reading a trail. The Hennings case presented a particularly messy trail.

Drake was certain Hennings was the killer and that he had been drunk, abusive and threatening. Angela was fresh from the shower, that was easy to see. From the blood splatter she was standing at the foot of the bed with her feet planted. The shot was unexpected, the force of the impact knocking her off her feet and back onto the bed. Then Hennings emptied the gun into her already dead corpse. The pattern was erratic, the angry actions of a drunken man hell-bent on destruction.

Mrs. Hennings posture was grotesquely alluring, her legs apart and her perfect figure exposed, one breast firm and unyielding to the pull of gravity, the other punctured and oozing silicone. Drake saw only the details, the angle of entry wounds and the partial bloody footprint that marked the killer's exit. Joshua Hennings left in a hurry. Drake saw that as a good thing, since an intoxicated man running from murder leaves a trail of desperation that Drake could follow like a bloodhound.

At that time Drake was highly respected and colleagues came to him for advice. His marriage was solid and his career stellar. Back then Lou Drake carried himself with a quiet self-assurance that made other cops take a closer look at themselves. He was bullet proof.

Then the case came apart. Solid evidence was deemed tainted, witnesses recanted their statements and other Detectives had meetings with important figures. Each witness told a story diametrically opposed to Drake's. The solid granite case against Hennings crumbled like a block of sugar in the rain. Slowly the evidence was discarded until the District Attorney dropped the charges. Then another suspect confessed, was incarcerated and committed suicide.

Thibido was one of the cops who sat behind closed doors and told his part of the story regarding the case against Hennings. Thibido was only a patrolman at the time, but his word must have been taken seriously because for Lou Drake the result had been terminal.

Case closed and career over.

Drake shrugged off the bitter memory and went to the kitchen for a beer. The Budweiser was cold and scorched his throat as he chugged it down. He unfolded the letter Serena gave him and read it again. His face was red with anger and his heart filled with fierce frustration as he pondered the words on the photocopied memo. The rough text was made coarse by the copier and the NYPD logo taken down to a monochromatic, corrupted representation of itself.

03/24/1998

Dear Captain Holloway,

I am writing because I am disturbed by the outcome of the Hennings murder investigation and the subsequent allegations of mishandling of evidence, the accusations of falsified and planted material and the suggestion that the case was compromised by the actions of Detective Lewis Drake. I have examined the findings, and though compelling, I have a difficult time believing an officer as qualified and respected as Drake could be responsible for the actions detailed in this report. I have followed the Detective's career and know his work on other cases. It is hard to accept the allegations. Though there is no doubt the case was poorly handled, the suggestion that Detective Drake intentionally sabotaged the evidence and the integrity of the case is outlandish. I am requesting additional investigations into this matter and will be present when Detective Drake is questioned at the inquiry on April 12th.

A special board of impartial investigators will be appointed to handle the processing of the findings. This special coalition and my office will decide whether any disciplinary actions should be taken against Drake or other involved officers.

Besides this concern, I am confused by your department's refusal to reexamine the evidence and attempt to make a new case regarding the murder of Angela Hennings. Despite the unavoidable dismissal of much of the current evidence, there is more than enough to still effectively prosecute Joshua Hennings.

Please address these issues and be prepared to explain your actions and this case when we meet on April 5th. I am frustrated and concerned and will personally walk this situation through channels until the truth is discovered and justice served.

Regards,
Alvin B. Fitzpatrick
NYPD Chief of Detectives Precinct 1
New York, NY

On April third, 1998 Fitzpatrick suffered a massive heart attack and died in his Manhattan home. The investigation was postponed in lieu of the memorial service and when the case did proceed, Captain Holloway of precinct six became the new managing investigator. Andrade and Collins became his right hand men.

As Drake took another swig from the Bud, he was sure the letter had never seen the light of day. How it survived was, most likely, a matter of oversight. Holloway transferred to precinct one and took a step up in the force. Andrade became lead Detective with Collins at his side.

The whole affair ended when a petty criminal with a past history of false confessions, most likely craving attention, confessed to killing Angela Hennings. He gave enough information to be taken seriously for once. Though many were suspicious, Walter Spader insisted he was guilty and wept over his shame for killing such a beautiful woman. Spader signed a detailed confession, and then hanged himself in his cell.

The letter and the memory infuriated Drake. He found himself grinding his teeth in frustration and willed himself to stop. He walked to the kitchen and rummaged through a messy cupboard until he found a dusty box of business size envelopes. He sat at his small Kitchen table and in careful print with a black pen, copied the address from the Chief of Detectives card. Rolling a fresh sheet of paper into his typewriter, Drake wrote a short note to the Chief. He referenced their talk in the station, thanked him for his kind words and then listed his concerns regarding the case against him a decade ago.

Drake read it over, put it aside and wrote several more versions until it felt right. He signed the bottom, folded it into thirds, placed his letter and Fitzpatrick's letter together in the envelope and sealed it. Drake was in a sweat. His stomach churned as he stared at the envelope, which suddenly seemed to weigh a ton. The potential fallout of the words seemed heavier than he could handle.

Drake looked at the clock on the kitchen wall. It was time to go meet Collins. He went to the bathroom, splashed water on his face, changed his shirt and pulled on a jacket. As an afterthought he clipped his small holster and his off-duty thirty-eight revolver high on his belt and put his badge in his pants pocket. With the letter tucked securely in his inside jacket pocket he felt troubled and exhilarated, frightened and happy, fat but light as a feather. As he left the apartment, an inner voice asked the only question that really mattered.

Can you mail it?

Molly's was a small, intimate café that was always crowded on Saturday. Drake made himself a mental bet that Collins had picked the place so Drake would be less apt to make a public scene if things got heated.

Drake spotted Collins at a small table in the far west corner, sipping from a white mug. The place was loud with students and Drake knew he and Collins would have to speak up close to hear each other; their heads leaned into one another like conspirators telling secrets. Drake waded through the haphazard tables, careful not to knock over a water glass or worse. Collins gave him a half wave as Drake settled onto a small iron chair.

Whatever he says, whatever he demands or accuses you of, Drake thought, *just go along with it. He cannot be trusted. His words are lies. The letter, remember the letter.*

"Thanks for coming," Michael said.

"No problem."

Collins waved to the waitress. She gave him a nod as she finished writing an order at a nearby table.

"Just like the old days, huh?" Collins said. "The coffee is still the best in town."

"I like Dunkin's better."

"As you should. How is Robin?"

"Great. Can we cut the small talk and get to the heart of the matter?" Drake said. "Why are we here?"

"Let's eat first," Collins said as the waitress approached.

"Ready boys?" she asked, her hair coming free of her ponytail.

"The special," Collins said.

"Ham and eggs over medium, fruit and cottage cheese, no toast or potatoes," Drake said.

"Protein diet?" the waitress asked with a smile.

Drake nodded. "And I'll have a coffee too."

The waitress moved away and Michael said, "You're trying to lose weight. Good for you."

"So," Drake sat back, the chair too small for his wide butt. "What do we talk about while we wait for our food? The weather is nice for October. Shame about the leaves going off so soon and so fast. Killed the tourist season. How about politics, or maybe the current economic situation. Or there's always what's going on in the Middle East."

"Funny, laugh it up," Collins said in a harsh whisper. "I called you out because I'm trying to keep you out of trouble, so if you want to drop the sarcastic bullshit I can tell you what this is about."

"Okay," Drake said with a noncommittal tone.

Remember the letter!

"Andrade called me in and said he found out you have been looking into the murder cases. Said Serena gave you access to the files."

Drake snorted. "That's bullshit."

"I sure as hell hope it is," Collins spat. "You're working the cage because of how badly you botched that case and you've already nearly ruined Dodd's career, so don't fuck with Serena's too. Or do I need to remind you of that young officer walking with a limp?"

Drake just stared at him.

"You're on dangerous ground," Collins said. "If I come back from this meeting and tell Andrade that you were defensive or an asshole he will cut you loose early, charge you with misconduct and leave you with nothing. Do you get that?"

"Yeah, but you've got this all wrong. I'm not working a case or anything like that. I'm working on a new book and I was using the Petre case as inspiration is all, for the novel."

"Drake, that is exactly why you are in the cage. Using the case for own personal gain is a gross breach of protocol. My God, if Andrade knew that, that alone would be grounds for suspension and firing."

Drake glared back him. "Look, what I do on my personal time is none of your business, or Andrade's. And I'm not disclosing anything about the case. Hell, how could I disclose what I don't know? The case is just inspiration, nothing more."

They both stopped talking when the waitress returned with their meals.

"Let's eat," Michael said, "then we'll talk."

Drake finished his breakfast before Collins, excused himself and went to the restroom. He took slow breaths and dabbed at his face with a damp paper towel.

Just agree with anything he says, he thought, *get this over with and then be more careful with your actions.*

Drake's plate was gone when he returned and Collins was eating his last bite of sausage. Michael pushed his plate to edge of the table and leaned forward.

"Look, a lot of shit has gone down since the old days. You think it has been easy for me to sit by and watch you balloon up and slide down? Jesus, Drake, you're working the cage! That's for women and old men who don't know when to retire."

"Okay, you made your point."

"Have I? When we were partners you were the guy everyone looked up to," Collins hissed. "We all saw you as Chief of Detectives someday. But that Hennings business almost took my career as well, you know that? I was in that seat with the flames of hell in my face just like you. That asshole is free today and you and I both know he did his wife!"

Collins' voice was hoarse, his eyes a bit wild.

"I know you went through it too," Drake said. "What do you want me to say?"

"That you will stop screwing around, stop sticking your fat ass where it doesn't fit and leave what is going on to the real cops. Okay? Just sit back, coast out the next couple of months and retire with some dignity and a pension. Otherwise you'll go down in history as one of the biggest fuck ups in the NYPD."

"Nice," Drake said with sneer. "Who writes your material?"

Collins leaned closer. "It makes no difference to me. I can go back and say I think you're a trouble-making rabble-rouser and watch you take the long walk goodnight. That what you want?"

"No," Drake said and lowered his head.

Just give him his power. Take what he's dishing out and know it is not true. Let him have this and then be careful. The letter, remember!

"Drake?" Collins gave him an angry stare.

"Yes, okay, I'll sit on my ass and stop being a screw up."

"Why don't I believe you?"

"What the hell would I do if I lost my pension? I'd be on the street in a month. I'll lay low, I promise."

"Good boy," Michael said and tossed a twenty on the table. "See you Monday." He got up and walked out.

Drake took his time finishing his coffee, thinking hard as he did so. Collins' words were heavy on his mind. When he left Molly's he walked along Glen Street and turned up University.

Damn Collins. Forget him and his holier-than-thou attitude and his fierce need to put Drake in his place. But wasn't everything he said true? When the circus started all those years ago, Drake had listened in dumbfounded shock to the evidence presented against him. Before the fall and the weight gain, Drake could handle himself in the field against perp and pimp, take a hit and take a fall. But in the arena of confident peers and angry superiors, he found out that his doubt was more powerful than his surprise and anger.

The letter felt hot in his pocket. The words might carry enough power to help him reclaim some personal honor. All he needed was a stamp and the possible truth could be in the hands of a man who could make a difference.

Drake's wandering brought him to the Hallmark Store on Justin Place. A display of Halloween knick-knacks and early Thanksgiving trinkets filled the windows. He pulled the envelope from his pocket and stared at it for a full minute. Michael's voice reverberated in his head and his eyes stung with anger. Drake set his jaw, entered the card store and walked to the small Post Office in the back.

"One stamp please," Drake said and pushed the envelope across the counter.

The tall, old and friendly-faced Postmaster tore a single stamp from a roll, dabbed it with a sponge and pressed it home. Drake felt an urge to reach out and tear the letter from the old guy's grasp, to opt for safety and the status quo. Instead he just watched as the Postmaster nonchalantly tossed the letter in the outgoing mail bin and wished Drake a happy Halloween.

"You too," Drake said and slowly walked back through the shelves of greeting cards, porcelain figures and novelty gifts. Halfway through the store he dropped in behind a short Puerto Rican girl with a large butt. She walked with a quick pace, her buttocks swinging with alluring heft. Drake was oblivious.

What if Smythe refused to believe? What if the Chief was part of the conspiracy? Drake's mind fought with screaming regret and he nearly ran back and demanded the letter.

Robin's voice whispered in his mind. *Oh Lou, listen to me. Have faith. I have faith in you.*

Drake fought to calm down. After all, what was the worst that could happen? He could get slapped down, called a nut case and kept under constant surveillance for the next three months.

Or he could get fired.

Have faith.

The store's front door opened and stayed that way. The young woman was holding it for him. Behind her a short, stocky black man leaned against the outside post, watching as Drake left the store. Drake knew the type. He had busted many of them in his career.

"Thank you miss," Drake said with a smile.

He turned right, still fighting the panic inside, his unhurried footsteps carrying him to nowhere in particular. A rough hand grabbed his shoulder and abruptly scattered his thoughts. When he turned back he was face to face with the stocky black man.

"That ain't cool," the guy spat.

Drake realized the man was younger than he first thought, the youth of his face hidden by an agitated hardness that Drake had seen on a thousand young black men just like him.

"Excuse me?"

"Knock it off, Leroy," the girl yelled.

The young man ignored her. "That ain't cool you staring at my lady's ass."

"What? Oh, trust me," Drake laughed, "I was not staring at your girlfriend's ass."

Drake took a step, dropped his head and continued his thoughtful walk but his arm was grabbed again. Drake turned and faced Leroy. Their eyes locked.

"Look," Drake said but the words were lost in the empty air between them. Eyes dark and shoulders tight, the boyfriend's entire body silently warned of attack. Drake blinked and broke the visual deadlock as Leroy threw a wide, right roundhouse.

Drake had no time to think. His body reacted as an old file in his mind automatically engaged from the ancient depths of his forgotten life. Drake raised his left arm, deflected the incoming punch and stepped into Leroy's momentum. He dropped his left shoulder to pin the kid's arm under his. Off balance from his own wild attack, Leroy dropped his right shoulder as Drake wrenched up with his left arm, spinning the kid in a half circle. Drake jammed his knee into the side of the attackers right leg, rendering him helpless. Any struggle caused Leroy pain and Drake tightened his grip.

"Stop moving," Drake said, "or I will dislocate your shoulder." The calm certainty in his own voice surprised Drake.

"Fuck you."

"Wrong answer," Drake growled and pushed harder.

Leroy howled in pain.

"Listen asshole," Drake said, "one of two things is going to happen. I will beat the goddamn shit out of you, or I will let you go and you will apologize to me for assaulting me and to your girlfriend for embarrassing her. What's it going to be?"

"Let me go," Leroy demanded.

Drake placed his balled fist against the young man's cheek and gave the arm one more wrench.

"All right, all right," the young man said, "I'll back down. It's cool."

Drake let go and shoved him away.

"Ha," Leroy laughed, though his eyes showed genuine fear. "Fuck you, you asswipe! You're lucky I was off my game. I woulda' kicked your ass!"

"That's too bad," Drake said and unzipped his jacket. "I figured you to be smarter, but I guess you're just stupid enough to take a swing at an off-duty police officer."

Drake pushed back his jacket to reveal the off duty revolver holstered high on his hip, he showed the kid his badge.

"Still want to kick my ass?" Drake asked. "I could haul you in right now for assaulting an officer."

"C'mon baby," the black kid sneered and walked his girl away, mumbling a stream of obscenities.

A few gawkers had stopped to watch the scuffle.

One of them called out. "You really a cop?"

Drake was trembling. His face was hot and he felt like we were going to be sick.

"Yes," he managed and sat down on the curb. "I'm a cop."

That simple declaration welled up inside him. A few short weeks ago he would have taken the punch and done nothing. But today he read the attack and reacted. The move came from his old Judo days, the commanding voice from when he was a Detective and the rational thought from a cop with experience. Drake looked at his shaking hands and started to laugh.

"You okay man?" a bystander asked.

"Never been better," Drake said.

He stood and turned back toward home. Let Collins make his threats. And screw the assholes that wanted him to shrivel up and blow away with a monthly check. The letter may lead to no more than extra trouble, but it was sent and now he was glad.

"Goddamn," he said with a happy edge in his voice.

He replayed the experience in his mind as though he was a spectator. His feet carried him with purpose and he felt like he could take on the world. He decided right then that he and Robin were going to use Halloween to celebrate the rise of a spirit – that of the once-dead Detective Lou Drake.

Gary White scrolled down his email list and sat back with a grunt. He had reviewed over three hundred messages in half a day and not found one he really cared to read. It was not that the queries were bad, though some were. It was the sheer futility of it all. No publisher wanted to hear from him. His contacts at the publishing houses had dried up or quit the business but he still received between a thousand and fifteen hundred queries from authors every week.

"Damn," he sighed when he refreshed the server and thirteen new queries added themselves to the deluge.

The most frustrating reality was that many of the ideas were actually quite good, ideas that he could have nurtured into saleable manuscripts five years ago. Today it was like casting lines with succulent bait into waters with no fish.

When his wife demanded that he should get a real job, he refused and she left. Then came the drinking and the eventual collapse. He was once a reasonably successful independent agent, and now he rented a street-level apartment next to the university with a view of the access steps to the upper street.

More queries came in through his mail server and he laughed.

"Sorry folks," he said and took another drink from the vodka bottle beside the computer. Tonight was Halloween and he looked forward to the revelry as a blessed distraction. He was prepared for trick-or-treaters as well as the assorted University students looking for a sweet handout. With a quickly carved pumpkin on the landing and a spooky CD running in his CD player, he would take part in the celebration and forget about his failed life, if only for a few hours.

His doorbell started ringing as staff from the campus came around with their children. Gary happily handed out generous wads of miniature candy bars. A few teenagers showed up and he made good-natured remarks about their age as he loaded sweets into their plastic grocery bags. Kids dressed in hellish garb drove by on the way to parties and Gary gave them all a friendly wave. By eight the revelry dissipated and he watched the street go quiet. Music wafted from homes as parties geared up, usually lasting until early morning. Gary felt a wave of regret. He was too old to join the fun. His ex-wife might disagree, but he suddenly felt a hundred years old.

At that moment nothing seemed more eerie than the post-rush loneliness as the visitors deserted him on Halloween night. Gary often imagined that this time of desolation was when the true ghosts of the holiday filled the streets to frolic in late October darkness. Eight to midnight, the time real ghosts danced in graveyards, long forgotten bones wailed for discovery and children screamed frantically in their beds, afraid of the dark. He imagined this as the time of real-life hauntings, when lonely spirits and giddy demons were brought out by the one night when society accepted them. The four most frightening hours of the year.

His jack-o-lantern smelled of burned cap and the candle was down to a struggling flicker when he switched off the porch light and poured himself another deep drink. Gary sighed as the bell rang. Latecomers. He took a swallow and opened the door to a trick-or-treater dressed in a hooded sweatshirt, a boney reaper mask and gloves with finger bones printed on the backs. Gary smiled and retrieved his candy bowl.

"I'll give you what I have left," he said, slurring the words slightly.

Gary turned and choked on a misty cloud, coughed and felt instantly woozy. He saw the figure pointing a small spray bottle, the red-tipped nozzle still dripping from the blast.

"What the hell?" Gary managed and then dropped to his knees.

With a grunt, Gary teetered to the right and fell with a slow, languid slump. He felt nothing when his head bounced off the parquet wood floor.

The skull-faced figure pulled a garish clown mask and a roll of duct tape from his sweatshirt. Gary caught these details with unfocused eyes as he slowly lost consciousness.

Gary's cheek felt bruised and his head throbbed as he regained consciousness. He was tied securely to one of his kitchen chairs. His mouth was gagged with what felt like a rag and his lips flattened beneath what must be duct tape. His eyes were shut and he could not open them. With each attempt he felt a sharp pain where his upper and lower lids met.

"I have glued your eyes shut and gagged you," a hushed voice said behind him. "If you struggle or try and get free I will cut your throat. Do you understand? Nod if you do."

Gary nodded vigorously.

"Good. You and I are going to have a little chat," his captor hissed. "I will ask you questions and you will nod for yes and shake your head for no. That clear?"

Gary nodded again; a whimper escaped his muffled mouth.

"Good boy. You know what's about to happen, don't you Mr. White?"

Gary nodded. The stories about agents being murdered lurched into his mind. He whined and instinctively struggled against the bindings as his stomach rolled. He gagged on the rag in his mouth. Sweat poured down his body and the room grew rank with fear and perspiration. He retched as his stomach tried to purge itself of the alcohol he had consumed earlier.

"Puke and you'll drown in your own vomit," the voice warned.

Gary swallowed hard. Trembling with fright and the effects of the sedative, he made fearful sounds through his nose. The breath of the masked attacker was at his right side and Gary whimpered as the words tickled over his ear like ants crawling on his skin.

"Okay now?"

A nod.

"Are we going to have any more problems with you losing it?"

A shake.

"That's very good."

Gary heard the killer move to sit in front of him.

"Your pumpkin was poorly carved and your drunken generosity is a black mark on the institution of Halloween. More than that, you are a poor excuse for a literary agent. You know that?"

A nod.

"Well," the sickeningly low voice said. "That is in itself a crime punishable by death. I see many query letters here, and your computer is filled with email queries as well. I know you have not sold a book in four years, but you still advertise yourself as an agent looking for new talent. Are you really looking for writers?"

A shake.

"That's what I thought," the voice said in a flat tone. "Gary, you are a sham and a liar. I was hoping I'd find you genuinely working to make something of yourself and the writers who for your help, but apparently you lure them in under false pretenses. Do you think it's fair for an agent to act that way?"

Gary knew there was nothing he could do. He prepared himself for whatever may come next and quietly prayed to a God he had not spoken to since the eighth grade.

"Gary, please take some solace in knowing you are becoming a part of the common good, a part of the revolution to inspire people to read again. You are becoming a story to be told, a tale spun around coffee tables and in local diners. The NYPD will make your name timeless. You will become a martyr for the cause. Your death will be glorious and part of the lasting mark I will put on the souls of all who struggle against the business of creativity in New York."

Gary drew a deep breath through his nose. Something stifling darkened the light coming through the thin flesh of his eyelids. It smelled of talcum powder and plastic.

"You're a clown Gary," the killer said as he secured the garish clown mask over White's head. "You are a joke and you have no vision. You stopped seeing the big picture. You ceased to have the sight necessary to carry the talent of the writer to the eyes of the publisher."

Gary breathed in great gulps and jerked when he felt something jab against his eyebrow.

"Stay still," the voice demanded. Gary locked his body, bathed in sweat and did not move when he felt a sharp poke on his eyelid. As delicate as a surgeon wielding a scalpel, the assailant pushed the point of an ice pick against the twitching and wrinkled skin of Gary's left eye and pushed forward with slow intent. Muffled by the tape and restrained by the rope, Gary swooned as a searing sank deeper into his core. By the time the killer addressed the second eye Gary was unconscious and his only movements were a few involuntary twitches.

"Do you see now?" the killer asked.

He expected no reply.

CHAPTER TWELVE

November clouded up again and freezing rain began around six in the morning. Collins caught himself dwelling on his meeting with Drake as he wheeled his Mustang carefully through the slick streets. The fat prick had pissed him off yesterday with his pathetic attempt to defend himself. What a loser. Collins could not believe Drake took the offensive out of the gate and how quickly he shriveled when challenged. Only three months more and it would all be over. After that Drake could eat himself to death, drink himself into a stupor or marry that fat doughnut girl and settle down in Jersey for all Collins cared.

By eight Collins brought his mustang to a stop in front of the Brownstone and pushed through the crowd milling outside 1264 Keller Avenue. Reporters filled the sidewalk above the scene and two television vans parked across the street. Reporters stabbed microphones like menacing sabers as Collins pushed past them and said nothing.

Below the street the well-heeled tenement offered four basement-level, rent-controlled studios. Access to the subterranean flats was down a flight of concrete steps to a master hallway that ran parallel to the street. Smelling of urine and mildew, the mossy walkway was lined with weather-scarred doors. One door stood open, crowded with uniformed officers.

"Collins," Thibido called from inside. "We've been waiting for you."

"I just got the call. What do we have?"

"It's bad," Thibido said in an unsteady voice.

Collins could see white around his eyes.

"Get some air, Thibido. Excuse me."

Collins elbowed his way in.

"Collins." Detective Reynolds gestured him over. "I want you to see this before the crew starts bagging things up."

"Christ almighty," Collins said and stared at the corpse.

The dead man was face down over a brown corduroy ottoman. He was naked with his arms hanging to the floor. His hands held bloody blobs in each palm. There was a great deal of blood dried to the color of rusted iron. The victim's legs were tied into a kneeling position and secured around the ottoman with yellow nylon rope. Gagged with duct tape, the victim's eyes were closed tight, as though still in throes of intense pain. The killer had opened the victim's back with an Exacto knife from the base of the head to the tailbone, the skin drawn back and held open with long nails driven into the shoulders, sides and hips. Exposed with careful surgery, the man's spine was morbidly white and splayed with tissue gone dry in the time since the guy had died. The small utility knife was left beside the victim on the bloodstained green shag carpet.

"Pretty gruesome, huh?" Reynolds said.

Collins looked carefully. "What's in his hands?"

"Judging from the amount of blood around the groin and buttocks, I'd guess it's his testicles," Reynolds said.

"Jesus," Collins said.

Collins stepped aside as the Coroner arrived. "All yours Harold."

The Coroner whistled. "Holy moley."

Collins and Reynolds walked up the stairs and helped the beat cops move the crowd back to establish a wider perimeter. Reporters called out questions. They seemed to have information not yet released. Either they were tipped off or some beat cop got a look and grabbed some airtime. The reporters begged for more information, but Collins blocked out their cries and leaned toward Reynolds.

"Any idea who this guy was?" Collins asked.

Reynolds handed him a card. "Right here."

Michael read aloud. "Thomas C. Mueller, Literary Agent."

"Ain't that a kick in the balls?" Reynolds asked.

"Fuck." Michael sighed and handed the card back.

Exposed spine and severed balls. The message seemed clear to Collins. Somebody considered this guy to be spineless, to have no balls.

The scene was days old and Collins shook his head. There could be others and he bet each and every one would have the same profession. There was no way around it; Malcolm had its own serial killer. This could not have come at a worse time.

"Gonna' call Andrade?" Reynolds asked.

"When I get back to the car."

"Lucky you."

Collins walked slowly to his Mustang, flipped open his cell and dialed Andrade's private number.

"Yeah," Andrade growled.

"It's another agent."

"Oh God, you're kidding. Okay, what's the scene?"

"Guy is bound naked. His spine has been exposed and his nuts cut off and put in his hands. The coroner is here. It's goddamn ugly."

Collins pinched the bridge of his nose.

"Come on in," Andrade said. "We need to talk about how we are going to handle this."

"There's press."

"Then we don't have too many options." Andrade's voice sounded flat and mechanical. "Just get back here."

"I'll be there in ten minutes," Collins said.

He flipped the phone closed and keyed the ignition. He stomped the gas and squealed his rear tires, raising smoke and leaving dry patches on the damp asphalt as he pushed the muscle car to the redline.

Things were going to get dicey.

While Collins sped back to the station, Lou was enjoying his day off by having breakfast with Robin, Sandy Anderson and Sandy's girlfriend Kelly. The four talked about writing and work. Eventually Sandy pushed Lou to tell the story of his altercation at the card shop. With a dramatic flailing of his hands Drake regaled them with the confrontation, dramatic struggle and Lou's victory over the punk.

"I wouldn't want to tangle with you," Sandy said. "You'd break me like a twig."

"Well, if I could get a hold of you. I'm pretty slow," Drake said.

"Well, I congratulate your restraint with the kid," Sandy said.

"Did that make you feel powerful?" Kelly asked.

Drake paused and then was honest. "Yes, it did."

"That's great. I bet you scared that punk straight as an arrow," Sandy said.

Later, once they were back home, Lou grabbed Robin from behind and they fell to the bed with urgent passion. Afterward Lou traced small circles on Robin's naked back and she made small noises of contentment.

"Oh," Robin said and rolled over. "I have to go to work. I'm doing a double so I won't see you later. Are we having dinner tomorrow night?"

"Yeah, sure," Drake said.

He watched her get dressed. Though Robin was forty years old most people thought she was ten years younger. She carried her weight like she was meant to be that size, with no sags or unsightly pockets of flesh. She was light on her feet and strong. She could almost beat Drake in arm wrestling.

"Take a picture," she said.

She wiggled into her pants, her breasts bouncing, and then restrained her bosom in a lace brassiere.

"You know you're sexy as hell," he said.

"Charmer," she said.

Robin pulled her purple Dunkin Donuts polo shirt over her head, kissed Lou, slipped into her shoes and left.

Drake laid back and dozed for an hour. He awoke with a troubled head, showered, and watched some television. 176 channels and nothing on so he tried to write but nothing came. Lou felt crowded in the small apartment so he pulled on jeans, slipped on a jacket and wandered into the village.

Drake reflected on the scene at the card shop. It was one for the books so he decided to do just that, to put the experience in his novel. His feet chewed up the blocks as he worked out how he would write the scene.

Half an hour later he found himself south of University in the older tenement district in front of officer Dodd's building.

Smythe's voice murmured in his head. *Been down to see him? I suggest you do that.*

Drake slowly climbed the steps, searched the names and pushed the button for Dodd.

"Yeah?" Dodd's voice crackled through the ancient speaker system.

"Dodd, it's Drake."

"Oh, I thought you were the pizza guy."

"Can I come up? I was out for a walk, so I decided to drop by."

Drake's voice was tentative, edged with apology.

"Uh, yeah, come on up."

"Hey, the Pizza's here too," Drake said into the speaker as a rusted Yugo pulled to the curb. A scruffy college kid got out and approached the door.

"Going to Dodd?" Drake asked.

"Yeah, apartment 412. Large pepperoni."

"How much?"

"Are you Dodd?" the kid asked.

"Just going to see him. I'll take care of that," Drake said.

"Okay, long as it's paid for."

Drake tipped five dollars and pushed through the old door to the landing. The elevator was out of order so Drake climbed the stairs and knocked on Dodd's door. Dodd opened it a crack, then took off the security chain and stood in the doorway on crutches. His right leg was in a full cast. He was unshaven and looked pale.

"Your pizza. I got it, the least I could do, right?"

"Sure, come on in," Dodd said.

As Drake stepped inside, his mind was working hard on how best to apologize. He figured he was going to have to eat crow along with a slice of pepperoni pizza, even if neither was on his new dietary regime.

CHAPTER THIRTEEN

"Another one," Serena whispered in Drake's ear when he arrived Monday morning. He gave her a questioning look as she feigned reading a report and nodded toward a sheet of paper on the counter. Drake quickly read through the report.

"Holy God," he said under his breath.

"Uh huh," she said.

She took the sheet and went back to the office.

Any Detective worth his grit could see the continuing message of the killings. Metaphoric references to all the body parts represented as sources of strength, pride, ability and spirit. Drake had no doubt that the killer was a writer, and a pissed off one at that. Hack or wordsmith, this individual must be fed up enough with the publishing game to lash out and make a statement.

He remembered what Franny had said: *they had it coming.*

Drake went to the bathroom. As he relieved himself he imagined the violence and the ease with which the killer performed his brutality.

Thibido came through the door with his usual lack of grace.

"Oh, hey there chubs," he cackled. "Hope I didn't catch you jerking off."

"Screw yourself," Drake said and walked to the door.

Thibido passed and intentionally brushed shoulders with Drake.

"Damn, wide load," Thibido mocked as he walked to the urinal.

Drake pushed back.

"Collins said you've been slacking when it comes to sucking his dick," Drake said. "He wants you to take a few more lessons from your mother."

Thibido went red and splashed himself with urine.

"Nice piss job," Drake laughed.

Childish, yes, but it gave him a sense of satisfaction to see Thibido's pants wet from the knee down.

"Screw you fat man," Thibido said as he zipped his fly.

"Keep your pants on asshole," Drake growled. "I'd break you like a twig"

Drake meant it and Thibido knew it.

While Drake returned to the cage Collins sat at his desk in the detectives office and scowled at the results of the forensics reports. There was zero evidence regarding the killer's identity; no prints, no fibers, no fluids. These scenes were absolutely clean of anything but the victim's body. The killer was like a ghost with a sick sense of retribution. No mystery why he killed. This perp seemed to be getting even for being rejected and, most likely, many, many times.

No forced entry. Two of the victims had been overpowered with a sprayed solution of strong tranquilizer and one had been tazed. Then all were slowly killed. How could anyone do this to another human being? It would take a strong stomach and a twisted psyche to be this methodically brutal.

Of course Michael had witnessed his own share of atrocities. When he was partnered with Drake they often stepped over horror to get a better look at a corpse and examine a scene. Thinking of Lou took Collins aback and he shook the head to clear the doubt. He focused back on the coroner's report and chewed his cheek.

"Jesus," Thibido yelled as he came through the door. His left pant leg was wet from the crotch to the knee. "Fucking Drake."

"What the hell happened?"

"Asshole Drake caused me to piss on myself. Son of a bitch," Thibido said and sat down at his desk.

"I won't ask," Collins said. He went to the coffee pot for a refill.

"Anything on the report?" Thibido asked as he dabbed at his leg with a ball of paper towels.

"Nothing," Michael said. "How did Drake make you piss yourself?"

"He's an asshole, that's how."

"Whatever," Collins said and closed the file.

"Son of a bitch," Thibido said. "What a way to start the week."

Pathologist Kathy Morey wrote at her desk in the basement morgue. Hollingsworth Memorial Hospital was originally built in 1930 as a white plague institution on what was an isolated patch of waterside land. That's why it was located far away from the population of New York City. The squat structure was sequestered on a sheltered cove only half a mile from the university. In 1930 it was only accessible by boat.

The building was five stories high and had a wall of windows on the seaward side, which were designed to be opened to treat the infected with the *fresh air* cure. Later proven to be ineffective, this supposed cure often contributed to the patient's demise from exposure in cold weather.

Kathy sipped coffee with her hand trembling as a result of examining the latest murder victim. The paramedics had brought the dead man in on his stomach so as not to disturb the mutilation. She hid her shock and conducted herself in a professional manner while there were others present. Once alone, though, she allowed herself a good cry. Prior to the murders her job was more administrative and this was more than she could handle.

When her phone rang she jumped, then answered with an irritated tone.

The emergency nurse said, "Captain Andrade is here to see you."

"Send him down," Kathy said.

She went to the restroom and checked herself in the mirror.

"Kathy?" Andrade called.

"Hi there," she said.

"Hey, you okay?" Andrade asked.

She nodded, her lips white from pressing them together. Tears continued to leak from the corners of her closed eyes.

"This..." she stammered, "this is inhuman."

"Yes," he said.

Kathy shook her head and took a wet breath.

"You should call in someone else besides me on this, you know that?" she said. "Sorry, but this is out of my league."

"No apology needed," he said. "I hate that you have to be a part of this."

Andrade gathered her in his arms and she clung to his broad shoulders.

She gave him a quick kiss. "But just because my lover is the Captain of the precinct doesn't mean I'm shielded from the atrocities of the world."

"This is freaky for all of us," Andrade said. "I already put the call into the main station and officially surrendered this whole mess to the Chief of Detectives Smythe. They are sending a crew to work the investigation and the FBI is sending down a special agent named Thatcher. I guess he has handled this kind of thing before."

"What forensic pathologist are they sending?"

"A doctor. Melvin Prichard. You know him?" Andrade said.

"Oh yes," she said.

Kathy broke the embrace and sat down on a stool beside the examination table. Around them aluminum gleamed, bottles shone under the lights and the antiseptic smell of treated death permeated everything.

"Prichard's the best there is," she said. "He has written half a dozen books, and works with TV and Hollywood as a consultant to make sure the fake doctors sound real. He has broken more cases than Perry Mason and I studied under him at Harvard."

"Heavy hitter," he said.

"When will they be here?" Kathy asked.

"First thing Wednesday morning. This is officially out of our hands." Andrade gave her a concerned look. "You okay?"

"Fine," she said. "It will give me time to look this over again, review what I wrote on the last two victims and have a semblance of a clear report when Prichard arrives."

"See you tonight?" Andrade asked. "Sharon and the kids are visiting her sister in Albany for the weekend."

"Sure, yeah. I'll be done here in a few hours and we can have dinner."

"Perfect," he said.

"I'll see you later," she said.

Andrade left and Kathy stared at the poor soul on the metal table. His life had been extinguished and his mind was free of the worries of the world.

Sure, he was split from head to tail bone and his testicles were in a plastic bag, but at the moment of death she wondered if the horror was worth the release. Can a soul find peace after a hideous trauma?

Kathy felt her own torment. Hers came from Captain Andrade who lied to her daily. He lied about leaving his wife, about his love for her and the future they would supposedly have together. She lamented the wasted time, wasted life and wasted heart. She stared at the long galvanized nails holding the victim's skin back from the wound and felt the same steely punctures in her self esteem.

Pulling on a fresh pair of latex gloves Kathy leaned over the dead man and pushed her disgust into the same dark place she put her self-respect. An hour later she was finished categorizing the traumas and called the coroner. She knew he was waiting in his office on the fifth floor for Kathy's preliminary examination before he could perform the autopsy.

"Harold?" she said.

"Hello beautiful," he said.

For a man who dealt with death all day, coroner Harold Olson was strangely upbeat and notoriously giddy.

"I'm done. Mr. Mueller is ready for you."

"Tell him to keep his pants on," he joked.

Olson could always make her feel better. Though she never experienced it herself he was known for his antics in the field.

"I'll ask him to be patient," Kathy said.

"Be right down," Olson said.

Kathy gave the corpse one last glance and went to clean up for her date with Captain Andrade.

CHAPTER FOURTEEN

Monday morning brought freezing rain and miserable conditions to the coastal towns as snow fell upstate. Malcolm's streets were vacant as most people stayed away from the university unless they absolutely had to be there. An occasional shuttle carried a shivering student from housing to the campus, and then the streets fell back into the desolate loneliness of freezing isolation.

The black Lincoln Navigator had no trouble with the wet highway as it carried six men toward Hollingsworth Memorial. Along with the driver, the five passengers were Henry Smythe, NYPD homicide Detectives Thames and Johnson, FBI special agent Kenneth Thatcher and Dr. Melvin Prichard. Compared to the detectives, Agent Thatcher looked too big for the space given him. He was six foot five inches tall, and his height was only overshadowed by his size. Thatcher looked comical in his suit as his muscular frame strained against the cut of his clothes.

"We're nearly there," the driver said. He pointed through the gloomy weather to the mist-shrouded hospital.

"Drop us off at the emergency entrance," Smythe said.

The driver drove into the back lot and pulled up to a red painted curb where a bold illuminated sign hung above a set of double doors leading into a well-lit reception area.

"Thank you," Smythe said.

The five exited the SUV and quickly headed for the dry building. The doors swished open and closed slowly behind them. Warm air washed over them and Kathy Morey greeted them. She asked them to follow her to the morgue.

"Is Captain Andrade here?" Smythe asked.

"He's waiting for us."

"This is special agent Thatcher," Smythe said.

Kathy gave the agent a smile.

"It's a pleasure," Thatcher said.

Staff members watched the giant walk by and he gave each of them a pleasant smile. Thatcher was used to this. It happened everywhere he went. His former partner, now retired, used to call him the hulk. It fit.

"We'll take the elevator," Kathy said and pushed the button at the end of the hall. "It's only one flight down, but the stairwells are not heated."

They descended the single floor and exited into a long hallway with a gray tiled floor. Double doors led to the morgue and the pathology department.

"Right this way," Kathy said as she opened the door to the dead.

Andrade popped a breath mint as Kathy and the team came into the morgue. Kathy made fast eye contact with Andrade, then she blushed slightly and looked down. Andrade was practiced in politics, the consummate diplomat. He extended his hand to Smythe, who was leading the group.

"Captain," Smythe said with a nod. "You know Detectives Thames and Johnson. This is special agent Thatcher from the bureau. And this is Dr. Prichard."

"Welcome," Andrade said.

At six foot three Andrade nearly looked Thatcher in the eye, but the sheer volume of space Thatcher occupied made the Captain feel small.

My God, Andrade thought, *his hands alone are twice the size of mine.*

"Well, let's make this official," Thatcher said. "As of the discovery of the third victim and the obvious nature of these cases, the FBI is considering taking over the investigation of these murders. Thames and Johnson will examine all the collected evidence and Prichard's forensics team will be here in an hour to start cataloging the material. For now I am strictly an observer until the evidence proves undeniably this is a serial case and needs to go federal."

"You have our fullest cooperation," Andrade said.

The double doors opened and Coroner Olson made his usual convivial entrance.

"Sorry I'm late. Busy, busy, busy. Holy Christ, you are a seriously large specimen," he said with a laugh when he caught sight of Thatcher. "Can I ask what you bench press?"

"Nice to meet you," Thatcher offered.

"No, seriously, what do you bench press?"

Thatcher smiled. "Four hundred and twenty-five pounds."

Olson whistled.

"May we see the bodies now?" Prichard urged.

Olson and Kathy opened two of the wall drawers and slid the corpses out. Andrade watched Kathy for signs of distress but she was the pinnacle of professionalism.

"We still have victims two and three," Olson said as he unzipped the black bags. "Victim one was claimed by his family after our preliminary investigation. We have full files on his case, complete with autopsy photos and the recording of the procedure. We kept full samples. His family has already buried him in their plot in Buffalo but agreed to allow exhumation if required. Our third victim has no family we could reach. His ex wife cared less; no kids and a brother that we learned is cave diving in Central America. All efforts are being made."

"Thank you," Prichard said.

He began the tedious chore of examining the bodies, reading through the reports and asking questions of Olson and Kathy. Thatcher took off his jacket and rolled up his shirtsleeves. Kathy watched as Thatcher listened intently to the discussion and made notes on a legal pad.

"We are dealing with a classic sociopath, most likely pathological, focused in his tasks," Thatcher said. "I have faced these types before and I have a scar on my abdomen as a reminder. In 2001 my partner and I worked a case in the California mountains. I underestimated the killer then and I'll never make that mistake again."

"I can imagine," Kathy said.

Smythe looked at Andrade. "Where is the rest of the evidence taken from the crime scene?"

"At the station," Andrade said. "We boxed it up and have it in a locker in our secure facility."

'Do we have access to the crime scenes,?" Prichard asked.

"Absolutely. I would just need to make a call."

Another black Navigator pulled up to the hospital, followed by a large panel van that held a mobile command center digitally connected to the entire NYPD database. Within an hour the staff of six was sorting through the paperwork, as well as the evidence taken from each murder site.

Drake was miserable in the cold. The walk from the station to his car was punishment and the trek across the parking lot to the bookstore was just as tough. Drake, now twenty-two pounds lighter, pushed through the door and pulled off his gloves to rub his hands together while blowing on them. His scalp tingled beneath his cap and he felt a shiver up his spine as the store bathed him in relief. His cell rang and he flexed his fingers before answering. It was Robin.

"Hi honey," she sang in his ear. "I'm taking a break. Where you at?"

"Bookstore," he said.

"Visiting your writer friends? Good for you. I'm working until eleven then going straight home. I have to be back at six, Helen called in sick."

"Okay. I'll drop by in the morning. Call me after your shift and we'll have phone sex, okay sexy?"

"Drake." She laughed with girlish glee. "What's gotten into you?"

"I just feel good. Too much for you?"

"Got me hot as a pepper."

"I went to see Dodd," he said. "I bought him a pizza and we sat and talked. After a couple of beers we got to laughing and he accepted my apology and shook my hand."

"And you feel better now?"

"Yeah, I guess that has a lot to do with it," Drake said.

"I'm proud of you," she said. "When was this?"

"Couple of days ago, should have told you sooner."

"I'll call and you'll have the best phone sex ever," she said.

Drake made his way to the coffee bar.

"Officer Drake," Sandy called with a wave. "Come join our motley crew and let us talk of the day's events."

Drake waved back. "Be right there. I need a coffee."

"Hey Drake," Shakespeare called out as he surfed the net on his laptop. "What's the hub-bub down at the station about this latest killing? News said the guy was another agent. That right?"

Drake carried his cup to an open chair and set his bulk down with a sigh. All afternoon he had passed his time in a state of agitated expectation, because he knew the writers would ask about the murders. He shrugged off his jacket and shook Sandy's hand.

"The new victim is indeed an agent," Drake said. "Guy named Thomas Mueller. The news announced his name an hour ago. Anybody know him?"

Shakespeare said, "That's the bastard who signed me and dropped me because I wouldn't cut my book."

"So you killed him?" Pooter jibed.

"Yeah, then danced over his corpse," Brian said.

Sandy put up is hand. Like Jesus calming the seas he quieted the raucous voices and rubbed his chin.

"Three agents are dead," he said. "That means one of us has gone wrong."

"One of us," Franny asked and put her hands to her chest. "In this group?"

"A writer, I mean," Sandy said. "Someone has taken it personally and has decided to do something about it. I heard a reporter say it was the likes of Jack the Ripper. Tell us Drake, is all this true?"

"Afraid it is," he said, feeling important. "I've seen the reports. I can't tell you the details but this perp is brutal. The victims are mutilated and defiled. The killer is making a statement, and I would guess whoever it is has gone pretty nuts."

"Or has the ultimate clarity of thought," Sandy said. "Insanity, maybe, but the intent is as clear as a bell. Do they have any idea who it is?"

"No."

"That says a lot," Shakespeare chimed in. "It means the killer is careful not to make any mistakes. If they had evidence, fibers, prints, hair, that sort of thing, they'd have an idea by now."

The group stared at him blankly.

"You seem pretty sure of that information," Drake said.

"I watch that TV show, you know, C.S.I.?" Brian explained in a small voice. "And I read a lot of Patricia Cornwell."

"You could put that in a book and sell it," Franny jibed.

"I have," he answered. "They didn't buy it."

"Imagine it," Sandy said and folded his hands behind his head. "Right now one of us could be sitting here with the proverbial blood on our hands and smiling in the faces of the rest. It could be me, Brian, Pooter. Even Franny,"

"I went out with Tom Mueller once," Franny said, her face pale. "We met at a book signing in Greenwich. I thought I could make friends and maybe get him to look over my work. He wasn't impressed and he stopped calling."

"She did it," Carl Nesbit said and slapped the table.

It broke the tension and got a laugh.

"Or maybe I did," Nesbit said with a laugh.

"No, it was me," Pooter said and there were more laughs.

Drake took in the ghoulish satisfaction these writers were getting from the deaths. If he were to think like a Detective, Drake realized any one of this group could be the killer.

CHAPTER FIFTEEN

The Station 10 staff emptied interrogation room 2 for the forensics team. The janitor scrubbed all surfaces and cleaned the ceiling with a special water trap vacuum system. He even blocked off the building ventilation system and installed an air purifier to scrub the air before hauling in the evidence from downstairs. A covering of fresh white butcher paper for three long tables completed the job, along with rolling box of drawers filled with instruments of discovery for each table.

Dressed in white 'clean' suits, their eye behind goggles and hands covered in latex gloves, three teams of two people categorized the evidence into bins. A separate table held every piece of paper taken from all three sites. As each of the victims were page merchants there was a great deal to process. Each scrap was scanned beneath a special light to detect any fluids, hidden messages or telltale markings. A spray solution exposed fingerprints and there were many, each to be cross-checked through the national database.

Though the work was tedious and laborious, the droning hours of processing the tiniest piece of evidence was a labor of love for these people.

As one paper-sorting technician scanned for yet another fingerprint, she skimmed the text of each page. Taking in the text broke up the monotony and kept her mind sharp. It was a game, a way to convert the tedium into a brain tester. Catch a line, recall it before she placed the sheet in a sterile box and put the next page through the digital scanner. As the blue light from the machine traced down the paper, she ran her eyes over the text and grabbed another cryptic message.

... came through the window, the man wept as his wife slowly passed away...

... as the sun rose over fields of gold, the clouds drew back like curtains...

... the opportunity to present myself for representation for my novel...

.... Drew rave reviews from the judges at the LAUN Writers conference...

So many messages on so many sheets about the same thing, about different stories.

Scan and read and box and scan and read and box and scan and read. Two hours went by and the team collectively stayed focused on their specific tasks.

Then the technician stopped and stared at the paper as it was copied into digital pixels by the traveling blue light. Spattered with blood, the text was as ordinary as any sheet she had scanned so far. The size and quality of the print was identical to so many others she had already tested. What caught her eye was what she read and took to memory. This batch of paper was found at murder scene number two, the Paul Orland case.

... the killer pulled against the rope and hefted the limp bulk of the man until he was within an inch of the pull up bar. His neck bulging upwards to the jaw from the pressure of the dog chain, the bone-shaped license jingled sickly against the metal noose. 'Answers to Rufus' was etched in the red aluminum and the victim gasped as he slowly choked to death...

"My God," she said. "I found something."

"What is it Andrea?" Prichard asked.

"Smoking gun. You won't believe this."

His hands held high so as to not cross contaminate anything, Prichard leaned over and peered at the paper. He read aloud as the entire team listened.

"My God," he said after finishing the reading, "this is a detailed written account of the killing. A complete description. Everyone, drop what you are doing and look for more like this. There must be more."

The team abandoned their present tasks and carefully looked through the remaining reams of paper from the Orland scene. Unfortunately they found nothing else of apparent value.

"Okay," Prichard said, "now let's go through the paper from the other murder scenes."

For the next hour all eight technicians sifted through the stacks. They took a break and came back to the tedious task of skimming the contents of hundreds and hundreds of pages. Another hour lumbered by before another member of the team called out that she found a page describing Petre's murder.

"Listen to this," she said. *"His mind clear but his body unresponsive, the victim could do nothing as the blade made its terrible pass along his abdomen and cut away the muscle and flesh holding in his intestines. Petre thought of nothing but the odd sensation of his guts spilling onto his legs and the unfamiliar tug from deep inside. There was no pain, only surprise. He wondered how long a man could live with his intestines outside of his body. Not long, he feared."*

"Again, a perfect match," the tech said.

"It certainly is," Prichard said. "Keep looking."

Another hour.

"Found it," one of the shrouded searchers called out excitedly. He held up the single sheet of paper. "It reads like the others. My God, do you realize the ramifications of this?"

"Absolutely," Prichard said.

He excused himself to call Captain Smythe.

"I'm surprised this clue wasn't discovered before," Chief Smythe said. He sat back in Andrade's chair.

Andrade was uncomfortable sitting on the wrong side of his own desk. He knew that Smythe was flexing his seniority. Taking a cop's desk was like a dog pissing on another's turf. Special agent Thatcher sat quietly in a chair by the door, his face placid and his eyes alert. Even though the human mountain did not say much, his silence spoke volumes to Andrade regarding his authority.

"Well sir," Andrade said, "these were single pages mixed in with all of other pages in the three apartments. Besides, the search was not for evidence in the text, but an examination of the surfaces regarding fingerprints and possible fluids. It was luck that the tech scanning the pages read the words to break up the tedium of her repetitive job. This was about luck, not skill."

"You're telling me the content of those manuscripts and the correspondence in those stacks would never have been reviewed?"

"Not by my office," Andrade said. "Later by forensics, probably. Chief, we shouldn't look at this as a deficiency in the investigation. We should be grateful this unexpected evidence came to light."

"Spoken like a true politico," Smythe said. He tapped his right index finger against his cheek. "I suppose you're right about that, but we're getting some serious heat now that the press is all over this. And now it is officially federal."

Thatcher surprised them both with his voice. "My guess is the killer was looking for exactly this kind of press coverage. That would be consistent with the standard profile of a clever serial killer. Most perps like this become bored with the thrill of outwitting the police and develop an unrelenting need to start taunting us. These killers are generally attention junkies and will eventually start a dialog of some sort. Usually by mail."

"Maybe now that he has the world's attention he will stop," Smythe said. "The message he is trying to relay about literary agents is pretty obvious. It certainly has people talking. Last night I watched a newscast where they focused on what literary agents do and how the publishing world has changed."

"I doubt the attention will halt the killings," Thatcher said. "It will, most likely, feed a need for more of the same. That would fit the profile to the letter."

"So, what next?"

"I suggest we follow the broadcast focus," Thatcher said. "Do some research of our own into publishing trends."

"Meaning?" Smythe asked.

"Talk to some agents and publishers. Get some hard data on what has this crazy asshole so pissed off."

"That's a great idea," Smythe said. "Do it right away and have a report for me within the week."

"Yes Chief," Andrade said.

"Listen to this," Thatcher said and read the last page found.

"The killer tugged on the yellow nylon rope, checking to be sure the victim could not escape. With the dosage of sedative he was carrying, it was unlikely the naked man could move, let alone struggle free.

Taking his time, the world asleep and his actions as secret as a confession, the killer put the blade at the base of the naked neck and pushed in until pearls of blood squirted from the flesh. The red drops ran in streams down the to the corduroy ottoman. Firmly and slowly the killer's hand drew the blade down the victim's back and marveled at how the skin opened, exposing the pink wrapped backbone like a lover opening a robe."

"I know, I read all three," Andrade said.

"There is even a page number at the bottom," Smythe said. "They are in order, as though the killer is writing a book about the murders. Page 47, 68 and 156. To write something like this you have to know the place, the furniture and everything else at the scene. So this killer cases the victim, writes this out, comes in, does the deed and then leaves this behind for anyone to find. What's that about?"

"Pretty original," Andrade offered.

"Certainly dramatic," Thatcher said. "The report says the paper is ordinary bond and printed with a laser printer in 12 point Courier. As common as anything. Gone are the days where we can identify the make and model of the typewriter used. The digital age has washed away all individuality with regard to crime."

"Indeed." Smythe said with a sigh. "Well, look into what we discussed and get me a report."

"I'll put Collins on it," Andrade said and stood up.

"And I suggest Drake," Thatcher added.

"Drake?" Collins asked, his voice up an octave.

"He's a writer and a cop. They used to be partners. He seems like a capable man and I would like his take on all this."

Thatcher gave Andrade a glare of conviction. It was not a request but an order.

"I agree," Smythe said with a nod, "Collins and Drake."

"Yes sir," Andrade said.

Smythe surrendered the chair, shook Andrade's hand and left the office with Thatcher.

John Andrade took his seat behind the desk and resented the warmth left behind by his superior.

Drake? He guessed it made a certain semblance of sense but Collins would not like it. Too goddamn bad, that was the deal. Besides, that hulk of an FBI agent was not to be argued with.

After returning to Station One, Smythe sat at his desk and read through the photocopy of the letter Drake had sent him. The letter expressed the late Chief Fitzpatrick's concern regarding the Hennings case, and reading the words made Smythe eager to give Drake the opportunity to prove himself. He thumbed the page and read over the short typewritten note from Drake asking for Smythe's attention. The day they spoke in the station Drake had a sullen and angry look to him. Smythe had the sense that the fallen career was a bitter taste Drake could not remove from his tongue.

Smythe prided himself on his ability to read cops. He felt like he knew their inner intentions despite their spoken words. He saw no conflict in Lou Drake, sensed no hidden guilt or shame in his soul. Instead he saw only a tired and self-doubting man in a holding pattern to retirement, confused as to what derailed his life.

This was certainly not consistent with Drake's previous reputation. Smythe understood that many things could take a cop down. Booze, greed, loss of faith and stress can render a cop ineffective. So often officers, especially detectives, crashed from the stress the job brings.

Smythe didn't feel this was the case with Detective Drake. During the Hennings investigation Drake was the image of professionalism and confidence. Smythe saw him become genuinely shocked and demoralized when the case crumbled and he was called on the carpet. No, this was a not a cop taken down by the rigors of police work. Drake was torn down.

Smythe once watched a TV special on the job of demolition experts. He was fascinated by the science and deliberate system of placing charges in holes drilled in supports and bearing walls. When blown, the structure collapsed under its own weight. That was Lou Drake. Someone had placed charges to make sure Drake was taken down like an old building.

"Helen," Smythe called through to his secretary. "I want to see whatever we have on the Hennings case."

"Hennings?" she sounded surprised.

"Yes, Joshua Fairbanks Hennings. I want to see whatever we have on that case."

"Yes sir," she said.

Then he dialed down to the Detective's department and asked to speak to Paul Kellerman.

"This is Kellerman." Paul's voice sounded distracted.

"Hello Detective Kellerman, it's Smythe."

"Yes Chief."

"Two things. Do you have time to come up and have a chat?"

"Certainly sir," Kellerman said.

"Good, and I also need your dad's home phone number. I want to talk to him as well."

"My father?" Kellerman's tone shifted to worry.

"Relax son," Smythe said with a chuckle. "You're in no trouble. If you were, your father would be the last to know."

"Yes sir." He told Smythe the phone number. "I'll be right up."

"Thank you."

Yes, the God's honest truth needed to be uncovered regarding Hennings. Smythe wanted to have a clean conscience as he watched Drake exit his police career into civilian life. Whether it was a set up or a screw up, Smythe needed clarity on this one.

CHAPTER SIXTEEN

"Drake?" Collins yelled into his cell phone. "They're pairing me up with Drake?"

"That's right," Andrade said from the other end.

Collins fumed. "You have to be shitting me!"

"Afraid not. We need this ASAP."

"Jesus Christ," Collins hissed. He keyed his ignition and the Mustang's angry growl matched his own. "Fucking Drake, that fat asshole just won't stay down."

Collins returned to the station and went straight to the cage. Drake was busy tapping an arrest report and looked up when Michael cleared his throat.

"Hey partner," Drake said and smiled. "Gonna' be just like old times, huh?"

Collins glared at him in exasperated surprise. "You already know about this?"

"Got the word from the big man himself. Chief Smythe called and told me we were partnered to go interview some publishing folks. I'm jazzed."

"Jazzed?" Collins mocked. "Jesus Lou, this is not a field trip. And it's not an opportunity for you to talk up your writing either. Strictly business."

"Yeah, I know. Don't worry. I got us an appointment this afternoon with big time agent Nancy Callahan at Roth & Associates, and we have a meeting tomorrow with Jerry Shapiro, managing editor with Halberson Publishing."

"How did you manage that, exactly?"

"I dropped Dr. Prichard's name," Drake said. "Both agreed immediately. The meeting with Nancy is in two hours. We see Shapiro tomorrow afternoon. The Chief wants me in civilian clothes so we don't make anybody nervous. I'll run home and change and we should leave in an hour."

"Whatever," Collins said and walked away.

"Don't mention it," Drake said and spun in his chair.

"Mmm-hmm," Serena said. "Back on the street, I see."

"You're not leaving us, are you?" Edna asked.

"No, just got an assignment for the afternoon," Drake said.

"Good for you," Regina said and helped herself to another doughnut.

Drake took his time and picked out an outfit that would project professionalism. His weight had dropped a total of twenty-six pounds and he was happy to fit into some of his older clothes. He pulled on khaki pants, buttoned his shirt with excitement and slipped on a corduroy sport jacket with leather elbow patches. Tasseled leather shoes finished the ensemble. Standing before the mirror he looked nothing like a cop and exactly like a writer. Drake was fine with that.

Back at the station he waited for Collins to come out of Andrade's office.

Thibido looked in as he passed the cage. "Look at you," he chided. "Got a hot date with a hippo?"

"No," Drake shot back. "Your mom and I are going to get the results of her AIDS test. She said next time you should use a rubber."

"Jesus," Regina said with an admiring smile. "That was cold. I didn't know you had that in you."

"Blow it out your ass," Thibido said.

Drake gave him a vicious smile.

"Drake," Collins called from down the hall. "Let's go."

Avenue of the Americas stretches out like the movie set of a quintessential New York landscape. Here business and commerce embrace the swirling lifestyle of the printed word. The place is lousy with magazines, book publishers and high rent offices, all connected by text message, phone lines and power emails that jump from one side of the concrete canyon to the other. Careers are made and lost in the high buildings as agents and editors take calculated risks on the words written by hopefuls, veterans and newcomers.

So often the sure-thing books are backed by generous advances and marketing strategies, only to languish on bookstore shelves. Those authors disappeared like snow from the streets come spring. The majority of authors were paid paltry advances on books with minimal sales targets, which occasionally and inexplicably rocketed to international sales and film options.

With each deal futures were made and lost. Queries and proposals flew through the windows as though they were flocks of birds, each hoping to find a perch. The majority flew back from whence they came from. This journey to greatness nearly always began on the steps of Roth & Associates and other agencies like them.

Nancy Callahan started out as a junior agent in a small office in Greenwich twelve years ago. Her beauty and marketing background gave her an edge and she used both to slowly negotiate the maze that was the publishing game. Besides her easy manner and ability to schmooze, she had talent for guessing the trends that are often as flighty as the authors that milled them. Nancy predicted the teenage vampire craze and was the first to take a chance on a relative nobody, reaping the rewards that made her client a household name and made Nancy a genuine player. Her twentieth floor corner office allowed her a view of the entire marketplace.

Today she stared out those powerful windows and saw nothing, her mind on the latest news and the policemen on their way up to speak with her. They came looking for insight. She knew she could give it to them, since she was no stranger to unstable writers with any number of delusions or neuroses. More than one restraining order was implemented over the years. And the threats of death? They came on a regular basis, rarely taken seriously as it was the last resort of the frustrated creative.

"Nancy," her assistant came through on the speaker. "Officers Collins and Drake are waiting for you in the conference room."

"Thank you, be right there."

Nancy checked her hair, touched up her lipstick and flashed her signature smile in the mirror. Her navy blue suit was cut to flatter her shape. The open-neck cream silk blouse plunged just enough to expose the curve of her bust without being inappropriate.

"Okay, let's do this," she said to herself.

The two cops stood as she entered.

"Hello officers," she said and extended her hand.

Collins introduced himself and she gave him a nod.

"That makes you officer Drake," she said as she gestured for them to sit down. "I understand you are working with Dr. Prichard. One of my associates is his literary agent. What can I do to help you today?"

"You are aware of the killings in Malcolm," Collins said.

"Yes, horrible situation. The news is making a spectacle of it."

Collins said, "We are here because we were hoping you could give us some insight into what we are dealing with. I've done some preliminary investigating into the book trades and I was amazed to see just how many agents there are, and also how many writers are trying to get published."

"Yes, there is a flood of inquiries out there. Unfortunately it is much like acting where there are a thousand actors for every part. Hollywood is the same. Too much talent for the marketplace, I'm afraid. But it wasn't always like that."

"In what way?" Collins asked.

'Technology has shifted the face of publishing," she said.

She made eye contact with Drake. He was quiet, though his face projected an air of knowledge, as though he knew some of the answers the thin cop asked.

"Would you agree with that, Officer Drake?"

"Oh, yes," he answered.

Collins gave him a sideways glance.

"See," Nancy continued, "in the old days a writer was someone who had the tenacity to sit down and type out a manuscript on an old fashioned typewriter, or by hand."

"Why is that different from today?" Collins asked.

"Oh, it's night and day. When I graduated from high school and was working toward a journalism major, there were no resources like today. Computers were expensive and even word processing systems were too costly for the average starving writer. No Internet, no Microsoft Word, no auto spell checkers and easy saving programs or writer's resources and easy access to agents through web sites."

She took a breath and allowed a dramatic pause.

"There was a time where writing a novel was a back-breaking chore that required writing and rewriting and endless changes and editing that required more writing and typing of several drafts. What came to the agent was rough but inspired and it was considered a great achievement. The chance of getting published was pretty good because only the truly driven had the ability to go the distance. Those writers, real writers, put blood, sweat and tears into their work."

"That's true," Drake said. "I found it a tough road even ten years ago."

"So you write?" she asked.

He nodded.

Collins looked displeased and Nancy recognized the power struggle that was going on between the two. She liked Drake and found Collins abrasive.

"What do you write about?" she asked.

"That's not important," Collins said. "Could I ask you if..."

"Officer Collins," she interrupted him, "to say that Officer Drake's insight as a writer is not important is closed-minded of you. I think his opinion has a great deal of bearing on this discussion. So, please, don't allow your own ego to get in the way of accomplishing what you came here to do."

"Okay," Collins said. "Getting back to the point."

"I think Officer Drake can help me explain this more clearly," she suggested.

"Fine," Collins surrendered. His voice was as sharp as broken glass.

"What Nancy means," Drake offered, "is now any shaved monkey with a computer can take the time and use the resources to create something they think is great. The market is flooded. It has become counter-productive for agencies to sift through the mess to find the real talents and the good books."

"Well put," she said. "He's exactly right. My boss says that when she was making a name for herself in the seventies, most writers came from or moved to New York. The industry was here. She was lucky if she saw twenty ideas a month and the publishers were always clamoring for new talent. Back then, people who read, well they read a lot and we had to work this business to fill the demand. Imagine this, I now get between five and six thousand queries a week even though my web site says I am not accepting new talent."

"A week," Collins said as though he suspected an exaggeration.

"Wow," Drake said.

"Yes, and in January I receive more than that. Half of those come by email and most of what I get is absolute drivel. And I don't get that volume because of who I am. The lesser agencies get more because new writers think if they go with a hungrier agency they have a better chance. But those agents have less influence and fewer connections with editors at the publishing houses. That makes publishing through those agents an even more difficult proposition."

"I am affiliated with a writer's group," Drake added, "and all the members talk about the difficulty of trying to get representation. It seems to be universal."

"Back in the day getting an agent was the easy part," Nancy said. "Then getting sold was the issue. Now all the arenas are too crowded and there is just not room for all who want to be the next big thing. Ironically, the very thing that makes writing and marketing a book easier is also the reason it is harder to get published."

"So writers spend years beating their fists against the door and nobody opens up," Drake said. "There must be a lot of animosity out there."

"That's it in a nutshell," Nancy said. "The simple truth is there is too many hungry mouths and just not enough food to go around."

"But wouldn't you say these killings are an aberration?" Collins asked. "Most angry or frustrated writers don't take this sort of revenge."

"Oh, I get plenty of hate mail, insults and death threats," she laughed. "Writers are artists and many are unstable and suffer from all kinds of things. See the security downstairs? People think that was installed after 9-11. Truth is we've had armed security ever since a writer suffering from some affliction shot a junior agent in our lobby in 1994. This writing business is a very emotional thing. As for the killings, yes obviously it is extreme, even for an angry writer."

"I see, well, we appreciate your time and thank you for the information," Collins said.

"I haven't told you anything that Officer Drake could not have made clear. Are there any leads? Do have an idea of who the murderer is?"

"We have leads and are working all the angles," Collins said. "This has helped us enormously."

Nancy gave him a calculating look. "Thank you for saying so, but I feel that is not true. Call it a habit of the business savvy agent, but I can detect bullshit like a mouse smells cheese."

"Well, we do thank you for your time," Collins said and stood to leave.

"My card," she said and handed one to each cop.

She knew Collins had no use for it, but Drake? It was a highbrow case and he seemed a sharp guy. Who knows, something just may come along that would benefit both of them.

"Thank you," Drake said.

Nancy smiled widely for him. Collins looked sullen and put the card in his pocket, most likely to throw it away later. Nancy knew Drake would put it somewhere safe. She watched them leave the office.

Out in the hallway Collins glowered at his former partner.

"Jesus, Drake. What the hell was that all about? You know each other?"

His voice was edgy and Drake thought he was probably more embarrassed than angry.

"I just knew what she was talking about. I've done some research."

"I did the research too, " Collins snapped. "Tomorrow you keep your goddamn mouth shut and let me do the investigating. My God, you made an asshole out of yourself up there trying to kiss her ass."

"That's how you see it," Drake said quietly.

"What?"

"Whatever you say," Drake said.

Collins cursed under his breath.

CHAPTER SEVENTEEN

Prichard frowned as the crime scene photos reflected off his glasses. They were garish and nearly obscene in their terrible imagery. His forensics team had failed to find any physical evidence, not a single hair, fiber, or even a partial fingerprint. Traces of talcum power were detected so they were nearly certain the perp used latex gloves, but they had nothing else. This one was a pro. In their discovery meeting, investigator Debra Vickers threw out the suggestion they may be working against an actual professional.

"Maybe it's a hired killer," she said.

"It would explain the lack of evidence," investigator Alice Bernard said.

Smythe discounted it. "There are too many messages here. No self-respecting pro would take the time to follow some cockamamie plan this complicated. There is too much at stake, and it's too far out."

"Unless the killer is a writer *and* a professional assassin," investigator George Tillman suggested. "Maybe it's a frustrated killer who wants to be published."

"That's a new one," Prichard said with a laugh. "I bet if a professional killer came forward and wanted to publish, that would be a bestseller."

"So, what then? We have a writer who has the skill and time and knowledge to pull off three murders with this much finesse and leave no trace?"

"Yes," investigator Mei Yang said. They all gave her a surprised look. Her Korean features were generally stoic and she seldom spoke unless she had something important to contribute.

"Go on," Prichard urged.

"With the wealth of information on the Internet, any intelligent person with the desire to commit undetected murder could just follow the available instructions. Writers are smart people and love to do research. This one took the time to stalk the victims, learn their habits and prepare the scene. He also wrote about the intent behind each murder and left these descriptions for us to find. To pull off these killings involved a great deal of patience and care."

"That's true," Vickers added.

"So," Prichard said, "based on the number of names we found at the scenes, on paper and emails, as well as the records we have seen from the mail servers, we can narrow the possibilities down to about ten zillion people."

"The killer probably writes crime fiction," Yang suggested.

"That would slice the list down considerably," Vickers nodded. "It is also, most likely, a man."

"Maybe it's a cop," Yang offered. "That would explain a lot. Many policemen are writers."

"Like Lou Drake," Vickers almost whispered, "the patrol officer that was at the first discovery. I heard he's a wanna-be writer."

"Exactly," Yang answered.

"Okay. Since we have nothing else to go on, let's pull the data and start categorizing the names that have come in and out of the victims' email servers as well as all the snail mail records we can find," Prichard said.

The team rallied to action. As they left the office Prichard picked up his phone and called up to the desk sergeant.

"Desk," McDonald answered.

"This is Prichard in the evidence room. How would I reach Officer Drake in processing?"

"I can transfer you, hold on please."

The girls smiled as Drake told them about Collins' anger at the meeting with the agent. They all agreed Collins was a jerk and Drake should not listen to a word he said.

Serena picked up as the desk phone twittered. She asked the caller to hold and handed the receiver to Drake.

"It's for you," she said.

"'Lou Drake," he said into the phone.

"Officer Drake, this is Dr. Prichard in evidence. If you have a few minutes could you come down here?"

"Of course," Drake said. Serena raised her eyebrow as Drake shrugged and left the cage.

Drake knocked softly on the door and Prichard's voice invited him in. Prichard shook his hand and gestured for Drake to sit on an examination table. Prichard leaned against the table and stood over Drake. Lou recognized the tactic of instilling friendly confidence while exhibiting dominance, a prelude to sneaky interrogation. If there had been another officer present, Prichard would be playing the role of the *good cop*.

"Thank you for coming," Prichard said with a smile.

"Happy to," Drake said.

"I understand you are a writer?"

"Oh, not professionally," Drake said.

Drake understood the insinuation. It was smart. If the tables were turned Drake knew he would have to take the same course of investigation. When a husband or wife is killed the first suspect is always the spouse. When faced with a killer who knows the law, knows forensics procedure and is a pissed off writer? Easy, first ask the writer cop.

"Why write, then?" Prichard asked.

"It's just a hobby."

God, Drake thought, *it is so good to be thinking like a detective again!*

"You have an interest in getting published?"

"Sure, that's always the goal, I suppose. Mostly I do it for fun. It may be something I do seriously after I retire. Give me something to do."

"Are you working on something now?" Prichard asked.

"Yes, a crime novel about corruption in the Indian gaming industry," Drake lied. Drake smiled as he realized it would make a good book.

"Sounds interesting. Before you were a beat cop I understand you were a detective," Prichard continued. "It must have been hard on you when you were demoted."

"Definitely."

"But you were out in plain clothes with your old partner yesterday, and based on how you are dressed I'd guess you are going out again today. That must feel good for you."

"Yes, it feels like I am my old self again," Drake said. He played the game. "I liked it very much."

"You were a good detective, weren't you?"

"Yes," Drake said.

"A very good detective. You had a reputation for reading a scene, right?"

"They gave me an award," Drake said.

"You know what I am doing, don't you?"

"Trying to draw out any sense if I may be a suspect, I assume," Drake said. "And I don't blame you. Perfect scenario; an angry cop writer taking his twisted anger and frustration out on those who symbolize the barriers in his way. I'd think the same thing if I were you. And I could be harboring unresolved resentment about what happened to me ten years ago. I may have hit an emotional bottom a while back and may even appear to be a bit too anxious to retire. But am I a killer? No, I'm not."

"I don't believe you are either," Prichard said "Thank you for humoring me. Do me a favor though."

"What's that?"

"If you do turn out to be the killer, don't tell anybody I said that, okay?"

"I promise," Drake said and shook the Prichard's hand. "If you need anything else from me, anything at all, please ask."

"I just might do that," Prichard said.

The afternoon was cold and the sky threatened more rain as Drake and Collins stood outside the Fuller Building on Fifth Avenue. The distinctive wedge shape and bull nose protrusion into the intersection of fifth and Broadway was designed by Chicago architect Daniel Burnham. At twenty-one stories, it was often called the first skyscraper in New York. Subtly elegant and faced with terra cotta and stone, the building was an attempt to bring the business district out of the city's core into the predominantly residential area. Due to its triangular shape and the lore of the original lot, the Fuller building became know as the flatiron.

The business minds ignored the distinctive address except as a source of conversation. It remained nearly empty on the small island of ground created by Broadway, Fifth Avenue and 22nd and 23rd Streets. Most critics of the time felt the building too odd and outlandish to be considered well designed, but most offered gracious compliments for the terra cotta façade. The opinions of the building changed over the decades. Flatiron eventually became as much a landmark of New York as the Empire State Building and the Statue of Liberty, immortalized by the photographic works of Edward Steichen and Alfred Steiglitz. Today the Fuller houses an eclectic gathering of companies in publishing and the arts. On the fifth floor Halberson Publishing called the Flatiron home.

Collins shielded his eyes and stared up the towering structure. "I've never been here before," he said.

"Beautiful," Drake said.

They checked in at the lobby desk and took the elevator to five. Beautiful curved ceilings arched over their heads as they walked the short hall to the Halberson suites. The company logo was etched into chipped glass doors, a flourished capital H. Collins pushed the button and announced their arrival.

"Mr. Shapiro will be with you shortly," the receptionist said.

Soon they heard a voice come from the hallway.

"Tell that asshole if he shows up here again, I'll chase him out with a gun!" The voice was gruff. "No, if he had anything I wanted I would have called him."

The door to the back offices opened and a man came through wearing a wide smile and eyes clear as a summer morning. He laughed and stroked his bottlebrush mustache with long fingers.

"Good afternoon officers, General account manager Gerald Shapiro," he said and greeted them with a hearty handshake. "Welcome to Halberson Publishing, will you follow me?"

Shapiro was broad through the shoulder and barrel chested. His suit fit him as though he was more comfortable in a polo shirt and loose slacks. His was hair gray and thin. He made small talk as they walked the hallway to a comfortable conference room. Drake figured him to be in his early sixties but he had the energy of a younger man. As they walked Shapiro pointed out details of the decorating; emphasizing the great pains taken to restore the suites to their original splendor after an unfortunate remodel in the mid eighties.

As they filed into the conference room Collins said. “I’m Detective Michael Collins and this is officer Lou Drake”

“Please, sit down,” Shapiro said, indicating the chairs around a massive table. “Can I get you anything?”

Shapiro’s words were deliberate, his vowels elongated and his last words clipped with a smiling quickness. “How about Coffee?”

“Sure,” Collins said.

Shapiro cut him off with a raised hand and looked around the table, then the room.

“Wait a minute. Estelle! Nuts! Where the hell are the nuts?” Shapiro bellowed. “Can’t function without them, got to have my nuts.”

“I see,” Collins remarked.

“A minute. Estelle, did you hear me?” Shapiro winked at Drake. “And you guys want coffee?”

“Yes, coffee please,” Collins said.

Collins was confused by Shapiro’s odd behavior. The strange man held up a finger and punched the speaker button on the phone on the table.

“Estelle, you didn’t answer me.”

“Were you hollering from the conference room again?” she said. “You know I can’t hear you unless you use the phone. And even if I could hear you I would ignore such a vulgar display of arrogance.”

“Where are my nuts?”

“I just put nuts in that bowl in there this morning,” Estelle said through the speaker.

“Good for you. However, the bowl and the nuts are not here. The intern must have absconded with them again. Now bring me some more, please. Thank you sweetie,”

Shapiro said sarcastically.

“Right away,” Estelle said.

"And send that intern in here with some coffee. Make him do something for that salary we don't pay him."

Drake suspected this was a well-practiced and well-tolerated form of communication between Shapiro and his fellow co-workers.

Nodding toward the phone Shapiro whispered. "I have to be careful with that sweetie shit. I can't say that anymore without risking a sexual harassment suit. What kind of world is this, anyway?"

"I see, okay, if we can get focused," Collins suggested.

"You see?" Shapiro smiled. "It was a question, officer. I'm looking for answers."

"All right." Collins stifled an accusatory laugh. This was deteriorating quickly in Collins' mind and he suspected this man was a buffoon or insane.

"Now," Shapiro said. "I understand you want to discuss these grisly murders that have taken place in the borough."

"Not exactly," Collins said. "We are more interested in what you could tell us about the current status of the publishing industry. We are convinced these killings are a statement of frustration regarding the inability of this particular writer to get in the bookstores."

"The state of publishing? It's in the shitter," Shapiro said. "I don't blame him. If I were a writer trying to get published today I might resort to murder to get attention. These days it takes an act of terrorism or a flagrant episode of inhumane cruelty to get noticed. I'd like to say I jest, but it's true."

"I guess," Collins said.

Shapiro stared in the direction of Collins, not looking exactly at him, but through him as though observing something taking place within the Detective's skull.

"Do you?" Shapiro smiled widely and shook his head. "Trust me. I've been in this racket for too long. It's become unrecognizable to a Neanderthal like me."

A tall woman made more so by impossibly high heels entered with a glass bowl filled with mixed nuts.

"There are the nuts. Gentlemen, this is Estelle; she's my foil, the real brains of this operation. Without her I might as well stay home and watch reality television. Nothing happens at Halberson's without her assistance.

At least that's what she thinks. It's probably true," said Shapiro.

"Oh, it's true," Estelle said. "He would be lost without me."

"Estelle, this is Detective Collins and Drake. Collins is the one doing all the talking, at least so far. Does Drake talk? It makes me nervous when somebody sits and just stares. It makes me wonder if I have mustard on my tie or something. Or are you guys playing good cop – quiet cop today?"

"Nice to meet you," Estelle said and excused herself.

"Mister Shapiro," Collins said.

"Please, it's Jerry. Have some nuts gentlemen. I get these directly from the nut farm in California. Did you know that California is the Saudi Arabia of nuts?"

"Jerry, please, can we be serious? Any input you have would be greatly appreciated," Collins urged.

"Only if he says something," Jerry said, looking at Drake. "And I'm serious when it comes to nuts. They're incredibly good for you. All kinds of important nutrients and oils - except for the peanut. I shouldn't be so tough on the goober. Where would baseball and the circus be without 'em, huh?"

"Jerry?" Collins said.

"Okay, but only if he says something," Shapiro said. "Is that so hard?"

"Your help could be very beneficial," Drake said.

Jerry responded with a wink. Collins moved uncomfortably in his chair as though he felt the interview was a waste of his time. Drake leaned forward and took a handful of the nuts and gestured for Collins to do likewise. Collins dismissed the overture.

"Detective... may I call you Mike?" Without waiting for an affirmative response the publisher continued. "Mike, you really should eat a handful of nuts everyday. That's not my idea, it's a fact. Check it out for yourself. You'll live longer. Trust me. Plus all your parts will work better, know what I mean?" Shapiro made a back-and-forth pumping motion of his fist. He winked again. Drake returned the smile and immediately felt he had established a friendly nonverbal relationship with Shapiro.

"Can we get on with this?" Collins asked with palpable irritation.

"No problem, Mike. Nuts aren't for everyone, especially when you have to deal with them everyday... in your line of work so to speak."

"Right," Collins said.

"Well, this whack job you're looking for is correct about the publishing industry. Never before have we seen a downturn like this in sales and readership. The pundits say we are seeing a thirty percent reduction, but I would say it's more than that. The whole game has changed. In the old days we had readers. Today we have skimmers. What with the Internet, all those doodads that you can carry that bring you video blips and songs and all that other nonsense, right from your pocket phone. "

A young man knocked and brought in three coffees and all the fixings. The conversation paused while sugar poured and spoons stirred, then Jerry continued.

"So we lose readers because the world is so damned entertaining and the time it takes to sit and read a novel is just too dear for the average person. Because we have lost readership we have to make the most of what we have left. That means we can't afford to take chances. If we can't take the chance then neither can the agents. If we aren't buying then they have to try to find something we will buy. Even then we have more coming across our desks than we can ever consider."

Drake saw an opportunity to jump into the conversation. "An agent explained there is also a disproportionately high number of new writers because of the computers."

Jerry rolled his eyes dramatically. "Oh God yes, those goddamn computers. Anybody with a PC thinks they are a writer. Then the Internet sites publish every agent's contact info and the wires start humming. Then the river of crap flows over New York. The agents push back the worst and the better comes through. But we can only say yes to a few and the rest flail around. It's absolutely crazy."

"That sounds very much like what we were told by the agent," Collins said.

"There's more to it. In the glory days there was a sales structure and local bookstores thrived and there was enough to go around. But with the tighter market, the big warehouse stores and the humungous retailers started to demand deeper wholesale discounts on new releases. It cuts so deep that we had to invent cheaper ways to produce books to meet the discount demand. Soon the big stores were selling new releases for less than the independents were buying wholesale. As a result, gone are the neighborhood stores and if you want the latest bestseller, it's off to Wally World."

"I've heard that," Drake said.

Shapiro gave him an exaggerated gesture to continue.

"I also heard that the publishers have to be more careful with advances and promotion," Drake finished.

"Give the man a see-gar," Jerry said. "With profit margins so small, new writers see smaller advances compared to twenty years ago. More is offered only when a book does make it big. As for marketing budgets and promotion, it used to be typical for a certain amount of money and time be put into making sure a book got good press. Now we have to leave that up to the author. And we produce smaller first runs and distribute close to the writer's hometown. Careful is the word here."

"Sounds difficult," Collins said. "What about these print-on-demand companies I've read about? How do they fit in?"

"Don't get me started. Technology found a way to take the art of book production and reduce it to the level of flipping burgers. Computers and digital printing, automated bindery, it boggles the mind. I've seen the machines and they remind me of those ACME contraptions the coyote used in that cartoon. Damn things pull up a file on a computer, the order is placed and shazam - bound books roll out the end. We use it for our low budget runs and paperback releases. But those POD groups, they offer packages so anybody, and I mean anybody can hammer out a hundred pages, pay a grand and they will send you five books and link you to all the online book sites. We traditionalists consider the POD trade the desperate vestige of the poor slobs who are just good enough to finish a book but not good enough to get any attention."

"But some print-on-demand books make it and get picked up by regular publishers?" Drake asked.

"In some cases print-on-demand success is almost a prerequisite for a regular publishing deal. Let the writer prove how eager and willing they are! If the author can make the damn thing sell, then the publisher steps in and takes over. But the market is overrun with the shit these companies have been willing to produce. Every once in a while I visit one of their web sites and read how they are celebrating their millionth title published. Imagine that, one million books sitting in a database and waiting for somebody to order them. These companies will fire up the contraption, roll out one book, box it up and ship it to Timbuktu. They charge high prices and pay the author fifteen, twenty percent royalty and the whole convoluted scheme has diluted the very soul that used to be publishing. I've looked at some of these books and the covers look good, but inside is a nightmare of bad writing, misspelled words and poor editing. It makes the heart weep."

Drake whispered, "I had no idea."

"Yeah, well, it is a sign of the times. We still try to uphold the grand old tradition, but we have to keep the fires burning so we go with the trends. Know any writers?"

"Lou here is a writer," Collins offered with veiled sarcasm.

"Wonderful, write cop thrillers?"

"I've written one," Drake said. "Just started another one."

Jerry smiled. "Joseph Wambaugh! The Onion Field, New Centurions, Choirboys, now those were novels. Yep, I would give my left nut to get hold of something like those," Shapiro said with a sense of excitement. "Did you try to get it out there?"

"I tried."

"Tough, wasn't it?"

"Sure was."

"Listen to this. Three years ago the New York houses published over three hundred books by previously unpublished authors. In that number, only one was a thriller written by a man. One!" Jerry held up his index finger. "Want to be published? Get a sex change and write books about kid wizards."

"I think that gives us what we need," Collins said. "Thank you for your time and the information."

Collins looked over to Drake as if to say *we're done here, let's go.*

Jerry shook their hands and walked them back to the front door.

"Thanks again," Drake said.

"You need to speak up more," Jerry offered. "Can I give you some advice from a publisher to a writer?"

"Of course."

"Don't give up. The writer who never gets published is the one who gave up just before the miracle happened. Write what you know. Write with conviction; write whatever falls out of your head and your fingers. Take this case your working on, turn it into your own *In Cold Blood* or *Serpico* or *Choirboys*. Write something like that and give me a call, I'll tell you if it is saleable."

"Thank you," Drake said.

"I know I won't get killed by some whacked-out writer. My reputation precedes me and they are all afraid. Know what I mean?" Shapiro said with another wink.

"Thanks again," Drake said.

Collins was silent down the elevator and back to the car. Through traffic his face was flushed and Drake knew he was angry. Drake watched the city go by as the clouds made good on their threat and rain began pelting the windshield.

"You knew, didn't you?" Collins finally said.

"Knew what?"

"Everything that clown just told us about what's going on in publishing."

"Yeah, pretty much," Drake said. "Some of it was news to me, but not much."

"Then why did we have to do this? Why didn't you save us the time and having to sit with that nut case?"

"Because," Drake said in a flat tone, "you would have told me I was full of shit and you wouldn't have listened."

"What a bunch of happy horseshit. And I didn't care much for that guy's attitude. I don't think he respected us, what with all that nut shit."

"Mike, I think he gave us an appropriate amount of respect. Respect is all relevant and more a matter of expectation than fact. Didn't he answer all your questions? Wasn't he polite and hospitable? What more could you ask for?"

Drake stared at the rain.

"Whatever," Collins said.

They spoke not another word on the drive back to Malcolm.

CHAPTER EIGHTEEN

"Sounds bleak," Andrade said after Collins summarized what he had learned in the meetings. "Now we know why this guy is so pissed off."

"Can we be sure it's a guy?"

"Forensics completed their investigation and they came back with a profile of our killer. They figure there is a ninety nine percent probability the killer is a writer, eighty five percent that he is male, educated, intelligent and lives within a ten-mile proximity of here. He also has to be reasonably strong between the ages of 25 and 50. Narrows it down to about a million people."

"We can stake out the bookstores, coffee houses, libraries, Internet cafes and the university. We'll bust him in no time," Collins said sarcastically.

"How'd it go with Drake?"

"Pain in the ass," Collins said. "He talked his goddamn head off when we met with the agent and made himself look like a big dumb brute at the publishers. It was waste of time, nothing I didn't already know."

"What else is new?"

"Bullshit, is what it is."

As Collins shared his opinion, Betty Jade walked from the university to her apartment building. Not quite night, the weather was biting and clouds threatened freezing rain. Her coat was warm and a woolen scarf protected her face. With the talk around the campus about the murders she felt uneasy but not frightened. If the stories were true the killer preyed on literary agents, not regular people.

Not that agents weren't regular people, she thought, but this madman was targeting specifics and she was far from the literary type. Betty worked as a nurse at the university infirmary and spent her days stitching cuts, applying cold compresses and dispensing condoms. Two nights a week she attended classes to finish her RN certification.

Off the campus commons she turned on Delmar Avenue and climbed the concrete stairs to Hale Street. As she reached the top of the steps she winced at the smell of something rotten. She knew that smell from nursing school. There was nothing else like it, the undeniable smell of death. Betty pinched her nose and breathed through her mouth as she looked around. Nothing was on the hillside or in the ditch.

To her left the bottom units of the apartment complex were set with windows at ground level, the living quarters built into the hill. She was on eye level with the end unit and peered in the dimly lit window ten feet from the stair railing. Inside she could make out a shape slumped over and wearing a Halloween mask, one of those gruesome clown things with the large teeth and mottled skin.

A dummy, she thought, a prop left over from Halloween. It was tied to a straight back chair with coils of yellow rope. As she stared the wind stirred and again the odor was strong and repugnant. A chill ran up Betty's spine and it felt as though the cold night stole beneath her clothes and froze her heart. The clown mask stared back and the lean of the body was too natural. It did not look like a dummy, but a dead body.

"No," was all she could manage. She ran the steps while rummaging in her jacket pocket for her cell phone. With her gloved hands she managed to dial 911 and found her voice gone when the operator answered.

"911 emergency. Hello, are you there?"

"Yes," she said softly. "I think there is a dead person in an apartment on Hale, the ones by the steps. I'm sure, I...uh... I..." She lost herself and cried.

"Can I have your name?" the operator asked but Betty closed the phone, shut her eyes and opened her mouth in a wail. She ran home and was weeping on her couch when someone knocked at her door.

He's an agent, her mind said over and over, *he's an agent, and I know it.*

She nearly screamed when the knock happened again, this time louder and more insistent.

"Ms. Jade," a voice called out. "I'm Officer Santino with the NYPD. Are you home? They traced your cell call and got your address through your carrier. Ms. Jade?"

Betty managed to approach the door and lean against the wall.

"Is he dead?" she asked.

"Yes, we discovered a body. I need to ask you some questions."

"Is he an agent?" she asked.

"I'm sorry miss," the cop said back. "I can barely understand you. Could you please open the door?"

"Okay," she whimpered.

Betty turned the knob and opened the door just enough to see out. Officer Santino was handsome and his face ruddy from the cold night. He wore his uniform well and Betty thought he looked Italian.

"Thank you," he said with a smile. "How did you discover the deceased?"

"I smelled him," she whispered. She struggled not to cry. "I smelled him on the stairs."

"Do you walk that way often?" Santino asked.

"Only when the weather is bad and I want to get home quickly," she said. "Tonight it felt like rain. Otherwise I go the long way around and stop at the bakery."

"Is there anybody I can call for you? You seem very upset."

"No," she said. "I'll be fine."

"Okay then. We may have to speak with you again and don't hesitate to call if you feel there is something else you remember." He handed her a card.

"Thank you," she said and closed the door.

She realized two things about herself just then. She would never forget the handsome, caring face of the cop at her door and she would always have an irrational fear of clowns.

Collins watched through the window as the coroner cut the latex clown mask from the seated figure. The stench was overpowering, so each officer and tech inside the apartment wore a bio mask. Collins took updates through his radio from an attending officer as the forensics team tended to the horror.

"Detective Collins?" Prichard called from the apartment. "We have found a page describing the murder, just like at the other killings."

"Can you bring it out for me to look at?" Collins called back.

Prichard exited the apartment and with a gloved hand extended a clipboard toward Collins. Agent Thatcher, looking like a futuristic warrior in his coveralls and mask, stepped up and grabbed the clipboard before Collins could.

"Thank you detective," Thatcher said to Collins, "but we'll take it from here."

"Hey asshole," Collins said, "who died and left you in charge?"

Thatcher ignored him and wandered away, studying the paper on the clipboard.

Collins turned back to Prichard. "Can you at least tell me, was the paper already on the clipboard when you found it or did you use one of your own clipboards?"

"It was already on it," Prichard said and left Collins alone on the sidewalk.

"Did it have a page number on it?"

"Yes, 156," Prichard said as he walked away.

"Thanks," Collins said with a sarcastic smirk.

Collins' presence was obviously unnecessary so he walked down the step to the University common and took refuge from the light rain beneath a large evergreen. He dialed Andrade's cell and the Captain answered with an abrupt "*Yeah.*"

"The dead man is victim number three. More of the same," Collins said.

"We already had three."

"Three murders, but by the page numbers we had one, two and four. They found the description on a clipboard near a stack of query letters. The page number is 156. Victim four, the last scene was 183. Trust me, this guy has been here since Halloween. He's tied to a chair and dressed like a clown. He was killed with a stab through both eyes with an ice pick. We found the weapon on the counter by the fridge. His eyelids were glued shut and the pick was pressed through the skin. He probably lived a while under the mask and, well, he was there a while."

"And the girl that discovered him?"

"She smelled him first," Collins said. "Then saw him through the window because a small light was on in the kitchen. I talked to some neighbors and they said he drank a lot. Plenty of people saw him alive Halloween night, but nobody saw a thing after that. I'll go door to door and ask for witnesses."

"Know any more about the victim?" Andrade asked.

"I ran the address and got the name. I checked the public record and the publisher resources online. Divorced, used to be a pretty successful agent, sold some books. Hasn't done shit in years and still advertises himself as an agent looking for new talent. He obviously pissed off the wrong writer."

"Is the team on it?"

"Like flies on shit," Collins said. "Chief Smythe is pleasantly displeased. He was angry we had another victim but happy his boys and girls had another chance to see if the killer left any evidence."

"Okay come on in."

"Ten four," Collins said and hung up. He caught the attending officer's attention and told him he was returning to the station.

"Okay," the beat cop said and went back to watching the techs process the scene.

Collins returned to the station where he and Andrade talked behind closed doors for an hour.

CHAPTER NINTEEN

Andrade stood in confused impatience as Kathy refused to let him touch her. She wasn't ready to go out and he checked his watch. Their dinner reservation was in less than an hour. He begged her to explain what was going on but Kathy just sat on her bed, silent and angry.

"Baby, talk to me."

She gave him a look that would freeze fire and he sighed deeply.

"What does that mean?" she snapped.

"I'm just confused. I thought we had plans that we were both looking forward to."

"You mean another night of pretending, denial and a good lay?"

"Whoa," he laughed nervously and put his hands up in defense. "Where the hell did that come from?"

"From all of this shit," she said and threw her hands up. "Murders and cops and us and, well, everything!"

"Sweetie."

"Don't sweetie me!" she said. "Don't you dare! I need to know something, and I need a real answer. John, when are you going to leave your wife for me?"

"Oh man," he said and stepped back. "Are you serious? You want to know that right now, this instant?"

"It's been a long time, John. The first time we had sex you swore you were semi available, your exact words." She used her bowed fingers as quotation marks. "You swore it was over, you no longer loved your wife and promised, you promised, John, that you would leave her and be with me."

"I still mean that," he said.

"No John, you never meant it. I've always known that but I was too flattered, too indebted to you for getting me this job and too comfortable in knowing you would never make any demands on me. It's as much my fault as yours, probably more so."

Andrade stood silent as the conversation deteriorated to her tears and his anger. She turned her back on him and sobbed. When he touched her shoulder she shrugged him off.

"Fine," he said. "I'm going."

"You better make sure you don't drag me into your mess," she said. Through tearful gasps she begged. "Please John, don't do that."

"What does that mean?"

"Oh Captain Andrade," she said and wiped her eyes. Andrade felt her sadness turn to loud accusation. "Did you think I was really that stupid, or naive?"

"Kathy, what are you talking about?"

"I spoke with... " She stopped herself.

John's face went red and she lowered her voice.

"Oh, don't worry Captain, I won't say anything to anybody. Come on, you really think you can screw me and not expose yourself? I saw how nervous you were when Smythe was down here and I've heard your talks with Collins and Thibido. I wasn't always asleep when your phone rang. Hennings, the future, Lou Drake? What did you think, that I would not understand you had something to hide?"

"Who did you talk to? What do you mean?" Andrade demanded.

"About the secrets and whispers and your precious promotion and transfer." She laughed through tears. "Then what? I was expendable, disposable and you'd find another side girl in the city?"

"Kathy, you have no idea what you are saying. Whatever you think is going on, you're wrong," he said carefully and took a step forward.

"Okay, I'm wrong. But please, just make sure you don't take me down with you. I have a life I would like to finally start living. Can you promise me that?"

"I'm going now," he said and stalked angrily out of her apartment.

Freezing rain came down from the black sky and struck Andrade's windshield. The falling ice formed small ridges of slush that were pushed away by his intermittent wipers. His face flushed by anger and his

Cadillac's tailpipe pushing vaporous exhaust into the cold night, he glared up at Kathy's apartment.

Her questions took him by surprise and raised the suspicion somebody broke the bond of silence. If it were true it had to be Collins. No, he stopped himself, they were both just as guilty and if he did talk he was putting himself in an equal degree of jeopardy.

Besides, what did she say, exactly? She implied vagaries and shared cryptic suspicions, nothing specific. But why the dramatics and the sudden change of heart? She did say she spoke with somebody but that could mean anything.

C'mon John, he said to himself. But she said some specific fears.

She mentioned the promotion and transfer, a new mistress. All expected, he thought, stop being so paranoid. A woman will say anything to justify her behavior, twist the facts and mix truth with suspicion to allow her to break it off with some personal power and satisfaction.

Or did he share more than he meant to? Did he talk in his sleep or become lazy in his discretion? No matter, it was over, that was clear enough.

"Face it John," he said aloud. "She just dumped you and you hate being rejected."

Andrade put the car in gear and drove slowly away. With one hand on the wheel, he used the other to answer his ringing cell.

"Andrade."

"Hello Captain," Chief Smythe said. "Sorry to call at this hour."

"No problem, what's up Chief?"

"I have some questions and felt it could not wait until tomorrow."

Smyth's voice was edgy and held a subtle accusatory tone.

"This about the murders?"

"In a way, but not so much," Smythe said. "John, I have a copy of a letter written to my predecessor about his concerns regarding the Hennings murder case ten years ago. It was mailed to me by an anonymous sender. It's a letter written from Fitzpatrick to Holloway, your predecessor. Kind of eerie. It is adamant about his concern regarding the evidence collapse and events surrounding Hennings. Names are mentioned. I think it would be a good idea for the two of us to have a sit down."

"How does this relate to the agent murders?" Andrade asked.

"I don't know, maybe in no way at all other than it involves former Detective Drake. It raises questions that I feel need answers," Smythe said.

"I'll call you in the morning and we can set something up," Andrade said. The Chief bid him a good night.

"Goddammit!" Andrade screamed. He threw his phone against the dashboard and cracked the face of his stereo.

Robin stepped out of the shower and wrapped her hair in a towel. Her curves were wet and they shone in the overhead light of Drake's small bathroom. Her place was no bigger and she had a roommate. They once went back to her apartment but found herself unable to feel free in her sexual release. After that they always came home to Drake's place.

"Be out in a minute sweetie," she called and he grunted back.

His fingers were busy clacking out the words that occupied his mind. His writing was an odd fascination for her, how he could trust his hands to tell a story he swore was beyond the scope of his inadequate mouth. Drake explained that his fingers could tell a better story than his lips.

"That make any sense to you?" he asked.

She shrugged and gave him a lost look.

"Think of it this way," he said, "When I was a Detective if I thought too much about a case I got lost. But if I let my instincts take over, it was like the scene just spoke to me. When I write I clear my head and allow my hands do the work and I'm amazed at how well they do."

"You don't think about the story?"

"Yeah, but not like you think. I know the story and I know what I want to say but if I think too hard it escapes me. So I trust my fingers and they go on a wild trip and the rest of me is along for the ride."

She decided to not understand it, just support it. Since starting the book his mood was so much better, more like the man she met seven years ago. But Drake became so morose in the last two years, then downright depressed after getting the cage detail. Now he smiled, stayed in touch and gave her the hope he might actually retire and feel good about it.

"Lou," she called out to him as she rubbed herself dry.

"Hmmm," he hummed.

"I'm craving Molly's. Let's go to dinner. I have a hankering for their chicken fried steak, mashed potatoes, and cherry pie. Oh, and a strawberry shake."

"Okay," he said.

She came out to the living room naked but for the head towel.

"Are you listening to me or just mumbling automatic responses because your head is off and your fingers are working?

"What?" he said and smiled at the vision before him. "Oh, yeah. Molly's."

"Be ready in a minute."

The restaurant was busy but not crowded. They got a seat by the window. Outside the night was damp and cold, with occasional wind gusts that creaked the windows as though it wished to join the diners in the comfortable eatery. Drake ignored the menu.

"I'm having the Cobb salad," he said and waved to a couple at another table.

"Who's that?" Robin asked.

"Writers from the group."

"Wow, he's short," Robin whispered. "And the woman looks a bit hard."

"Right on both counts," he said.

The waitress came to the table.

"That must be Drake's girlfriend," Brian said to Franny. "He's talked about her a few times. She's kind of pretty, in a farm girl sort of way."

"Daisy Mae on steroids," Fran said.

"She's tall," Brian mused. "They make an interesting couple."

"No more interesting than we would," Franny said.

"But we're not. Besides, I'm not your type."

"Yeah," she laughed. "You're gay. Besides you wouldn't fight with me."

"Looks like they are doing just that," Brian nodded toward Drake.

Franny watched Robin stand and hiss something to Drake with her finger pointing accusingly. Drake struggled out of the small chair as his date turned on her heel and made her way through the restaurant.

"Robin wait!" he called over the chatter of the other diners. The room went quiet and everyone watched the blond push out the door, her head down against the weather. A few murmured and somebody laughed as Drake hurried out and called to her. The blond did not look back and Franny shook her head.

"Men. How typical. Not one who knows how to treat a lady," she said.

"How would you know, you ain't no lady," Shakespeare said.

"And you are only half a man," she said and backhanded his shoulder.

It was all in good banter and soon the restaurant returned to its natural volume. Brian asked for more coffee while Franny stirred sugar into hers.

By the time Drake retrieved his car Robin had flagged down the university shuttle and dropped angrily in a seat near the driver. Besides the driver she was alone on the bus.

"Damn him," she said.

She resented her missed meal. To berate her for ordering exactly what she told him she wanted? *Carbs*, he warned, *too many carbs*. This new diet was fine for him but to start preaching at her, suggesting she could benefit from what he called *his new regimen.* It was rude and embarrassing. And the way the waitress looked at them? Damn him!

"Next stop please," she called out and the driver gave her a nod. She climbed down from the warm bus and shrugged against the cold as she climbed the steps to her place. A turn of the key and she was home. She dialed Felipe's pizza and asked to have a medium pepperoni delivered.

"Be there in half an hour."

As she hung up the phone rang. It was Lou.

"What do you want?"

"I'm sorry," he said. "You took what I was saying all wrong. I wasn't trying to say – what I mean is –"

"Oh, I know exactly what you meant." She cut him off. "You said I was a fat pig and if I stopped eating like one, then maybe I'd lose some weight. Well, what a great time to bring it up and make me feel like shit, with the waitress standing there waiting for my order. Tell you what Lou, run your own damn life and stop trying to run mine. Besides, who the fuck are you to give me advice about weight loss?"

Robin slammed down the phone, went to the refrigerator and opened a beer. Let him know what it's like to wait for a call. So many times his mood had taken him to a dark place and her calls and needs went unanswered. He feels good about his life right now? *See how it works without me,* she thought and flopped on the couch. With a punch of the remote the TV came to life and she waited for her pizza while watching an old horror movie about giants ants invading Los Angeles.

Drake went home and felt so bad he comforted himself with a piece of peanut butter toast, which blew his whole carbohydrate count for the day. He couldn't sleep so he took a pill. Alone is his bed, the sleep aid starting to kick in, he found himself rationalizing his behavior. The writer's group, his quiet investigation and his lost weight all made him feel better. As though he was reclaiming his old self. That is what he would say to Robin in the morning, that his intention was trying to help her by explaining his need to find his old self.

She must understand that. He had seen old photos of her when she was thin and young. He had a similar shot of himself on his refrigerator as positive incentive to stay on his new diet. It was not a condemnation of what she was now, but a suggestion she could be like she was again. How could that be a bad thing?

The pill stole his focus and soon his mind was a jumble of odd thoughts and distracting images. With sleep he dreamed of a teenage boy walking a blood splattered dog down a dark street. Moments later he was snoring like a bear.

CHAPTER TWENTY

The ringing phone interrupted the movie Collins was watching on TV. It was Andrade so Collins let it go to message. His mind was occupied with the increasing pressure from Smythe and his team of super human evidence collectors, not to mention the big gorilla from the FBI.

For the life of him Collins could not put a single dent in the case. It was as if this perp had read all the manuals and knew police procedure better than all of them put together. Most odd was the small voice in the back of his head that kept wondering if Lou Drake in his prime would be able to make some sense of this.

Funny, Collins thought, *we take action that makes sense at the time. But then years later those actions can come back and bite us on the ass. But it had been necessary. It was.*

Hennings had been guilty as shit. Collins knew it because Drake knew it. The case was airtight; Drake's magic was infallible. Then Hennings' attorney, Hal Norwich called and asked Collins and Andrade to meet him at the Rose and Crown tavern in Greenwich.

Andrade explained that it was highly inappropriate to have such a meeting.

"It could be construed as a conflict of interest," he said.

"It is a simple meeting to discuss a matter completely separate from the case," Norwich assured him. "Just a friendly discussion."

Andrade agreed to meet but insisted that he and Collins wear wires in case the bastard lawyer tried anything or said anything incriminating. It would be worthless in a court of law, but it was still a careful precaution. They met and the lawyer said Joshua Fairbanks Hennings had a proposition for them.

"Mister Norwich," Andrade said. "If this an attempt to influence us in any way I will place you under arrest and charge you with obstruction, bribery and criminal intent. Be careful what you say next."

"I have nothing to say," Norwich said. Instead he pulled two letter sized manila envelopes from his briefcase and handed one to each of Collins and Andrade.

"Mind explaining this?" Andrade said.

"Please take time to look these over and call me when you are ready to meet again." Norwich snapped his briefcase closed and walked out of the bar. Collins fingered the edge of the thick folder and Andrade looked worried.

"What's this?" Collins asked.

"It's call intimidation and bribery," he answered. "Michael, we need to make sure we are very careful. This asshole lawyer will try any trick to get his client off, so look over what he gave you and we will compare notes later. If this is what I think it is we will have that asshole in cuffs by morning and the additional charges of attempted bribery and obstruction will ruin Hennings chance of getting off."

But the envelope did not contain a bribe. Instead it contained a record of every improper, questionable and downright illegal thing Collins had done since becoming a cop. When he first made Detective it went to his head, skewed his perception and he started gambling. With the habit came the debt, the itch and the cycle of insanity. Collins found himself facing people you did not want to owe money to. Cliché, yes, but then so was his macho ego. Desperation drove him to squeeze some people for information about drug deals. He busted and skimmed money from the dealers to pay off his debts. He swore off the cards and horses and football and never looked back.

It was all in there.

Collins saw what unlimited resources and coconut-sized balls could accomplish when there was nothing to lose. Surprisingly, the report also included a copy of his service records, list of commendations and a photocopy of a memo from station one regarding Andrade's consideration for Captain and Collins' promotion to lead Detective. The message was clear, Hennings had the contacts and influence to make careers or destroy them.

Next morning Andrade called and they met. At first they were each reluctant to share what was in their folders. Then they made a pact. It was better to know each other's dirt and work together than it was to work against each other. An hour later they agreed that fighting Hennings was professional suicide. If they refused the unspoken ultimatum and Hennings did go down, their lives would still be destroyed. It was a matter of self-preservation. They were ready to sell their souls to the devil for the greater good. On the count of three they exchanged packets and read through them.

"Gambling and drug shake downs? Michael, how cliché," Andrade said with a smirk.

"Massage parlors, high priced hookers and cocaine?" Collins shot back. "Like you can judge."

The next meeting with Norwich was in a very dark corner.

"So gentlemen, this is an opportunity to get something you need in exchange for your cooperation. The contents of these files would end what, by all accounts, are exemplary careers. Detective Andrade, you would lose more than your career if this became public. Your wife would, most likely, be very displeased."

Bottom line, Hennings would be forever grateful if the case could be, well, compromised. If not, it meant personal and professional disaster, maybe even jail.

"To ruin the case we would have to discredit the evidence," Andrade told the lawyer. "We would have to provide a scapegoat."

"We'd have to destroy Drake," Collins said and they all were quiet for a moment.

"You okay with that?" Andrade asked.

Collins gave him a tight-lipped nod. "What choice do we have?"

It was investigative sabotage. Thibido was a willing participant in exchange for a gold and blue shield. What followed was systematic discrediting of the case. Collins played the shocked and concerned partner.

Both he and Andrade walked with a healthy bonus and nice promotions. The envelopes of evidence against them were destroyed, but could be easily resurrected with a single call to a human bloodhound that worked for Joshua Fairbanks Hennings. Collins never knew how deep the corruption reached, but many seemed to benefit from the events. Then a suspect confessed and killed himself in his cell. Case closed. The irony was profound.

CHAPTER TWENTY-ONE

Drake sulked in the cage. Since his fight with Robin he had not been able to write or sleep. Robin refused to answer her phone and his diet was shot to hell by grief-driven gluttony. He gained back eight pounds and hated himself for it. Robin went to the back office whenever he dropped by the Dunkin' Donuts store. He sent a dozen peach roses and wrote her a poem of apology, begging her to forgive him. Drake even admitted his suggestion was a result of his own holier-than-thou selfishness caused by his feeling of superiority from losing weight.

She did not respond.

"Sugar, you're doin' this all wrong," Regina said. "You got to show her she means more to you than just flowers and poems. All an apology does is make a sister more pissed off."

"So what do I do?"

"Bling! A girl knows her man is seriously regrettin' when he gives her shiny stuff that costs a lot."

"She's right," Serena said with a nod. "When my man does something real bad, he has to come crawling with something sparkly or it ain't on. And we ain't even married."

"Drake," Edna said and gave him a smile, "listen to these girls. Back in my day all it took was a couple of chocolate bars and some silk stockings. But today, it takes what they said. Can I ask you something?"

"Sure."

"You love this girl?"

"Yes I do," Drake said. "She's never done this to me before. I was always the one who stopped calling and she was always willing to take me in when I pulled my head out of my ass."

"So you do love her?" Edna asked again.

"Yes."

"How long this been goin' on'?" Serena asked.

"Six years," he answered.

"Oh Lord," Regina said with a laugh. "That fool girl has been carrying your ass for six damn years? And you wonder why you in the doghouse because you said something wrong?"

"What did you say?" Edna pushed.

"Oh, I said she might lose some weight if she tried eating differently."

"Oh my God," Regina cackled. "You called her fat? You?"

"Yeah," he whispered.

"Honey," Edna said and put her finger under his chin. "You fucked up big time. You do love this girl?"

"I do," he said.

"Then I suggest that shiny thing you buy be an engagement ring."

Is that a proposal?

"Okay," he heard himself say and began to sweat.

"That's a good boy," Serena said. Regina patted his shoulder.

Drake sighed. "Oh God."

Chief Smythe sat in his office at station one in deep reflection, thinking back to when the Hennings case was the talk of New York. Speculation had flown like a flock of angry crows, flapping and calling out abrasive rumor. The city was divided and Smythe, working as captain of vice at the time, watched in morbid fascination as the case deteriorated, taking Detective Drake's career and reputation down with it.

The newspapers blared bold headlined, as if reporting war. The local television and talk radio spoke of little else. Was Hennings a killer? Smythe had thought so, but he was vice.

Then the case was dropped and Hennings gave a press conference, his practiced sadness edged with arrogant satisfaction. At the time Smythe shook his head and sighed — the same sigh he heaved today over the same case and similar doubts. But this time he doubted the two principals at the Malcolm station.

After reviewing the testimony transcripts from the internal investigation one thing was undeniable to Smythe, Detective Thibido was somehow involved. His testimony seemed practiced. Smythe knew Thibido well enough to know he *never* used the words in his testimony, let alone knew what they meant.

It stank like a classic internal payoff, under-the-table promises that were kept through apparently proper channels. When the copy of the letter arrived his suspicion was confirmed, so Smythe bided his time, waiting for somebody, anybody to slip and expose the truth. He almost prayed the conspiracy was a fabrication of his own paranoia.

Scandal was never easy. The revelation of dirty cops fueled public hostility and stained the force. This was inevitably followed by a rallying outcry and diminished power of the law. There are many other cities with worse police corruption, but the Big Apple seemed to attract the most attention.

Smythe poured over the transcripts of testimony and the eventual confession by the low-life, petty crook. The suicide was unfortunate or a stroke of luck depending on whose side you were on.

And now the agent murders.

The mayor screamed behind closed doors, demanding progress and reminding Smythe that the finest police force on the planet was being made to look ridiculous by a rogue writer of all things.

"And not a very good one!" The Mayor raged. "I read the fucking pages!"

Another sigh, another thought. Smythe gave his phone a dirty look as it beeped and his secretary chimed through.

"Yes Sharon."

"Dr. Prichard is on line one."

"Thanks," he muttered and lifted the receiver. "Yes?"

"Excuse me sir, but I thought you would want to be the first to know. We have another victim. Another agent."

"And?"

"Name is George Hammerstein, 1475 Cove Drive. It is very bad."

"Be right there," Smythe said and hit the COM button. "Sharon? Call my driver, I'm going to Malcolm."

"Yes sir."

Maybe Drake was right. Retirement was good and bad, and some things would be missed. The present course of events would not be one of them.

An hour later Smythe's car pulled up to 1475 Cove Drive. Cruisers were everywhere and Smythe saw Michael Collins on his cell phone with one finger pushed into his other ear. Gray afternoon sky gave a pewter cast to the scene and the temperature had dropped enough to show Collins' breath as he spoke. Smythe joined Collins on the curb as he terminated his call.

"Chief," Collins shook his gloved hand.

"What do we have Detective?" Smythe asked.

"This is the most bizarre scene yet," Collins said.

Cove Drive was set up from a rural road on the north edge of Malcolm. The street was lined with small rental cottages that were once summer homes for the middle class from New York City. Covered in shingles and beneath ancient trees, the house at number 1475 had once been a charming two-bedroom hideaway. Now it was a run-down shack that looked like an old woman whose makeup has cracked. Uniformed officers stepped aside as Collins led Smythe through the shabby entry into the back bedroom.

"Careful of the dog shit," Collins warned.

Smythe watched his step.

"He was found when his neighbor complained about the dog howling," Collins said.

George Hammerstein lay on his back on the unmade bed. His eyes were open and his mouth gaped. A complicated mesh of knotted yellow rope, anchored to a wall radiator, held his arms, torso and legs securely. A simple pulley system was attached to the doorframe of the decaying bathroom opposite the radiator. The yellow nylon rope around his neck was taut. Hammerstein's throat was cut to the bone, and the pulley contraption had pulled the vertebrae apart, elongating the dead man's neck by several inches. The lumpy mattress was soaked with blood and the rope was splattered red.

"I get it," Smythe said. "This man would not stick his neck out."

"As explained by this," Collins said. He handed the Chief a printed page that described the murder. "This time the paper was left in plain sight."

"This would have taken some time," Smythe said, "so the victim was out or sedated. How long has he been dead, do you think?"

"Few days probably," Collins said.

Smythe and Collins stepped aside to let Prichard by. His team began to map the scene and Smythe gestured for Collins to follow him outside.

"Number five," Smythe said. "This is number five."

"Yes sir. The page is numbered 314, and most crime novels are between 300 and 450 pages. So, unless this is some insane, ongoing epic with no ending, the story could be close to the climax."

"Let's hope so. Any reference to that on the page?"

"No sir, just a description of the murder," Collins said.

"I'll leave you to it," Smythe said and waved to his driver. "Back to the station."

"Yes sir."

The tires slid for a moment on the wet leaves, then found traction and the black car left the scene behind, blowing its own breath from the rear pipes into the cold pewter afternoon.

Andrade sat in his living room and stared at the dark big-screen TV. His mind seethed as he fidgeted with the redial button on his cell phone. Collins had yet to return his calls from the night before. Facing the station was impossible. He knew the place was no longer his. Not that Chief Smythe, or anyone else had relieved him of it, but a sense of impending doom drove Andrade into hiding.

After his fight with Kathy his imagination took a bad trip to a dark and frightening place where irrational whispers lived. Andrade had enough time to contemplate Smythe's call, Kathy's cryptic attitude and her direct plea to be left out of his downfall.

Downfall? How did she say it?

Just make sure you don't take me down with you.

Who told her he was going down? Whatever the message and however she came to her opinion he had to consider that it was dangerous to pretend that nothing was going on. He had to face the possibility that she talked with someone, and only two people knew enough to be truly dangerous; Collins and Thibido.

Thibido was too dumb and too frightened of Andrade to betray the secrets, so it had to be Michael Collins. And if Michael betrayed him it meant Collins was driven by a force above Andrade himself, meaning he must have made a deal with Smythe.

His face red with fear and fury, Andrade jumped when his cell rang. It was Collins.

"Yeah," Andrade barked.

"Where are you? " Collins asked. "We've got a bloody mess on Cove Drive, victim number five. This is as bad as the spine shit but with a freaky new twist."

Collins's voice held the same professional intensity he always shared with Andrade.

When Andrade didn't answer, Collins said, "You there, John?"

"Yeah," Andrade said. "What's the story?"

"Neighbor called. Uniforms showed up and found a horror show. Same as before, only with a Frankenstein twist. I'm pulling out of here and heading back to the station."

"I'll meet you there," Andrade said. *I have to,* he thought.

"Jesus," Collins sounded frustrated. "This is just a goddamn nightmare. Hopefully we'll get something from forensics on this one so we can reclaim our balls and actually get back in the game on this case. Smythe and his super team, I feel like all I have is my dick in my hand."

"Yeah," Andrade managed and hung up. His mind was more muddled than ever.

CHAPTER TWENTY-TWO

Robin was fresh out of the shower when she heard her roommate Helen answer the phone. It was Lou and Helen was as cold as ice with him. Helen had listened carefully when Robin told her what happened at the restaurant. The two of them had an estrogen-driven rant session, both swearing all men were insensitive assholes and that Drake was a lost cause. For days Robin ignored Lou's calls and swore it was finally over. His gestures were pathetic, Helen said, and Robin agreed with her. This was not the first time Helen had answered the phone and told Drake Robin wasn't home, even though Robin sat six feet away. Each time Robin felt a pang of guilt, but she soon got over it.

"She doesn't want to talk to you," Helen said. "Besides, she's on a date and I don't know when she will be back."

Lou must have said Okay because Helen went off on him.

"That's it? *Okay?* Jesus Drake, you really are pathetic. I just told you she was out on a date and all you say is *Okay?*"

Robin imagined his shock and sadness when he heard she was out.

"I'll tell her. Bye-bye Lou – "

Robin felt this was too cruel. She grabbed the phone away.

"Wait, no, I'm here Lou," she said.

"Rob?"

"What do you want?"

"Helen said –"

"No, I am not on a date. That was mean and I'm sorry I let her do that to you. But, I don't want to talk to you."

"Just listen," he begged. "Can we get together? I want to talk and clear the air. Then you can do whatever you want and I'll go along with it."

"Fine," she heard herself say. "But I have something to say now."

"Okay." He sounded anxious.

"In one of your many messages you said you were only trying to help me see I could be what I once was, right?"

"Yeah."

"Why in God's great earth would I want to be what I was before?" she asked. "Yeah, I may have been thin, but I was a neurotic, screwed-up and lost girl who had no idea what to do with her life. You have to look ahead Lou. You want to lose weight? That's fine, but I'm not looking back. If that's where you want to go, it's a trip you take alone. Can you understand that?"

"Yes I can," he said.

"Okay then. Meet me at Molly's tomorrow at one."

"I'll be there."

The next day Robin arrived ten minutes early. Drake was already seated by the window. He wore his best clothes and looked good, less dark around the eyes. His weight loss showed in the way his coat fell off his shoulders. She could not help but smile as she took her seat across form him.

"Hello," she said and folded her hands on the table.

"Thanks for coming," he said, "You want to order something?"

"Lou, I didn't come here to have lunch and make small talk. I chose here because it was easy for both of us. What do you want to say to me?"

It hurt her to shut him down like that and she struggled with conflicting emotions. The waitress knew something serious was happening at table twelve and left the couple alone.

"Okay Rob," Drake said and took a breath.

"Lou," Robin said and he put up his hand.

"Let me say this," Drake said. "I had time to sit back and look at myself and I didn't like what I saw. I Finally took some positive action and when I saw it working I got big headed, suddenly my shit didn't stink and I became like every other former lost cause who suddenly made a difference, even a little one. I got arrogant, and I am so sorry."

"Okay, but it is more than that," Robin said.

"Yes it is," Drake said with a nod. "So much more. Robin, I love you so much. I know I've been selfish and wallowing in my own self-pity and sometimes I wondered how you put up with me? I was so selfish and so distant, but you never gave up on me. No matter how I pushed you away or isolated, you always came and knew how to drag me out and make me face the light of day."

"Lou-" Robin interrupted and he put up both hands and pleaded with his eyes.

"Please, let me finish and then you can say whatever you need to. If I don't get this out now I never will. Okay?"

"Go ahead," Robin said with a sigh and leaned her elbows on the tabletop.

"So, what I mean to say is it would kill me if, now that I see how much I appreciate you, if I couldn't spend my time proving it to you. Please Rob, can you find it in your heart to give this poor, pathetic and love sick man the chance to prove his love? Just one more chance?"

"I appreciate all that," she said. "Lou, we have been doing this strange dance for five years and I'm afraid the song and the steps will never change. You say you want things to be different but I have to look out for my own emotional peace of mind and make plans for the future."

"I agree," he said, "and I thought about what you said about not looking back. You're completely right."

She gave him a quizzical look, then looked down.

"I don't know, Lou," she whispered. Her anger evaporated and her heart suddenly ached for him, begged her to trust though her head knew not to.

"I do understand," Drake said and touched her hand. "I do."

"So, what does that mean?" she asked.

"Could we go for a walk? There is something I really want to ask but it's kind of crowded in here."

"Lou, it's freezing out there and I don't want to draw this out more than we have to. Whatever you have to ask me, here is fine. Okay?"

"All right," Drake said. He surprised her by getting down on one knee beside the table and pulling a small velvet box from his jacket pocket. He opened it and presented her with the ring.

Robin's breath caught in her throat. Suddenly there seemed to be no air in the room.

"Robin, I want to change the music and the steps to take this dance into a wonderful new level. I don't want to look back at what was, but to the future where we are happy and healthy together. If you say no, well, I will wish you well and leave you alone. But I want you to know that I am serious. I want to spend my life making you happy. Robin Sarah Bradley, I ask you with a hopeful and grateful heart to be my wife."

"Oh shit," she said.

Drake raised his eyebrows.

"My God," a woman said at the next table. "Well honey, what's your answer?"

"I... I - " Robin stammered.

She gave Lou a hard stare. This didn't feel to her like an act of desperation or a ploy. Lou was on one knee and his eyes were clear. His face was placid and she knew if she said no he would, indeed, wish her well and move on with his life. Her heart softened and she looked at the other diners, each frozen in expectation of her answer to this very public proposal.

Is that a proposal?

Isn't this what she always wanted? Yes it was.

"What's she going to say?" a young girl asked her mother four tables over.

"I don't know, we'll just have to wait and see," the mother whispered back.

"Yes," Robin said. "Yes, oh yes."

"I love you," Lou said. She nearly knocked the table over to kiss him. Then she let him slip the ring on her finger and smiled as the restaurant erupted in applause and whistles. Lou ordered a bottle of champagne and the crowd joined in the celebration.

Afterward they left the restaurant and rushed home to Drake's place, where they tore at their clothes and fell together on the bed. Robin wrapped her arms around Drake's thinner body and felt loved and happy. They urged one another to fulfillment and Robin rolled on top to push herself to climax. Her orgasm was profound, a body-shuddering and soul-touching level of sexual release than she had never experienced before.

She collapsed on Drake's chest and lost herself in the feeling of complete satisfaction. As she gasped for breath she drew her left hand close to her face and watched the light reflect off the diamond set in the simple platinum band on her finger.

"Wow," Drake said. "That was a good one."

"Yes it was," she whispered and kissed him gently. For a moment she felt guilty for how she treated him. She knew some of her anger was driven by the fact he was right, she was overweight.

"You seem a thousand miles away," Drake said.

"I was just thinking about this afternoon," she said. "That was so romantic."

"Molly's for grub, beer and a proposal," he said with a laugh.

"I'm sorry I was so mean to you."

"No, I know, you don't owe me an apology. You were right and now we can finally move on with our lives together."

"Mr. and Mrs. Louis Henry Drake," she said with a languid smile.

"I like the sound of that," he said. "When are you going to tell Helen?"

"She'll say I'm crazy. I'll show her the ring and she'll probably smirk it off."

"So when are you moving in?" he asked.

"When do you want me to?"

"A week ago," he said.

She smiled and kissed him again.

Dr. Kathy Morey contemplated a new life of her own as she waited for Andrade to arrive. The clock said twelve twenty in the morning. The apartment felt too small and Malcolm was no longer a safe place for her. Even the fire burning in her fireplace couldn't warm her. Andrade had called around eleven and said he had to see her tonight but could not come by until midnight.

"Safer that way," he said cryptically.

She pulled an afghan over her shoulders and sat on the couch. No, it was not safe, emotionally or otherwise.

She and John first met at a city employee Christmas party and he flirted with her shamelessly. He made a conscious effort to stay in touch and she was flattered by his attentions, even though he was married. When her job fell victim to cutbacks Andrade made it possible for her to slip into the position in Malcolm, and then he slipped into her bed. His attentions were sweet and the sex was mind-blowing, but at some point his will and his schedule started to control her life.

Then the body count began to rise and everything seemed to change between them. Andrade became darker and she became concerned. John ignored her silent desperation and used her as an escape from the horror he could not stop or solve. When Smythe rolled over him, Andrade took his frustration out on her in bed, his sexual appetites leaning toward the violent. As more bodies were discovered and Andrade became more nervous, she spent each day pretending she was okay. Inside she was dying emotionally from fear and desperation. Then Smythe called and asked to meet with her.

They met at the Coroner's office and Chief Smythe carried a thick file with the name *Hennings* across the tab. She remembered the media attention that case had received, not to mention the constant talk around the office. The tabloid newspapers showed gruesome photos and most New Yorkers were split on his guilt or innocence. The case was ironclad, or so everyone seemed to think. Then came the scandal and the investigation and the District Attorney dropped the charges.

"Miss Morey," Smythe said. "I would like to keep this meeting confidential. Is that okay with you?"

She nodded nervously. "Of course."

He held up the file folder. "Are you familiar with the Hennings case?"

"I am."

"I have a delicate question to ask and you are under no obligation to answer. I'll preface this by saying that I have been a Detective for a long time and have an eye for things most people would miss. When we met a few days ago for the body viewing with the forensics team I could not help but notice an unspoken dialog between you and Captain Andrade. He showed it more than you, but I noticed you blush."

She feigned ignorance. "I'm not sure what you are getting at."

"I doubt that is true, but I don't want to be out of line. It would help me to understand something that has me troubled. My staff thinks I am here to speak with you regarding pathology, so anything you share with me is completely confidential and I promise it will go with me to my grave."

"I understand," she said.

"Are you, or have you been involved with Captain Andrade?"

She bit her lower lip and looked into his eyes. Could she trust this man? It took her only a few moments to decide that she could. "Yes," she whispered.

"Take your time," Smythe soothed.

"Yes," she repeated, "Captain Andrade and I are ... well, lovers."

"Did he ever discuss this case with you? Or did you overhear him talking about it with Detective Collins or Detective Thibido?"

"He never discussed it with me directly, but I did hear him talk about it with Detective Collins."

"And what was the nature of the discussion?" Smythe asked.

Kathy hesitated. "Why do you need to know?"

"I am fairly certain," Smythe said, "that criminal charges will be laid regarding the handling of the Hennings case. I am also fairly certain that Captain Andrade had a role in what happened. Now you can tell me what you know and I will do my best to protect you." He looked at her gravely. "Or you can protect Captain Andrade by remaining silent, and you may end up facing accessory charges."

Kathy felt a cold sensation wash through her. “The conversations I heard were pretty vague mostly,” she said. “I just caught parts of references and whispers. John took calls from Collins when we were together, especially lately. Other than that I have no specifics. I can say that John has become very agitated since you arrived.”

“I see,” Smythe said and stood. He never opened the file, never showed her so much as a sticky note or grainy photograph. “Thank you for your time and trust me when I say I will never repeat a word we spoke here today.”

“Did we say anything?” she asked.

“Though it may not seem so,” he said, “we spoke volumes.”

She watched from the fifth-floor office window as Smythe exited the building and returned to his car. He made a call on his cell and sat in the parking lot for several minutes before driving away. He was a nice but firm man, she thought, a formidable person who wielded his power with grace and respect. This was the exact opposite of Andrade and she decided to end the whole sordid affair.

Now Andrade was calling from the parking lot.

“Come on up,” she said.

Let him come, she thought, and do his worst. She was done with him forever. She buzzed him through the back entrance, heard his footsteps on the stairs and his knock at her door.

“It’s open,” she said. He stepped in but remained rigid in the foyer, his hands deep in his overcoat pockets.

“I need to know who you’ve been talking to,” he said.

“About what?”

“Kathy, I don’t have time for this. Do I have to repeat back to you what you said last time I was here?”

“No,” she said.

“Kathy, it’s important. Who have you spoken to?”

“Nobody,” she said.

“We both know that’s a lie,” Andrade hissed. “Stop playing games.”

“John, all I know is you were acting strange. I heard you talking with Collins and you were obviously worried about something that was between the two of you. I heard you use the name Hennings and I know that since Smythe started coming around you've acted very nervous."

"So it was Smythe?" he said.

"No, I didn't say that," she said softly. "I didn't tell this to anybody. I'm not stupid, John."

"Neither am I," he said and took a step forward.

"John, take another step and I will scream. I'll hit the panic button on my phone and it will automatically call 911. I want you to leave now."

Andrade's voice softened "Kathy, you need to understand there is a lot at stake here. I am under some serious pressure and I need to know if you have talked to somebody. Maybe you accidentally gave the wrong impression. Just give me a name and I will go away and never bother you again. This is matter of my professional life. Please, who was it?"

"Nobody," Kathy said.

With her thumb poised over the phone button, she asked again to leave.

"Okay, if you say so, but if it wasn't Smythe than it had to be – "

Andrade stopped and took a deep breath. He shook his head.

"Okay, I understand," he said.

"Please don't call me," she said. "Just leave me alone."

Andrade opened the door and paused for a moment. "Whatever you say."

She watched John start his car, drive out the alley and make a right turn up University. She packed a bag and quietly left the same way, beginning a careful, early morning drive toward her sister's place in Connecticut. She would arrive before dawn but she knew where the spare key was hidden. She could slip in without waking the family. Her nieces would be thrilled to see their aunt Kathy and her sister would be a comforting ear. Kathy needed family. She drove and cried tears of remorseful relief, but also felt fear for who John suspected she spoke with. Her car pierced the night as she prayed for the life of Michael Collins.

CHAPTER TWENTY-THREE

Kathy arrived at her sister's as winter was determined to chill New York to the bone. Two clear and intensely cold nights followed and then surrendered to a snowstorm that was hell-bent on burying the boroughs to the eves. Now six weeks from retirement, Drake was thirty pounds thinner and he held his head high.

Collins could not hide his anger. He growled obscenity-filled whispers at Drake every time they were part of the same meeting. They nearly came to blows once in the restroom, though Collins backed down when Drake lunged. Collins barely escaped Drake's bear grip by stumbling back into a stall, locking himself in and calling for help while Drake pounded on the door. Since then Collins made sure Drake was boxed in the cage before hurling his insults. Drake took satisfaction in knowing Collins was now afraid of him.

Robin was visiting her sister in Vermont to plan the wedding so Drake worked as many hours as he could. He was putting aside all extra dollars toward his retirement fund. Even with Robin's salary, they needed his paycheck to maintain their current lifestyle. His new book was far from finished and the investigation into the agent killings was still active but producing no clues. Drake had some hunches but voiced his opinions only on paper, integrating the reality of the case into his fictional story line. He hoped the killings were done, that the murderer had made his point and taken satisfaction in knowing he would never be caught.

Drake was pulling a late night shift when his cell rang and the caller ID announced Chief Smythe.

"Hello?" Drake said slowly.

"Officer Drake, this is Smythe."

"Hello Chief, what can I do for you at this late hour?"

"Well," Smythe said, sounding tired, "I can't sleep because of you."

"Me sir?"

"Afraid so. Your letter opened a can of worms for me. They are crawling all over my life and I can't put them back in the can."

"Sorry sir," Drake said. He didn't know whether to be fearful or hopeful.

"I guess the ugly truth will always find its way into the light of day," Smythe said. "We are looking into the possibility there may have been some complicity in derailing the Hennings case. Nothing is confirmed and you did not hear this from me, I just wanted to make sure you kept out of the line of fire for the next few days. Okay?"

Drake felt like whooping with joy, but he tried to keep his voice even. "Sure Chief"

"Good then. Just keep your head down and don't talk to anybody about this."

"I won't," Drake promised.

"Good man," Smythe said. "You know, talking to you may just help me get to sleep. I almost envy your retirement. You'll be away from all this."

"Thanks," Drake said and they hung up

Drake's stomach rolled. He felt a wave of anxiety crash over him, and he had no idea what that incoming tide would wash up. Though he was sure no one knew he had sent that letter to Smythe, there was always a chance a lip could slip. Come morning he would speak with Kellerman and make sure he had not accidentally said anything.

By midnight it was looking like a quiet night at the station house, so Drake opened a novel he had nearly finished and poured a fresh cup of coffee. Radio chatter echoed down from the front desk and the video feed showed two bundled officers entering the station with a small arrestee. Their voices wafted up through the narrow corridor as they stomped the snow off their shoes and shrugged off their jackets. Drake stopped short as Officers Yarrow and Bloom presented their prisoner for booking. Brian Shakespeare was red-faced and glassy-eyed as the cops pushed him to the counter.

"We caught this gentleman weaving his way down University in his Porsche," Yarrow said. "He failed the field test and we explained we had to arrest him. But when I tried to cuff him he freaked out and hit me with his satchel. Look at this."

A red welt was visible along Yarrow's jaw line.

"We had his Porsche towed," Bloom said. "He's pretty hammered. Blew a point two five. For such a small guy he has a big attitude."

"I know him," Drake said. "Hello Brian."

"He's got a famous name," Yarrow said. "I asked if he was related to William and he called me a cocksucker."

Bloom removed Brian's handcuffs. "Book him on driving under the influence, open container and assaulting an officer. He had a half pint of tequila between his legs."

"He's pissed off because I took this away from him," Yarrow said and dropped the worn leather satchel on the booking counter. Drake knew the manuscript strapped with a rubber band was inside.

"Lou?" Shakespeare gave him a blurry stare. "Fuckers took my book."

"Take it easy, Brian," Drake said softly. "Let's just get through this."

"These assholes took my case, they took my book and then they messed with me. They pushed me 'round, fucked with me."

"I know, now listen to me. Just do what I tell you and we'll get through this."

"Goddamn cops," Shakespeare said, his voice growing louder.

Yarrow grabbed the back of his jacket and Brian supported himself with a shoulder against the counter.

"Give me a reason shorty," Yarrow said. "I got you on assault already. I'd be happy to teach you a lesson in how to be nice in my station."

"Brian," Drake said with flat authority. "Look at me. Stop the bullshit, okay?"

Brian gawked at him and Drake gave him a wink.

"Sure, yeah, okay," Shakespeare slurred and dropped his aggressive posture.

"That's a good lad," Yarrow said.

Drake asked Brian to empty his pockets.

The booking process went without further incident. Drake bagged all of Shakespeare's belongings, read off the list and had him sign the inventory sheet. Yarrow told Bloom to put Shakespeare in cell three after prints and pictures.

"Go with these officers," Drake told Brian.

Bloom escorted him down the hall.

"Hey" Brian yelled back. "What about my book?"

"It's safe with me," Drake said and lifted the satchel.

Bloom walked Shakespeare down a short flight of steps to the tombs. The cells ran in a straight line along the right side of the hallway. The drunk tank was on the left, open to the hall with a wall of bars and high impact plexi-glass. Tonight the tank was empty but Bloom put Brian in his own cell like he was told.

"You be good now," Bloom said. "There is a blanket and a pillow. Why don't you try and sleep it off, okay?"

"Fuck you," Brian said and gave the cop a woozy stare.

Bloom smiled and waved Shakespeare off.

"Back atcha" Bloom said. "See those cameras? Old Lou will keep a close eye on you, so don't try and squeeze through the bars and climb out the window. Okay short stuff?"

Shakespeare sat on the lower bunk and glared at Bloom as he left the tombs.

"He okay?" Drake asked as Bloom came up the hall.

"Yeah, he'll sleep it off. You know that freak?"

"Yeah, he's a member of the writers group I meet with every week. He's just drunk."

"So you write?" Bloom asked.

"I do."

"Anything I might have read?"

"No," Drake said. "If I was published I wouldn't be doing this anymore."

"My sister is married to a writer," Bloom said. "He writes historical stuff, text books, that kind of thing. Nothing I'd want to read. What are you writing about?"

"Murder," Drake said.

"Well, good luck with that."

Drake thanked him and pushed the video feed button for the cells. Six small windows appeared on the monitor. Shakespeare sat on the lower bunk in the lower left screen. His body was rigid and his eyes were hidden in the shadow of the upper bunk. He looked lost. Drake felt sorry for him, and wondered how he must feel after being arrested and then bumping into Drake. He imagined Brian was afraid that Drake would tell the group. Drake gave the monitor one more quick look then went back to his book. Only eight pages to go and hours left on the clock.

Collins jerked awake to his cell phone ringing on his nightstand. Sleep still had hold of his mind as he grunted and checked the caller I.D. It was Andrade. Michael shook his head and cleared his throat. Two thirteen in the morning. Andrade had better have a good reason for this bullshit.

"Yeah," Michael croaked.

"I need to see you."

"I'll see you in the morning."

"No, now," Andrade said.

"Now? Where the hell are you?"

"Right outside."

Andrade pounded on the door with a glove-padded fist.

"Why?"

"Just let me the hell in!" Andrade demanded. "Make it fast. It's cold out here."

Collins pulled on a shirt and was halfway to the door when he stopped dead in his tracks. He looked at the phone in his hand and cocked his head. What could Andrade possibly want that could not wait until five when Collins was up and ready for work?

Two thirteen in the morning and pounding on his door? Andrade had been acting weird lately. He was all twitchy and suspicious, with his panties in a bunch because Smythe had been hanging around. While Michael was running around and dealing with the horrors of the recent murders, Andrade had become more distant, even staying away from the station.

Collins pulled on a pair of pants and headed for the door. Just to be safe he put his Glock into the waistband at the small of his back and dropped his shirttails to hide it. He felt a little paranoid doing it, but if John was drunk it could get ugly. Andrade began pounding at his door again and calling his name.

"What?" Collins said through the door. "I was sound asleep."

"Open the fucking door," Andrade said.

"Jesus," Collins said and opened up. "You know what time it is?"

"I know," Andrade pushed past him. "I was freezing my balls off out there."

"Where's your car?"

"I walked. I was down the street at the bakery, had a late date."

"Cap, what the hell is so important that it couldn't wait until morning?"

"Just a second, let me warm up," Andrade said and rubbed his hands together.

Collins watched as Andrade flexed his fingers and rotated his neck. He unbuttoned his overcoat and put his right hand in the deep pocket. Collins watched the hidden hand for sudden movements.

"Okay," Andrade said. Collins smelled alcohol on his breath. "I need to know who you've been talking to."

"Huh?" Collins wiped his right eye with the palm of his hand. "What the hell does that mean?"

"Who the hell did you talk to? Was it Smythe?" Andrade said. His voice was a harsh whisper.

"I don't have a clue what you're talking about," Collins said.

"Did Smythe offer you immunity? You went to Kathy, didn't you?"

Collins laughed. "Why would I talk to anybody?"

"WHO THE FUCK?" Andrade screamed and pulled a small but dangerous revolver from his jacket. It dangled by his side as he rocked slowly from side to side. "Michael, what deal did you make?"

"Jesus John, calm down. I swear, I don't know what the –"

"Bullshit," Andrade hissed and pointed the pistol at Collins, the wide barrel of the small .44 aligned with Michael's right eye.

"Smythe called me and wanted to talk to me about Hennings," Andrade said. "He mentioned Drake and a letter about the case written by Fitzpatrick himself. How would that letter get copied and sent to Smythe unless it came from you? And Kathy just told me to hit the road. She said she wasn't going to let me take her down with me. Why would I be going down?"

"Wait." Collins stepped back. "Why would I do that John? If the truth about Hennings came out I'd be as fucked as you." He moved his hand around his hip toward the Glock.

"Not if you made a deal. I won't allow you to ruin everything I have worked for."

Andrade shook the revolver, the barrel bouncing dangerously in Collins' face. "I won't let you backstab me and step over me. Whatever deal you made..."

"There is *NO* deal," Collins said.

Andrade cocked the revolver and Collins reached for the automatic. Andrade read the movement and pulled the trigger. The explosion was deafening in the small room as the slug caught the meaty muscle in Michael's right bicep, blasting a gapping hole through his arm.

"Shit!" Collins screamed, pulled the automatic from his waistband with his left hand as he fell to the floor. He jerked the gun up in Andrade's direction and started firing wildly. Andrade recovered from the recoil of his first shot and pointed his gun down on Collins. Andrade squeezed off two more shots as seven rounds hissed by his head and pocked the cinderblock wall behind him. The eighth shot caught Andrade in the right cheek while his fourth shot struck Collins in the chest, knocking him flat on the carpet.

Andrade jerked back as the bullet punctured his face, shattered his teeth and exited through his neck, spraying the wall with blood. Collins gasped and writhed on the floor as Andrade fought to stay conscious, fell to his knees and crawled toward the door with the revolver still clutched in his right hand. He spit blood and struggled back to his feet, pulled open the door and stumbled out into the cold night.

Andrade gripped the iron rail of the steps as his legs gave out. He could hear the sound of sirens converging on his location. He lost his footing and collapsed in a heap as the gun bounced into the thin snow of the walkway. Neighbors were out staring and Andrade tried to announce himself as a police officer, but all he managed was a bloody gurgle.

"There's the cops," he heard a neighbor say as he lost consciousness.

Inside Collins managed a wet breath, exhaled and died.

CHAPTER TWENTY-FOUR

Desk Sergeant McDonald answered the 911 transfer at 2:42 and literally stood up in shock. The 911 operator relayed several calls regarding shots fired and a man down on the front stoop at what appeared to be the home of Detective Michael Collins. McDonald slammed down the phone and shouted the information to Yarrow and Bloom through the intercom. What followed was a series of obscene expletives and hysterical action as the two patrolmen barreled out the door. Tires hissing on the snow wet asphalt, the engine growled as the two cops raced toward Collins' address.

McDonald walked to the cage and stood with one hand on his hip and the other slapped to his forehead. Drake leaned on the booking counter and blew out an exaggerated breath.

"I checked," McDonald said. "That is Collins's address. Sounds bad, but I'm sure we'll hear soon. Sounds like, well, I don't know. I hope he's okay. What a nightmare."

"Did you lock us down?" Drake asked.

"Shit," Shamus said and ran back to set the auto lock, making entry into the station impossible unless buzzed in by the desk.

"I'll keep watch to see what comes in from patrol," McDonald called down.

Officer Bloom steered the cruiser through the snowy streets and turned the corner at University. The rear of the cruiser fishtailed and Yarrow supported himself on the dashboard. At the end of the block the residents were out in the cold and a woman in a pink bathrobe knelt next to a figure covered with a patchwork quilt. The car's lights flared and the siren died as they came to a stop. Yarrow pushed open the passenger door and ran to Collins's front porch. His shoes slipped on the icy steps and he grabbed the railing to avoid falling on the downed figure.

"Ma'am, you need to move away," Yarrow said.

"I'm a nurse," she protested. "This man is severely injured. He's been shot in the face."

"Sweet Jesus weeping on the cross," Yarrow gasped. It was Captain Andrade. "Bloom, the man down is the cap."

"What the hell?" Bloom said and made his way up the steps.

"It's Andrade. Call for backup!"

"Son of a bitch!" Bloom said. He slapped the radio on his shoulder. "We have an officer down, it's Andrade. We need medics."

"Got it! Sending help now!" McDonald yelled through the radio.

Yarrow grimaced over the Captain, Andrade's face was a mess. His lips were shredded on the right side and fragments of his teeth and jawbone plastered to his jacket with frozen blood. Beneath his head a blood saturated towel was stiff with frost.

"I put that towel under his head to help stop the bleeding," the nurse said in a shaking voice. "The policeman in the apartment is dead. I checked his pulse."

"Ma'am?" Yarrow asked.

"That nice policeman, Mr. Collins. He's dead inside. It looks like they shot each other. There's blood everywhere." She started to cry and the tears rolled down her cheek only to freeze on her chin.

"Bloom," Yarrow said, "check inside."

"Oh man," Bloom called once he was inside the apartment. "Yeah, he's dead. Shot in the right arm and in the chest. Holy shit it's a fucking mess."

Sirens screamed as cops, paramedics and a fire truck came single file down the narrow street. The frozen tree branches and snow-patched ground reflected the urgency of the flashing lights, turning the dark lane into a garish festival. Patrolmen urged people back into their homes as the medics examined Andrade. They called orders to one another as they worked to stabilize him.

Two firemen entered the house and came out seconds later to confirm Collins was dead.

“What the hell happened here?” Yarrow asked nobody in particular. “What the living hell happened?”

“Hell if I know,” Bloom said. “This one is for the Detectives, but they are the ones who need detecting,” Bloom nervously laughed. “This is beyond fucked up.”

Detective Thibido showed up and spent his time gawking at the scene and looking distraught. He eventually joined the patrolmen and watched with an expression of pure fear.

“You okay?” Bloom asked and Thibido shook his head in the negative.

Twenty minutes later Andrade was on his way to the hospital as the fire team called in Collins’ death, got a field confirmation and zipped him into a bag. They were loading his body into the van when a plain sedan with a flashing red light on its dash rolled down the shoulder and stopped. Chief Smythe climbed from the passenger seat.

“ I don’t care what time it is,” Smythe yelled into his cell phone. “I want everybody down here now.” His breath in the cold night looked as though he breathed smoke.

“Chief,” Bloom yelled. Smythe carefully climbed the steps in front of Collins’s house. “This is where we found Andrade.”

“Give it to me.” Smythe said.

“Not completely sure,” Yarrow said. “The call came in that shots were fired and a man was down. We realized it was Collins place and when...”

“I was asking Detective Thibido,” Smythe cut him off.

“Sorry sir.”

“Well?” Smythe pushed.

“Uh, “ Thibido said, looked confused and stared at his feet. “Like he said, we got a call and, well, like he said, we saw it was Collins and we...”

“Oh for Christ’s sake,” Smythe stopped him. “Who was here first?”

“We were,” Yarrow said.

“Where were you, Thibido?”

"Off duty, sir," he said with an apologetic whimper. "I was asleep when the call came through to me."

"Jesus," Smythe huffed. "Okay, you." The Chief looked at Yarrow. "You tell me."

"We hauled ass over here and found this. Andrade was laying on the porch with his face shot off and Collins was dead inside."

"So, did they shoot each other?"

"It looks that way but we can't be sure."

"What about you?" Smythe asked Thibido who looked cornered and said nothing. "My God, what the hell kind of Detective are you?"

"Sorry sir," Thibido managed.

"You're right," Smythe said. "You are one sorry son of a bitch."

Prichard's forensics van arrived and the driver carefully negotiated the snow on the shoulder. He parked behind Smyth's car. Tillman, Vickers, Bernard and Mei Yang exited the van and began unloading equipment. Prichard looked tired and angry while his crew created a barrier with crime scene tape.

"Doctor," Smythe called and Prichard joined them by the steps.

"Quite a mess and a fiasco, huh?" Prichard said.

"That about sums it up," Smythe answered.

"Any witnesses?" Prichard asked.

"Yes we do, absolutely," Yarrow spoke up. "The lady in the pink is a nurse who tended to Andrade and told us about Collins."

"Very good," Prichard said. "The team will work the scene. You two officers make sure these people stay in their homes and ask who saw or heard anything."

"I'll get out of your hair," Smythe said. "I'll get to the hospital and check on Andrade. Thibido, you come with me. Yarrow, gather up all these other cops and get everybody out of the area until we get this processed. Damn its cold out here!"

The team moved across the scene with machine-like efficiency, bagging and photographing every detail.

Digital cameras flashed from the doorway and windows of Collins' dwelling as though lightning flashed inside. Smythe half waited for the thunder that announced the shit storm on its way. He thought of the scandal he hoped to avoid and knew it would rain down with the power of public shock.

He walked back to his car with Thibido in tow. The two of them climbed into the back seat.

"Head for the hospital," Smythe said to the driver, and then he turned to Thibido. "So, what can you tell me about this whole messed-up situation?"

Thibido went white and lost his struggle with his emotions and Smythe waited until Thibido regained his composure.

"Are you going to start crying or are you going to answer my questions?"

"I..." Thibido tried and failed to respond.

"Just forget it for now," Smythe said. "We'll talk again when you find your testicles and get willing to tell the fucking truth."

When they pulled up to the emergency entrance at the hospital Smythe told Thibido to stay in the car.

"And don't let him touch anything or go anywhere," he told his driver.

The driver nodded and glared at Thibido through the rear view window.

"We're finished here for now," Vickers told Prichard. "We'll come back and make another sweep when the sun comes up. We have blood spatter on the wall in alignment with Andrade's height and wounds as per the probable line of fire. The wall was pitted with bullet strikes and we found flattened rounds on the floor behind where Andrade stood. Two deep gouges in the floor beside the chalk line for Collins and impact damaged brass slugs along the baseboard. There are ejected casings around Collins and none around Andrade's position. Slugs look like forty-four revolver rounds and a five shot, snub-nosed forty-four was found in the bushes next to where Andrade fell. The automatic was next to Collins. There is no doubt they were shooting at each other."

"Okay," Prichard said. "Let's get all this down to processing and I want everybody else to come back to the station with me. I want statements from everyone."

"Yes sir." Vickers said and began passing the word.

CHAPTER TWENTY-FIVE

Drake paced the cage. Shots had been fired and a man was down at Collins' place? His conversation with Smythe regarding the letter went through his head and a body-trembling shudder went up Drake's spine. He suspected the truth had come home for the conspirators and brought violent vengeance with it.

Drake went back to his reading but the novel soon ran out of pages. He finished an arrest report and sighed at the number of hours left in his shift. A few cops came and went, all talking urgently about Collins. Then the empty halls echoed the slow drip of the faucet in the coffee room, the pinging of the vents as the heater kicked on and the occasional cough from desk sergeant McDonald up the hall.

"Drake?" McDonald called through the speaker.

"Yeah?"

"Just heard that Collins is dead and Andrade is at the hospital, shot in the face. Witnesses say they did it to each other."

"No shit?" Drake said back.

"Can you believe it?"

No honor among thieves and liars, Drake thought, *and Karma can be a bitch.* Drake squelched his sick sense of satisfaction that the conspirators had turned on one another. He rubbed his eyes with the palms of his hands and felt suddenly exhausted.

"That's really fucked up," Drake said back.

"How is our boy in the can?" McDonald asked.

"Fine," Drake said.

Drake could see in the monitor that Brian lay on his side with his back to the camera. He was most likely still deep in a drunken slumber, and would eventually wake up to face a nasty hangover. Drake knew it well; he had spent many weekends that way after the Hennings case. He had spent several months swimming in the waters of oblivion, trying to quiet the incessant voice that plagued him with questions of what went wrong. Then when his wife left, Drake used alcohol to ease his shame and loneliness.

On the monitor Shakespeare woke and sat up. Sympathetic to the Brian's condition, Drake knew what the guy needed. Other than something for his head, Brian would need information and support. From the break room Drake pulled a Coke and a bottle of cold water from the fridge, then grabbed two packs of Advil from the medicine box. With his supplies in hand he headed down to the cell.

Shakespeare rolled over, put his feet on the floor and rubbed his face. He quickly walked to the stainless steel toilet and vomited. He swallowed hard and burped up sour gas as his head swam. It felt as if the mountings that held his brain in place had slipped so it floated free in his skull. His lips were tacky with dried spit and his tongue felt like a kitchen sponge. Throwing up helped.

On his feet Shakespeare went to the sink and splashed water on his face. It took the sting out of his eyes. He drank tap water from his cupped hand, which caused him to retch and vomit in the sink.

“Oh God,” he said and closed his eyes. His stomach settled and he went back to the bunk and sat down. There was the vague memory of drinking with Sandy and Pooter, then being arrested, a struggle and getting booked. His satchel was gone and his book was in the hands of strangers. No, not strangers he remembered, the manuscript was held by the fat cop from the writer's group. Drake, Lou Drake had his case. How long ago was that? Hours, days? His sat with his face in his hands and his eyes blurry with the hangover. He did not hear Drake approach.

“Hey Brian.” Drake said.

“What?”

Shakespeare opened his eyes. Drake stood outside the bars.

“Brian, are you with me?”

“Yeah,” he said. His voice was hoarse. “Hey Lou.”

“You remember being brought in?”

"Uh, yes. Two cops roughed me up some. You have my satchel, said you would hold it for me. How long have I been here?"

"About three hours, I'd say," Drake said and checked his watch. "Yes, three hours. You were out. You were pretty shit-faced. How you feeling?"

"Pretty bad. Can I get something to drink? Something cold?"

"Way ahead of you," Drake said and handed Brian the open soda can.

"Thanks," Brian croaked and drank deeply. He swallowing hard, belched loudly and drank down the rest as shook his head to clear his mind.

"Better?"

"Yes, thanks. You have my book?"

"Upstairs," Drake said. "It's safe in evidence. You know you're in some pretty serious trouble."

"Yeah, what's the damage?"

"Drunk driving, resisting arrest, assaulting an officer," Drake said as he slowly listed the charges. "Do you have a good lawyer?"

"The best," Brian said. "Uh. Just a minute." He rushed back to the toilet and purged the cola as his body trembled.

"Pretty bad?" Drake asked.

"Uh, yeah."

"Why did you drive?"

"Ha, well, why does any drunk drive? I was over that line and it was so late. I guess my shit-faced head thought I'd get home without anybody seeing me. Stupid, huh?"

Brian went back to the cot and sat down. He blew out a rancid breath and rubbed his temples with his index fingers.

"Want some water?" Drake said.

Brian took the bottle and sipped it slowly.

"Think you can hold down something for your head?"

"We'll see," Shakespeare said and took two of the Advil. He swallowed more water and sat with his elbows on his knees.

"Well, we have a situation here tonight, so I have to get back to my desk. Nobody will get to you until later in the morning. Try and get some more sleep and I'll check on you in a while." Drake said.

"Thanks Lou," Brian said and rolled back onto the cot.

"I'll leave you these other pills," Drake said. "You'll probably want them later."

Brian mumbled another thanks and Drake climbed the stairs back to the cage. As he settled back into his chair a harsh buzzer rang. The desk sergeant opened the station and pandemonium ensued. Leading the pack of raucous cops was Chief Smythe himself. They passed the cage and headed back to Andrade's office in a tangle of footsteps and competing voices. Drake watched in horrible fascination. In the mingled words it became clear that Collins was indeed dead and Andrade was in the hospital.

"Holy shit," Drake whispered.

CHAPTER TWENTY-SIX

By the time the sun announced the arrival of morning, the station was busy with patrolmen, detectives and forensics personnel from around the city. Smythe's camp was pitched in Andrade's office and the team interviewed each cop, detective and emergency crewman who responded to the shooting. Agent Thatcher was present with his usual quiet intimidation. Smythe questioned Thibido again about what he knew regarding the events at Collins's apartment. Again Thibido said he knew nothing. Smythe shook his head in disgust and informed Thibido he was a person of interest, asked him to surrender his gun and badge and had him sequestered under guard in an interrogation room.

Officer Yarrow was questioned longer than the rest and when he exited the office several other officers asked what he knew. He shrugged.

"I'm as confused as anybody," he said. "It's a fucked up situation."

Detective Kellerman arrived around eight and waved in through the window of the cage. Drake gave him a raised eyebrow and a nod in return. Kellerman entered the office where Agent Thatcher stood by the window.

"Good morning Kellerman." Smythe greeted him with a handshake. Agent Thatcher also offered a hand and took a chair by the desk. Kellerman joined him.

"Good morning sir," Kellerman said.

"Unfortunate situation," Smythe said as he sat behind the desk.

"Yes sir," Kellerman said with a shake of his head. "I can't imagine what could have happened to cause these two men to do something like this."

"Nothing?" Smythe raise his eyebrows. "I doubt that."

"Sir?"

"What do you know about the Hennings case?" Smythe asked.

"I wrote a paper on it in college."

"I know" Smythe said, "I read it. You made a good case that there was underhanded shit going on that caused the case to be dropped by the District Attorney.

"But that was the assignment, sir." Kellerman responded. "Pick a high profile case and argue from the other side. I picked Hennings because it was an option. It was nothing more than that, just doing the assignment."

"I suspect your opinion was more than academic," the Chief said and stood up. As he walked around the desk he placed his index fingers below his lower lip and bobbed his head as he spoke. "I got the distinct impression that your argument was more than theory. You had serous doubt about the results of the investigation. Am I right?"

"I suppose," Kellerman said slowly.

"Especially with Drake being your father's former partner, your Dutch uncle and longtime friend of your family?"

"Freedom to speak freely?" Kellerman asked.

Smythe nodded.

"I was appalled by what I found in those files. I researched Lou Drake's arrest history. He was obviously a competent Detective. I found the circumstances surrounding the evidence dismissal and supposed misconduct on his part very suspect. I've always thought he was set up so Hennings could be let off the hook."

"But someone else confessed."

"And then hanged himself in his cell. Awfully convenient. Teddy Simons was a known pathological liar, petty criminal and had a reputation for confessing to other crimes as well. I believe he was used and evidence was planted to collaborate his confession so he would be taken seriously."

"Interesting," Smythe said. "So how does that work into this situation?"

"There's no honor among thieves," Kellerman said.

The Chief smiled. "Exactly," he said, and then he nodded at Thatcher. "Go bring in Thibido."

Thibido crossed his arms on the interrogation room table and tried to hold a brave expression. He failed and dropped his face to his arms and shook his head. How had it come to this? For the past ten years he had been on track to follow Andrade and Collins out of the borough and into the city. He never said a word to anyone about his testimony in the Hennings case, never betrayed the trust that took him out of the patrol pool and made him a Detective. Not that he knew that much at the time, only what he was coached to say. And nobody questioned him, Andrade made sure of that.

Now this.

When he got the call Thibido could not believe that Andrade and Collins had shot each other. It made no sense. The scene at the apartment was surreal. When he saw Andrade lying on the ground in a bloody mess he became paralyzed with fear. And the sight of Collins was equally startling, with his face white and his chest torn open by the powerful round of the compact hand cannon. The rumor of his emotional paralysis spread fast through the ranks and now Thibido knew the officer gossip mill had him labeled as undesirable.

Thatcher opened the interrogation room door. "Chief wants to see you."

"Sure," Thibido said.

His passing through the station drew condemning stares. Thibido felt like the proverbial dead man walking. When a cop screws up so bad that the whole department knows about it, the long walk to the Chief is like climbing the gallows steps. Thibido kept his head down and prepared himself for what seemed to be inevitable. Most likely he would get an ass chewing, condemnation and the mandatory suspension pending investigation. They would give him the option of resigning, and given the chance, he would likely play that card.

"Come in, sit down." Smythe said when Thatcher and Thibido arrived at Andrade's office.

Thibido sat down beside Detective Kellerman, who was already sitting in one of the two chairs in front of Andrade's desk. Thatcher resumed his post by the window.

Thibido nodded solemnly to Kellerman, who returned the gesture.

"Have you gotten your act together?" Smythe asked. "Done with the dramatics, ready to have a real talk?"

"Yes sir."

"Last night was a full on clusterfuck. This puts the literary agent killing investigation in limbo and this shit is now our number one priority. Agent Thatcher will be the liaison while the case is reviewed. There is a lot at stake here and we are hoping you can shed some light on it."

"Yes sir."

"Good. You know Detective Kellerman?" Smythe asked and Thibido nodded. "We have some questions for you. There are some details surrounding this incident that we are very confused about. You were attached to these guys, worked with them for almost ten years."

"I did sir," Thibido muttered.

"Yet according to your jacket you personally have not broken a single case. No arrests, no decorations and no commendations. Collins made every case and you acted as support. Is that right?"

"Yes, but he was my partner. Collins was a great cop."

"Not to get too personal, but I see you are single, no family, nobody at all," Smythe said.

"I was an orphan," Thibido said. "The force became my family, I guess. And, well, I guess I just... " Thibido's voice failed him.

"Yes?" Smythe urged.

"He was a good cop. I was his backup, that's what I did."

"Batman and Robin," Thatcher said from the back of the room.

"Truth is," Smythe continued, "if it wasn't for Collins you would have never made Detective. Even your patrol record was mediocre. You're not a very good cop, are you Thibido?"

"I do my best," he said. "Look, I want to apologize about my behavior at the scene, but to see Andrade down and Collins dead, it just shook me really bad."

Smythe snorted. "Never seen a gruesome crime scene before, is that it?"

"No ... I mean, yes but—"

Smythe slammed his hand down on the blotter and Thibido jerked backwards in his seat.

"But the truth is," Smythe said, "you have a pretty good idea why two supposed friends and partners would suddenly gun one another down in the middle of the night, now don't you?"

Thibido was shaking his head even before Smythe finished speaking "No sir," Thibido said. "I have no idea."

"Detective Thibido, I have witnesses who will testify that you and Lou Drake were at odds and that Drake and Collins nearly came to blows in the bathroom. I have it on good authority there is grave evidence that Andrade and Collins may have intentionally sabotaged the state's case against Hennings. They did this to further their careers. Now while all this was going on you were joined at Collins's hip. How is it even possible that you don't know shit about why these two suspected conspirators shot one another?"

"I'm sorry sir," Thibido said, "that's the truth."

"I don't buy that for a minute," Smythe said. "You can't expect me to believe he never said anything to you about any conflict between him and Andrade."

"Collins had become more secretive lately," Thibido said, his eyes down. "He seemed more agitated, like he was pissed off about something, but I figured it was about the murder case. He talked about it a lot."

"And what was your take on the dead agents," Thatcher asked and Thibido jerked, as if he had forgotten the agent was in the room.

"Me?"

"Yes," Smythe said, "you."

"I, uh, well – I guess I was just following Collins and waiting to see what he came up with. I guess," Thibido said and slumped in his chair.

"No clue, huh?" Smythe asked.

"No, I'm sorry sir," Thibido whispered.

"I'm sorry too," Smythe said. "Okay, consider yourself on suspension as we look into this further. Now get out of here. And if I hear you even step a toe over the state line I will have you arrested for obstruction and flight. You understand?"

"Yes sir," Thibido said and left the office in hunched shame.

Thatcher closed the door.

"That was surprising," Kellerman said. "I thought that pathetic shit bag would sing like the proverbial canary."

"He would have if Andrade was dead," Smythe said. "I suspect with Andrade alive Thibido is too afraid to spill the secrets. He probably even hopes Andrade will make sense of this and save his ass."

"That's messed up," Thatcher said.

As the chaos continued upstairs, Drake checked on Brian and found him asleep in the cell. Drake's shift was over but he hung around the station trying to gather information on the night before. He wanted to know how Andrade was doing. Nobody had a spare moment to talk to him and all the most informed discussions were behind closed doors. Drake checked out with the desk sergeant and said he would be back in three hours to look in on Shakespeare. McDonald noted Drake's departure on the computer.

"Okay, you're all checked out."

"Uncle Lou," Kellerman yelled to Drake as he left the interrogation room.

They embraced and Drake shook his head in cynical exasperation.

"Some night, huh?" Drake said.

"Oh yeah. How about breakfast?" Kellerman suggested.

"Sure kid, how's your dad?" Drake said as they started toward Molly's.

"He was bored until the literary agents started getting whacked. Now he's going to get a job as a security guard at the university."

"You were in seeing the Chief, right?" Drake asked.

"Can't say too much," Paul said seriously. "This is a really bad situation. We had Thibido in for questioning and he said nothing. Now Smythe has to make some sense of this whole deal. The FBI will most likely step in."

"Thibido," Drake shook his head. "Poor bastard."

"You okay, uncle Lou?"

"Yeah, just tired is all. I worked a double shift and a friend was brought in on DUI. Did your dad tell you I got engaged?"

"No," Kellerman said, sounding genuinely pleased. "Robin?"

"Who else would have me?"

Kellerman smiled. "Good for you."

"All this activity has something to do with Hennings, doesn't it?" Drake said.

Kellerman punched his shoulder and said nothing.

Drake nodded. "That's what I thought."

CHAPTER TWENTY-SEVEN

Thibido took miserable steps through the thin snow as he walked towards Molly's Café. He had not eaten for eight hours. His freedom depended on staying in Malcolm and reporting in with Smythe every day. His answers to Smythe's line of questioning came easily as he was following Collins' orders, the same as he had doing for ten years.

As Thibido approached the café, he saw Kellerman and Drake come out and go their separate ways. Thibido ducked down and backtracked to avoid Drake as he came up the walk.

"Hey," Drake yelled.

"What?" Thibido said. He turned on Drake with mock anger.

"You're just the guy I wanted to talk to," Drake said.

"Back off," Thibido spat. "I don't have time for you,"

"You better make time," Drake said and grabbed Thibido's jacket.

"Or what?"

"Oh, how about this?" Drake said.

While Thibido tried to resist Drake dragged him to the back of the restaurant and pushed him into the delivery bay where the dumpsters smelled of old chicken fat and spoiled vegetables. As cold as it was, the smell was pungent. Drake pushed Thibido against the ripe trash containers.

"What the hell?"

"I just had a talk with Kellerman," Drake hissed. "He told me an interesting story about you."

"Fuck him and fuck you too," Thibido yelled but his frightened voice betrayed him.

"I'll fuck you up bad if you don't answer some questions," Drake hissed back and shoved Thibido back into the dumpster.

"Not a chance," Thibido said and tried to push by.

Drake dragged him back and Thibido threw a wide punch. Drake easily ducked the roundhouse and drove his fist into his gut. Thibido coughed and doubled over. Drake grabbed his lapels, pushed him back until they struck a stack of empty banana boxes and Thibido tumbled backward in a heap.

"You will answer some questions or so help me I will beat you to a bloody pulp," Drake said, his voice filled with venom.

"Naaa," Thibido whined. He struggled with the cardboard boxes and tried to crawl away. Drake put a foot on his back and pushed him down into the cold refuse. Drake dropped to one knee, grabbed Thibido by the hair and put his lips an inch from his ear.

"You know what happened with the Hennings case. They brought you in and you said what they told you to say. You helped that pile of shit Hennings go free and you were a big part of the reason I took a dive."

Drake's voice was driven by ten years of betrayal.

"No, I–" Thibido cried.

Drake shut him up a hard tug on his hair.

"Kellerman told me what the Chief thinks," Drake said. "He also told me you played dumb. But I know Collins. He loved to talk. You know the truth and if you don't tell me I will do you and make it look like a suicide."

"I don't know. I swear," Thibido gasped.

"Bullshit," Drake growled.

Thibido rolled on to his back, his face smeared with banana mush, his clothes filthy with wet garbage and his eyes wide with fear.

"Tell me or so help me," Drake said.

"I can't," Thibido wailed. "I can't!"

"Can't or won't?" Drake rasped.

"I CAN'T!" Thibido screamed.

"You're pathetic," Drake said and spat on him. "Pathetic."

"I can't," Thibido said with whimper.

Drake stood and glared with his chest heaving. Finally he said, "This isn't over asshole."

Then he turned and walked away.

Thibido's body shook with shame and terror as he slowly climbed to his feet and stepped out of the garbage.

He watched Drake lumber up University Avenue until he disappeared behind some trees.

A feeling of hopelessness washed over Thibido. He stood with mouth agape and tears streaming down his dirty face. He couldn't do this anymore. With Andrade down and Collins dead, he wasn't strong enough to keep the secrets alone.

He started walking back toward the station. His walk became a run. He ran toward Smythe to tell him everything, to purge the sin he now carried alone. He wanted to surrender the heavy load of guilt that clung to him like the stink of the restaurant garbage bins.

As he ran he realized that he was more afraid of what Lou Drake would do to him than Andrade and Hennings combined. Thibido ignored the stitch in his side and the burn in his chest as he pushed his out-of-shape body.

"I think I just messed up," Drake said to Kellerman on his cell phone.

"Meaning what?"

"When we left each other I caught Thibido trying to ditch me. I caught up with him and I flipped out," Drake said. "After what you told me I'm afraid I lost it. I smacked him, pushed him into the trash behind Molly's and threatened to kill him if he didn't tell me everything."

"Jesus, and what did he tell you?" Kellerman asked.

"Nothing," Drake said with a soft laugh. "He lay there covered in old bananas and dirty snow and said he couldn't tell me. *I can't,* he said."

"God. Wait, did he say he didn't know or did he say he – what did he say?"

"*I can't,* he said," Drake reiterated. "He acted pathetic and said *I can't.*"

"Then he knows but is afraid to talk, just like the Chief speculated," Kellerman said. "You didn't mess up anything, unless some University kid got it on video tape. Did anybody see you?"

"Nobody saw a thing."

"Then this could work in our favor. If you scared him enough, he may come in for his own protection."

"That would wrap things up in a nice little bow," Drake said.

They agreed to wait and see.

Drake took a shower and tried to take a nap. His cell rang. It was the desk sergeant calling to say the drunk in cell three was awake and asking for him.

"I'll be down in half an hour," he said.

Drake changed into a fresh uniform and left the house.

"Glad you're here," McDonald said when Drake arrived at the station. "The guy is acting nuts. He keeps saying you're the only one who knows him. I looked over his arrest report and he hasn't asked for an attorney or nothing. With this shooting thing we haven't given this guy any attention."

"I'll go see what's up," Drake said. "Is there anything new on Andrade?"

"He was in surgery. I guess he lost most of his lower jaw and the round took a chunk out of his neck. They patched him up but it took a few hours. He's in post op and sleeping it off. Sounds like he'll need a lot of corrective work."

"Jesus," Drake said.

He was still shaking his head in wonderment as he started walking down to the tombs.

Shakespeare sat on his bunk and looked nervous. His eyes were twitchy and his face was slack.

"Hey Brian," Drake said. "I heard you were asking for me."

"You still have my book? " Shakespeare asked. "I was worried when they told me you went home. Is it safe?"

"Yeah, it's safe. Don't worry. Besides, don't you have a backup copy of the manuscript?"

"Yeah, sure, but, you know. I'm not done with it yet and I don't want anybody messing with it. You know what I mean?"

"Sure," Drake said and leaned against the wall. "Are you ready to contact that lawyer of yours? Why don't we get you that phone call and arrange to get you out of here."

"Yeah, that would be great," Brian said. "Did you read it?"

"The book? No."

"Didn't think you would. Thanks for respecting my privacy."

Shakespeare's tone was growing agitated. He started walked around the cell, clenching and unclenching his hands while rotating his head. He reminded Drake of an animal in an enclosure at the zoo.

"That cop gave me some shit and I told him I wanted to talk to you because, well... these assholes don't know me like you do."

"Calm down," Drake said, "Don't want to attract any unnecessary attention."

"No, no, we don't want any attention. There's too much at stake, too much to lose, right? I mean, that could ruin the whole thing, that would ruin everything."

"Ruin what?" Drake asked.

"This is the one," Brian said and sat back on the cot. "This book, it's the one that will get me in the door. Nobody has ever written anything like this before. It has action, human drama, ironic twists and an embodiment of all that is wrong with the world. It speaks to where we are going as a race and the eventual destruction of society as we know it."

"Sounds great," Drake said.

"It is," Shakespeare said. "Desperation and clarity of purpose and the final resolution of all we strive for. The Red Ryder BB gun that arrives on Christmas morning. The eventual bliss of the long overdue prayers sent to God on the eve of our birth. To finally be granted the epiphany that to have what you want in this world you've got to go and get it for yourself."

"That's pretty profound stuff." Drake chuckled. "Are you still a little drunk?"

"Not at all," Brian said. "Come on Lou, you should understand what I am saying better than anyone."

"Why is that?"

"You're no cop, I know that. You're a writer, but what are you writing? You have a new book going, but what is it really about?"

"They say to write what you know, so I'm writing about being a cop, a Detective chasing a serial killer," Drake said.

"That isn't what you know," Brian said and shook his head. "That's what a thousand others have written about because you think it will sell. It won't, my friend. Today you have to write what nobody else knows, what the people secretly want to see but can't because they are sheep. Why do books about horrible lives sell? It's because most Americans have easy, fat, cushy lives where their idea of suffering is to have their meal come cold, their luggage lost or their cable go out. They crave real tragedy because they need to shock themselves out of pathetic obscurity."

"So, what exactly is your book about?" Drake said.

"It's about you and me, those out there on the street, the hundreds sleeping in cardboard boxes and sleeping in missions and passed out drunk in mansions. It's about how all of humanity is intertwined by fate and fortune."

"I see," Drake said. "I'm sure it will be great. Look, I'm sorry to derail our literary discussion but I think they want to get you out of here. Give me a number so I can make a call and get the ball rolling."

"Okay." Brian nearly pouted. "You do understand what I mean, right Drake?"

"Yes, I do."

"So keep the book safe, make sure you keep it safe."

"Don't worry, " Drake said. "I will take good care of it. Now give me that number, okay?"

"You'll have to look it up." Brian's eyes went dark, as though his own personal cloud rolled over his mind and blocked out his inner light.

"What's his name?" Drake asked.

"David Alan Barringer, in Manhattan."

"Okay," Drake said as he wrote it down.

"Lou? Why do you write?" Shakespeare asked.

"Because it makes me forget my pathetic life."

Brian smiled.

CHAPTER TWENTY-EIGHT

A few minutes later Drake was in the cage searching for the phone number for Brian's attorney. He saw Chief Smythe storm out of Andrade's office and bark orders at just about every person he saw.

"When can we talk to Andrade?" Smythe yelled to a Detective.

"I'll know in a bit," he yelled back.

"Sooner the better. Oh, Drake," Andrade said. "I need to speak to you now."

"Sure Chief, I just need to look something up," Drake said.

"No time, I need to see you right now. Interrogation room. Sergeant, take Thibido and put him in Collins's old office under guard. I want him cuffed and watched. Understand? Lou, now!"

"Yes sir," he said as he wrote down the lawyer's number.

Smythe ducked a few questions and waved away another cop. Thatcher joined Drake and the Chief in the interrogation room and locked the chaos outside. Smythe drew a deep breath and took a seat. He gestured for Drake to sit across from him while Thatcher stood by the door.

"Crazy shit, huh?" Smythe asked. Drake nodded. "Do you realize how much of this is because of you?"

Uncertainty stabbed at Drake's gut.

"You'll have to tell me, sir."

"It's really all about you, I'm afraid," Smythe said. "You sent me that letter and that got me making some calls. Now we know two seemingly good cops had an OK Corral moment that left one dead."

"I don't know what to say to that," Drake said.

Thatcher took over. "You were looking into the agent killings, weren't you?"

"Only as inspiration," Drake said. "I am working on a book. The murder cases got me inspired to write, that's all."

"Was it research when you threatened to kill Detective Thibido?" Smythe asked.

"I – " Drake started.

"You made a strong impression," Smythe interrupted. "Thibido showed up in my office, almost sick from running, and stinking of rotting fruit and begged me to hear his confession."

"Oh," Drake said. He fidgeted in his seat.

"So," Smythe continued. "Agent Thatcher and I listened to a story of deceit, betrayal, sabotage and ugly back-room deals. Thibido gave us a full confession about his role. This gives us enough to not only entertain the notion of reopening Hennings, but also to exonerate you."

A huge smile spread across Drake's face. Suddenly he felt lighter than air. After all these years! He felt like getting up and dancing a jig. "That's amazing," he said.

"I've placed Thibido under arrest. He promised to cooperate when we question Andrade. Lou, I – "

He was cut short by a sharp report from the hall, which was followed by an uproar outside the door.

"That sounded like a shot," Thatcher said.

The door burst open. McDonald was ashen-faced and swallowed hard.

"What?" Smythe asked.

"Thibido just fucking shot himself, right out here," he said.

"What the hell? Where did he get a gun?"

"His hands were cuffed in front of him, so he just grabbed the revolver from a patrolman and stuck the barrel in his mouth," McDonald said.

"Goddammit!" Smythe yelled.

"This is bad, " Thatcher said and followed the Chief out the door.

"Out of my way," Smythe said and pushed past the crowd of cops.

"Oh for the love of Christ," he said.

Thibido lay on his back, his eyes dull as old marbles and a pool of blood spreading beneath his head. Everyone in the station looked from Thibido's body to Smythe's seething face. Drake stood behind the Chief and closed his eyes.

"Has anybody called for an ambulance?" Smythe asked and people ran for phones.

Drake went back to a chair in the interrogation room and laid his head on the table.

Two hours passed and the station was once again quiet. Witnesses were questioned and it was determined that Thibido did, in fact, grab a cop's gun and shoot himself in the mouth. The slug exited the back of his head and was found near the base of the front desk. Smythe released the officer of any liability regarding the grabbing of his gun, but was warned to ensure the lock strap was in place in the future. The scene was photographed and the body removed. Smythe ordered the station cleared and the shootout investigation put off until the next day. Smythe told Drake they would pick up where they left off later.

Smythe said, "Drake, we will have to finish our conversation later. Go home, get some sleep and be back here for the graveyard. I need every man."

"Yes sir," Drake said and logged out, went home and collapsed into a dreamless sleep for four hours. He awoke stiff and lethargic, but after a shower and a shave he felt better and returned to the station. All evidence of the earlier drama was cleaned up and the station looked normal. He poured himself a cup of coffee and called Shakespeare's lawyer. The message service said David Benninger could not be reached until morning.

"But I have a client of his in custody," Drake said. "We're trying to arrange his release."

The woman said they had no way of reaching Benninger.

"Just leave him the message that Brian Shakespeare is in custody at the Malcolm station and charged with assault."

"I will sir," she said and Drake hung up.

His head was conflicted by the events of the last forty-eight hours. His heart, however, felt only a single emotion - satisfaction. What had Franny said about the dead agents? *They had it coming?* The same applied to the men who stole his life. What a day, what a week, what a messed-up situation.

Drake decided to distract himself with Shakespeare, to engage him in more rambling about writing and the meaning of life. On the monitor Brian looked asleep but Drake walked down anyway and found he was indeed out cold, the empty Advil pack and water bottle set outside the bars.

"What a day," Drake said and picked up Brian's trash.

In the break room Drake dropped the wrappers in the can and returned to the cage. The silence of the station was eerie. Drake looked at Shakespeare's satchel in the evidence bag and reflected on their earlier conversation.

Why do you write?

It makes me forget my pathetic life.

This is the one, Brian said. *Nobody has ever written anything like this before.*

It's about you and me.

Maybe he has really done it, Sandy's voice echoed in Drake's mind.

Drake shook his head at how protective and superstitious writers can be. How paranoid they can be, like Shakespeare afraid somebody would steal his book and pass it off as their own. More than that, how protective they are of what they have created. Understandable as the completion of a novel is an amazing feat, despite what the industry and the naysayer may think. Like a birth, it takes pain and blood to write a finished book. Then comes the real work. Will it sell? What if it has no friends? Food for thought, Drake mused, to those who are thinking of getting pregnant with the desire to write. As for Shakespeare's fear of theft, worse had been done in the world of publishing. Shakespeare's words got Drake thinking about his new novel.

That's what a thousand others have written about and you are too because you think it will sell.

So show me what is viable, Drake thought and reached for Shakespeare's manuscript, the one that Brian felt was so important he was willing to face jail time. He unzipped the mesh bag and pulled out the weathered leather satchel. Drake paused looked at the monitor showing the video feed from the cells. Brian would never know, Drake thought, and I can find out for myself if the pages in the bag are as profound as he claims. Shakespeare's passion was certainly convincing enough, but even the most horrible writers believe their work to be golden.

Drake opened the satchel and pulled the heavy stack of paper from its cocoon. Wasn't that what every unpublished manuscript was, a hopeful caterpillar sleeping in hopes of becoming a published book?

"He's a friend," Drake said aloud. "Maybe he would like my opinion,"

Drake knew this was nothing more than pure rationalization. He and Brian had never sat down and talked, never had a meal together. They never became friendlier than the jovial familiarity of the writer's group. Still, wasn't that the whole premise of the group? Common goals and supporting each other? Giving advice and constructive criticism when it was appropriate?

You're full of shit, Drake thought, *you just want to read it to see if it's any good.*

REJECTION was printed in bold across the title page in twenty-four point Courier font. Brian's name, address and phone number followed a few spaces down. Blue, red and flesh colored rubber bands criss-crossed the bundle, wrapped around the stack as though it were held hostage by a kidnapper. It was as though the words on the pages hoped the publishing industry would pay a ransom and release them with the stroke of the contract pen.

Nice one, Drake thought. *You'll have to use that in a book.*

Drake pushed a thumb under the first rubber band and slowly removed it from the manuscript. One after another Drake removed the bands until the pages were loose in his hands. He turned the title page and placed it face down. Page two was a cryptic acknowledgement, followed but a short paragraph paying homage to the desperate toiling of every writer and the goal of immortality through publication. There was a hand-written dedication to Sandy and the group as a whole.

Drake flipped to chapter one, page one. He sat back and read an overly-detailed scene of a man packing a duffle bag, checking and rechecking the contents and looking at his watch as the sun set over Greenwich Village. True to what was said about Shakespeare's style, it took twenty pages before the story began to suggest the character was up to no good. Not that is was poorly written. It was as good as many of the novels Drake had read.

He turned page 46 face down and began to read a laboriously descriptive image of the protagonist as he committed a brutal and sickeningly well planned murder of a full time waiter, part time literary agent.

"Oh shit," Drake said and sat up straight.

His mind clear but his body unresponsive, the victim could do nothing as the blade made its terrible pass along his abdomen and cut away the muscle and flesh holding in his intestines. Petre thought of nothing but the odd sensation of his guts spilling onto his legs and the unfamiliar tug deep in his body. There was no pain, only surprise. He wondered how long a man could live with his intestines outside of his body.

Page number 47.

"Holy Jesus."

He flipped to page 68 and read the brutality.

156 offered more insanity and hideous revelation. Drake jumped to page 183, and then 269 where he read the single-page description of murder number five. Still he searched deeper, and on page 345 he found number six. A quick read and Drake's throat went dry. It described, in torturous detail, a methodical decapitation after the draining of all blood from the body of Rothchild & Associates agent Nancy Callahan.

"Oh my God," Drake whispered.

She must be safe because her murder would have made headlines. He dug his wallet from his back pocket and pulled out her card. Should he call her office and leave a message? No, come morning he would call her to confirm she was safe. Through the station database he could track down her home number and call before she left for her office. At that moment Drake laughed at fate's sense of humor. Fact was indeed stranger than fiction, remarkably so. Ironic destiny takes many forms. Drake realized that Shakespeare being dragged into the station had dropped an opportunity square in his lap. The worn leather satchel was the hand of providence and the last few days' events were as serendipitous as finding a winning lottery ticket.

On the monitor Brian awoke, sat on the edge of the bunk and rubbed his face. Drake walked to the desk sergeant and acted nonchalant.

"Hell of a day, huh?" McDonald said.

Drake nodded. "You got that right."

"First Andrade and Collins, then Thibido. We really do live in a screwed-up world."

"That's for sure," Drake said. "I'm still spinning from all this shit. And I pulled an all-nighter last night. I'm beat and feeling kind of sour in the stomach. I'm going downstairs and get some Pepto from the first aid cabinet and lay down for a bit."

"Okay, you do look a little green around the gills. I'll hold down the fort and call you if anything comes up. Is the drunk still out?"

"I'll check on him," Drake said.

Drake walked the hall back to the cage where he put Shakespeare's manuscript inside his jacket and zipped it up. His feet felt heavy as lead but his mind was reeling. Drake picked up a wooden stool, took two Cokes out of the fridge and carried them down to the cells. Upstairs the monitor showed Drake place the stool in front of cell three and sit down. The camera documented Shakespeare's expression of surprise as Drake handed him a soda.

CHAPTER TWENTY-NINE

Shakespeare's forearms flexed with strength and Drake imagined those muscular arms hoisting a man up by way of a rope and choke chain. He recalled the testimony about the kid seen walking the dog by the park and the tall trick-or-treater coming late to the apartment by the stairs.

Not a teen, but a small man. A very clever, very strong, and very angry small man. A man who was focused on details and with the time and money to be thorough and careful. Someone who understood police procedure after endless hours of research.

"I'm feeling like myself again," Shakespeare said.

"That's good."

"So, what's up Lou?"

"Thought we would talk," Drake said and sat on the stool. "We had a seriously messed-up day here today. Some very weird shit went down and now the place is dead. I'm exhausted but I got stuck with graveyard. I couldn't reach your attorney but left a message. I came down here because I figured that sitting and talking to you would make the night move faster. "

"Okay, thanks for the soda."

"No problem," Drake said and put his can on the floor beside the stool. "I've thought about what you asked me, about why I wrote? You know, my answer was dramatic but not really all that truthful."

"And?" Shakespeare asked.

"I'm retiring in a few weeks and I was afraid of what my life will be like. I fantasized about writing a bestseller and spending the rest of my life as a rich big shot. Then you said what I was writing was not original, it had been written a thousand times. You were right and I was stuck, not sure where to go with the story. I was following these agent murders and working the cases from in here and found myself at a standstill. I fictionalized what was happening and strung a story together about a cop struggling to reclaim himself by solving the cases, becoming a hero and retiring on top. But something was missing and when I read over what I had, it just sounded false."

"I know that problem, " Brian said. "I've started and stopped about a dozen books because of that very reason."

"That many?" Drake said. "I've only completed one and I'm working on the new one. Two books in ten years, not a very good record."

"Imagine never writing a book," Brian offered. "I heard once that many people on their deathbed say their biggest regret is that they never wrote the book they always dreamed about. Imagine that, having a story inside you until you die and never giving it life. That would be a tragedy."

Drake nodded as though this were the greatest truth he had ever heard.

"My favorite author once said that writing a piece of fiction is an act of complete creation," Drake said. "We bring to life people and events that never existed before. I've always liked that."

"That is very true," Shakespeare said. "If you are writing fiction.

"Can I ask you a question?"

"Sure," Shakespeare said. He leaned one elbow on his knee and rubbed the back of his neck with his other hand.

"It's a question that Sandy asked me when we first met. Then you asked me and I now I want to ask you. Why do you write?"

"Oh, that's easy. I write because I have to. I write because it gives me freedom."

"Sandy said that we all take the high road and talk about writing as some sacred exercise done for the sake of the action, but he thinks we're all full of shit. He says we all secretly do it for the money. But you have money, isn't that right?"

"Yes I do," Brian said, his tone becoming sharp and his red-rimmed eyes narrowing. "Sandy can be full of his own shit most of the time. Yes I have money and I write anyway, because it's more than that."

"So, clarify that for me."

Shakespeare seemed to ponder that for a moment.

"Isaac Asimov once said he writes for the same reason he breathes - because if he didn't he would die," Shakespeare said and cracked his knuckles. "That's why I write. I was born with money and I've always had money. I can do what I want when I want. But even with the cash I was teased about my height, pushed around and made miserable. People didn't take me seriously and no amount of money or cars or whatever made a bit of difference. So I started to write and I found I could numb all of it for a while. Like you said so eloquently, to forget my pathetic life. Some people drink, others use drugs – I write."

"How long have you been writing?" Drake asked.

"Thirteen years. Ten books over a decade and I've never been published. I had an agent once, but he said my writing was too detailed and I would bore the reader. I pointed out Crichton filled his books with details and deep subplots and he was an international bestseller. He said I was no Crichton and dropped me when I refused to re-write the book."

"Why didn't you just do what he asked?" Drake pushed.

"Because he was wrong. He was lazy, unwilling to do the work to recognize the importance of what I had written. No balls, no vision, no spine."

"He was one of the murder victims, right?"

Brian hesitated for a moment and looked sharply at Drake, but then he nodded and slowly said, "Yes, he was one of them all right."

Drake went on as if he had not noticed Shakespeare's reaction. "Sandy and I talked about rejection, how it builds and collects and becomes like a weight we can't see but sure can feel. He told me he had hundreds of rejections and he finally realized he just couldn't do it anymore. He gave up."

"Being rejected always pissed me off," Shakespeare whispered.

"I can only imagine," Drake offered. "So why keep writing? I mean, besides the breathing bit."

"Because you always hope this will be the one. This idea, this plot, these characters will finally break down the office door and force the agents and the publishers to take notice. You hope they will finally see what you have to offer and your book will be on the shelves. It doesn't matter whether it becomes a bestseller or paperback pulp fiction, at least the book is in print and people can walk into the local shop and buy it."

"And," Drake said softly.

"Well, then you are somebody. Ever see that baseball movie where the old timer gets stuck teaching the hot head new guy how to make it to the show?"

Drake smiled. "Bull Durham."

"That's right," Shakespeare said with a nod. "Well Sandy is that old guy who was in the majors for two weeks and now acts like he can manage the destinies of newcomers. But there comes a time when we have to quit or become something more than every other writer."

"And you feel your new book does that? It breaks the mold?"

"Oh, it does," Brian said with a smile. "It kicks the shit out of the whole deal. I have found the perfect combination of timely plot, realism and personal complicity that will grab the agents by the balls. They'll be fighting over me. Whoever wins the honor of representing this novel will make a goddamn fortune."

"It sounds amazing. Will you tell me what it is about?"

"You want the five minute pitch?" Shakespeare asked.

Drake nodded.

"Okay, let's see..."

"Don't think," Drake said. "He who pauses in the face of the sale loses the respect of the buyer. We have seven seconds to make a good impression. Marketing 101. Take a breath and tell me, what's the book about?"

"Redemption," Shakespeare said. "REJECTION is about redemption and ultimate accomplishment, the realization of the goal of the masses and the absurdity of the quest. It examines the plight and struggle of humanity and the eventual desperation of a single visionary that is willing to break away from the pack and do what is necessary to rise above the mediocre. It exposes the evidence of the close-minded status quo, driven by fear and lack of vision. The book portrays one man willing to do whatever is necessary to become great."

"REJECTION. Good title," Drake said with a smile.

"Have more vision Lou, look deeper and realize the title could be anything, but the title is necessary to get the initial attention of the close-minded, spineless and shortsighted stepping stones to the final goal."

"You mean getting the attention of an agent so you can be published," Drake said.

"Exactly, but not for the money or the fame. It's all about the soul-filling personal satisfaction that you have become an author. Not just a writer – but an *author.*"

"Is the book finished?" Drake asked. "Are you ready to pitch it?"

"Almost," Shakespeare said. "I'm really close. I just have a couple of things left to do and then I can be done."

"To do?" Drake asked.

"Research" Brian said.

"Like I said," Drake said. "I'm struggling with my new book. Yours sounds amazing. Could I read through what you have written? Maybe by reading what you have accomplished it would help me get my own vision. Sandy says to be a good writer you have to read a lot."

"That would be a very bad idea," Shakespeare said. His voice trembled and his eyes darkened. "That would be a very bad idea."

"Why?"

"Don't read my book," Brian hissed.

"Brian, I wouldn't steal anything from you I won't tell a soul what it's about."

"No!" Shakespeare yelled and stood up. "You will not read my book! You will bring me my satchel right now. NOW!"

"Brian, calm down."

"NO!" Brian screamed and lunged at the bars. He reached through and the veins in his neck looked like electrical cords. His eyes were red and his breathing came in heated huffs. "Bring me my book!"

"I can't do that," Drake said and casually stood up.

"I will kill you if you read my manuscript," Shakespeare rasped. "Hear me?"

"Oh I hear you," Drake said and took a step back from the bars. "But I already have read the book."

Drake pulled the pages from his jacket.

Brian's eyes widened and seemed to bulge from their sockets. "You will die," he said in a hoarse whisper. He lunged and jammed his arm through the bars, his fingers like a claw.

"I was especially interested in a few particular pages, like 47 and 68. I know the case and I've read those pages before. Brian, I know who you are."

"You will never know me," Shakespeare said and returned to the bunk. "Nobody will ever know me."

"Oh, I know you. You are me and every other writer who has tried and tried and been rejected. It's a good title. In fact it's a great book, but it is also your condemnation, a confession that will put you in prison for life."

"I see," Brian said. He seethed and leaned back into the light. "So you show your true colors. You're going to put me away and steal my book, aren't you? You know the power of what I've written and you can't refuse the temptation to claim it as your own. Seduced by perfection you are willing to sell your soul to the devil."

"No," Drake said.

"DON'T BULLSHIT ME!" Brian's voice was a grating howl, a primal scream that came from the depths of a pain carried for life.

"Listen to me," Drake said.

"No, I will not listen to the lies of a soul thief. You will die, Lou. And I will be the one to stand over you and take the ultimate satisfaction, knowing I took back what is mine. You, Lou Drake, are a dead man."

"No Brian, I will be your messenger. I will deliver what you have worked so hard to achieve. If you can clear your mind of hate and fear, you will see that I have so much to offer you. I can make all your dreams come true."

Brian glared with an intensity of hatred that Drake had never seen before. Shakespeare's eyes were wild and his face was mottled with red.

"You lie," he hissed.

"Brian, I can carry your book and my new idea to the one person who will see what you've done. She will truly understand the magnitude and the media frenzy it will create. She will grasp the opportunity you just mentioned, and she will turn both of us into household names."

Brian's chest heaved with fury. "What the hell are you talking about?"

"It's not what you know," Drake said, "but who you know. Well, I know the one person who will open the door."

"Who?" Shakespeare said.

"The one person who is sure to publish your book, just like you said."

Much of the desperate anger seemed to drain from Shakespeare. A thoughtful crease formed between his eyes as he looked suspiciously at Drake.

"You mean ... you think you can get my book published?"

"I don't just think it," Drake said, "I know I can."

Brian stared at him through the bars, trying to regain his breath. His jaw worked convulsively from side to side. Finally he said, "How?"

"You'll have to confess. I will be the arresting officer. It would have happened eventually and you know it. You've done the research. How many serial killers have actually gotten away with it?"

Brian conceded with a small nod. "Since the advent of DNA technology, most have finally been caught. But I left no such evidence. There is no physical proof I have done anything."

"The book," Drake said.

Brian's face reddened.

"It describes the murders and the pages match those at the scenes," Drake said. "The manuscript has your prints all over it. It will lead to a search of your home and they will seize your computer."

Shakespeare seemed to deflate in on himself. "Yeah, I suppose," he said.

"But I can turn this into something great," Drake said.

"Great how?"

"Great as in finally getting your book published."

Brian looked at him sullenly. "But with your name on it, right?"

Drake shook his head. "No, you're not getting it. I'm going to help you become a well-known author."

Shakespeare's voice was now flat and lifeless. "But..."

"Look Brian, you've got to trust me. Neither of us will ever be rejected again. I understand what you've gone through and what you want, because I want the same thing. Work with me and I can guarantee you'll be a bestselling author, and so will I."

"So you're going to ride my coattails, is that it?"

Drake snorted in annoyance. "Aren't you listening? I'm saying you can have what you always wanted, and you're standing there arguing about stupid details. Now do you want to be published or not? Because if you don't just say the word and I'll walk out of here. Some other officer will ram your ass through the legal system and you'll never see your manuscript again."

Panic flooded Shakespeare's face. "No, wait, I didn't mean—"

"Face it Brian, you were always going to end up in jail. As soon as you showed the book to an agent this outcome would be inevitable. You're smart enough to know that. You're not crazy, just willing to do whatever was necessary. Am I right?"

Brian sniffed. "I'm not crazy."

"No, you're just methodical. And when you were brought in here ... well, that was an act of providence, wasn't it? It was the will of fate that I would be the first to read this book. Any other cop would misunderstand, so it had to be me. Don't you see? I'm supposed to deliver your book to the world. And then the literary agent will fulfill what you have been working toward. But you and I need to have an agreement, and we need to be true to our word."

As Shakespeare seemed to consider this, Drake had a moment of doubt. My God, he thought, I'm conspiring to get what I want at the cost of this man's life. No, that wasn't it. Brian would go to jail no matter what. Shakespeare condemned his own life the day he killed the first victim and left the page behind as evidence.

Drake wasn't like Andrade and Collins. He was simply taking the opportunity to become what he wanted more than anything in the world.

Did that make him like Thibido?

No, it was not a conspiracy. This was collaboration. No extra suffering would occur as a result, in fact one life would be saved. Brian was no scapegoat. His life would not be stolen. They would both benefit by fulfilling a common dream. Besides, for what he'd done, Brian definitely belonged in jail.

Shakespeare leaned against the wall, crossed his muscular arms across his chest, cocked his head and looked at Drake. His mouth worked as he chewed his cheek. Shakespeare hunched his shoulders, leaned forward and broke into a sneering smile that chilled Drake's bones.

"Well?" Drake asked.

"What agent?"

"Page 345," Drake said.

Brian Shakespeare was silent. Drake stood still and waited while a madman decided his fate.

It was late and the village of Malcolm was fast asleep. The two men faced each other and Drake knew Shakespeare was in a struggle between a writer confronted with dreams of fame, versus a killer facing capture. New York currently had no death penalty, so Drake knew Brian was considering the idea of life in prison. Time settled in like a fog and Drake barely breathed.

Shakespeare straightened up, his eyes softened and he gave Drake an odd smile.

"It would be pure irony, wouldn't it?" Shakespeare said with a chuckle. "Yes Lou, that is true and undeniable irony and you are a goddamn genius."

"Yes," Drake agreed with him. "So, do we have an agreement?"

"Oh yes," Brian barely got out.

The killer put his hands over his face and started to cry.

An hour later Smythe and his staff passed the cage and saw that Drake was still there, scribbling on a legal pad.

"Drake?" Smythe asked as he walked by. "Go home and get some sleep, we'll finish our meeting this afternoon."

"Yes sir," Drake said. "Sir, may I have a moment?"

"Not a great time. This shit storm is getting bigger. The press is making up their own story on what went down at Collins place and I have to do damage control."

"It's important," Drake said.

"Is it about Andrade and Collins?"

"No, something just as important, if not more," Drake said.

"Okay, interrogation room one, my office is occupied."

Drake looked flushed. His eyes were tired but bright as Smythe folded his hands on the metal table. Drake placed the leather satchel in front of the Chief and kept his right hand on it, his index finger fidgeting with the clasp.

"What's this about?" Smythe asked.

"We have the agent killer," Drake blurted with excitement.

"Excuse me?"

"Down in the cell three," Drake said. "He was brought in on a drunk driving charge. If it had not been for the Collins and Andrade situation he would have been processed and out on bail. But the perp's lawyer was unavailable and the guy was very drunk. By the time he sobered up I discovered the evidence. I talked with him and he made a full confession. I followed strict protocol. I entered the report into the database and filed it with the desk sergeant. I stayed the night to ensure the prisoner was safe and the evidence was secure."

"Drake, this is hard to believe," Smythe said. "If he only made a confession it is extremely suspect. You of all people should know that. What is the evidence?"

"Right here," Drake said and opened the satchel. He pulled out the thick stack of typed sheets and laid them in front of the Chief. "I think you'll find the tabbed pages of great interest."

Smythe opened to page 47 and read. He looked up at Drake and flipped to the next tabbed page, then the next.

"My God," Smythe breathed. "Have you processed this as evidence?"

"Yes sir. Like I said, I followed exact protocol. I reached his lawyer just before you came in and he will be here any minute. The prisoner gave me a full confession when I presented the manuscript and explained that I had to arrest him on suspicion of murder of all the victims."

"This Nancy Callahan, isn't she the one you interviewed?"

Drake nodded. "Yes, that's her."

"Is she all right? Did you reach her?" Smythe said.

"I did, and she is fine. I didn't explain my concern, only that we had received a tip she might be in danger. I assured her she was safe and I would contact her later."

"Well, Lou," Smythe said and actually laughed with surprise, "I guess congratulations are in order."

Drake handled the case after that with the finesse and competence of a seasoned Detective. Smythe met with the commissioner and they agreed that in the light of the evidence regarding Andrade and Collins, the circumstances warranted an evaluation of Drake's demotion. The examination ended with his reinstatement to Detective, effective immediately. Drake completed his work on the case in plain clothes and with a gold and blue shield.

CHAPTER THIRTY

A snake of flexible tubing joined a coupler feeding oxygen into a hole cut in Andrade's throat. His lungs inflated and deflated as a result of the ventilator keeping an ever-present vigil at his side. The feeding tube entered Andrade's abdomen while an IV kept him hydrated. The reconstructive surgery of his jaw, pallet and throat kept him from breathing, speaking or taking sustenance on his own. Chief Smythe sat beside him on a stool while the monster of an FBI agent stood by the door. Andrade's lawyer stood by the hospital bed and communicated through small nods and shakes of his head. All parties involved had agreed upon this meeting and today Smythe read Andrade his rights, officially placing him under arrest. Andrade could only blink his eyes to communicate. One blink for yes, two for no.

The slug had splintered when it hit his teeth. Shards of tooth, bone and bullet punctured his palate, smashed his jaw, damaged his temporal bone and caused extensive tissue damage as it exited the back of his neck. To avoid any further damage, Andrade's head was locked in a ring, held stationary by a brace. His jaw would stay wired until the bone grafts healed. His tongue was also lacerated so the doctors felt he would likely have a speech impediment after recovery.

Against her better judgment a nurse allowed him a look in a small mirror. John was obviously shocked at the extent of the damage. The bullet tore his lips and cheek as well. But he would recover, unlike Collins.

"John," Smythe called him back to attention. "You looked like you drifted away there for a minute. You with me?"

Andrade blinked once after his lawyer gave him a small nod.

"You understand the rights I have just explained to you?"

One blink.

"Okay then. The prosecutor is working the case with the FBI and your attorney is cooperating with our direction. So the best we can do at this point is wait until they let you out of this bed. Until then there will be a police guard at your door at all times. You understand?"

The lawyer nodded and Andrade blinked.

"Is there anything else I can do for you, anything you need or want to know?"

Two blinks.

"Okay then. We will be seeing you."

"Excuse me," a nurse interrupted. "We need to attend to mister Andrade."

"Sure, I was just leaving," Smythe said and Thatcher followed.

Walking side-by-side down the hospital hallway, Thatcher and Smythe wore matching expressions of satisfaction.

"We've frozen his assets and taken statements from everyone willing to come forward about Andrade and Hennings," Thatcher said.

"Kathy Morey will make a good witness," Smythe said. "Will Thibido's statements be admissible?"

"I'm sure his attorney will challenge it, but we will make it work," Thatcher said.

"I'll tell you," Smythe said. "I used to believe that this type of scandal just didn't happen in small towns, but this is one for the books."

"I once worked a multiple murder in a small mountain town in California," Thatcher said. "I found the strangest secrets live where the people know one another too well. Want to get a drink?"

"I just happen to know where there is a party," Smythe said.

They walked in silence. Down the corridors of the hospital Smythe glanced into the open doors of the rooms holding the infirm and traumatized, each a story of life's tragedy. Police work is full of traumas and tragedies, each one an act of human frailty driven by a thousand forms of desire and fear.

Smythe reflected that Drake had experienced those fears and traumas and deceptions, but his story ended well. Andrade's would not. If he confessed he would do life. But what kind of life is prison, especially for a cop? Every other prisoner would be gunning to make his life miserable, if not to kill him. If Andrade fought the charges, and Smythe knew he would fight, then there was a small chance that a jury might be stupid enough to believe a cop of his stature was above the accusations leveled against him. If he found that jury and they acquitted him, Andrade still faced expulsion from the force and his dirty secrets would be made public. The press would plague him for life. His choices were dismal, but then Collins had none at all.

Smythe answered his ringing cell phone.

"Are you going to make it to the station in time for Drake's party?" Yarrow asked.

"Yes, but don't wait for us to get started."

It was Drake's last day and Station ten buzzed with electric excitement. The women from the cage were well into their second glass of champagne. Loud voices resounded off the walls in a raucous celebration. The interrogation room was laid out as a banquet table, with potluck offerings ranging from homemade delectables to buckets of KFC. Nancy Callahan poured herself some red wine and carried the plastic cup back to where Drake laughed with fellow officers and his friends from his writer's group.

"Who would have thought?" Sandy said again. "Brian was always so good-natured and happy. If I had to choose somebody from the group to be a killer, I would have guessed it was Pooter."

"I could still be one," Pooter said. "You can be my first victim."

"Why not, it worked for Shakespeare," Fran jibed.

Nancy Callahan sat beside the publisher, Jerry Shapiro, and they chatted amiably about book rights. Shapiro surprised Nancy with an on-the-spot offer, which eliminated the need for Nancy to arrange an auction. Shapiro made a very generous offer for two books—Drake's true crime proposal about the agent killer, as well as Shakespeare's confession manuscript. The package amounted to a double printing and distribution deal that made Nancy's eyes water. With the media hysteria and the ongoing shock as more was revealed about the case, a fast deal and timely release would mean enormous sales. There were already whispers of interest from Hollywood.

After they shook on it, the two of them drifted back over to the group and Shapiro soon demanded attention as he regaled them with the story of Collins and Drake's visit.

"So these two policemen come to see me," he said, "and I asked Collins if he wanted some nuts. He gave me a look that would kill if it could."

Shapiro laughed at his own wit and the group joined him.

"It's true," Drake gasped and pounded the table. "Jerry kept on about the nuts and Collins was squirming in his seat. I thought he was going to freak out. Later in the car he was pissed as hell."

"Ah, it was fun," Jerry sniggered and took a drink of his beer.

"You know," Dodd said. "Drake is the only guy I know who can put a string of screw-ups together and come out with a promotion and a book deal."

Drake laughed. "And all I had to do was break your leg."

Dodd gave him the finger.

"Among other things," Yarrow said as he took a sip of his beer.

"Oh, that's nothing," Nancy interrupted. "Listen to this. I get this early morning call from Drake and he says he was calling to make sure I'm okay. I said I was fine and he gives me this cryptic shit about a tip I was in danger, but since I answered the phone there was nothing to worry about. He hangs up and I realize he is saying that the fact I answered my phone meant I wasn't dead. Now the only reason I would be dead would be if the agent killer got to me, and that meant he probably had the killer in custody. If I hadn't been more of a lady I would have shit my pants."

"God," Shapiro said. His face was serious and then he burst out laughing.

"Sorry," Drake said. "I was trying to wrap this case up in a few hours and I just needed to know she was okay."

"Well, I wasn't okay after that call, I'll tell you that," she said.

"Lou," Robin said and punched his shoulder, "you must have scared the bejesus out of her."

"He did," Nancy said. "Then he shows up with a photocopy of the confession manuscript, a true crime book pitch and presents me with a scenario about how we could all make a killing, pardon the pun, by capitalizing on this whole thing."

"And you said?" Drake urged.

"He showed me page 345 and I read my own murder. I have to say I was horrified and mesmerized at the same time. It is a freaky thing to realize the murder that was planned for you will be immortalized in what will be a guaranteed bestseller. Not in just one book, but two."

"Published by me," Shapiro added. "Oh, anybody want any nuts?"

The group howled. Kellerman finished his beer and watched his father relish in the festivities. His dad shared a few stories from the good old days and bragged about Drake's exploits.

"I always knew the Hennings thing was a set up," George Kellerman said. "Pissed me off to no end to know a good cop was beat down because somebody was telling a load of shit."

"Here, here," Paul Kellerman said. His dad raised his glass.

"Here, here," the crowd answered.

The party reached a pinnacle, the food eaten and the allotted amount of alcohol consumed. Police work still needed to be done, though. The station was still open and the borough of Malcolm still went about its business despite the auspicious occasion of Lou Drake's retirement.

"Okay, let's wrap this party up," Smythe said.

There were handshakes and hugs all around. Nancy and Jerry agreed to a strategy meeting and he left, but not before patting Drake on the shoulder and urging him to *write, write, write.*

"You got it boss," Drake said.

Nancy gave him a hug and said she would call him the next day. Robin helped Regina, Serena and Edna clean up the mess in the interrogation room while Drake had a closed-door meeting with Smythe and Thatcher.

"Sorry to see you go," Smythe said.

"Thank you sir," Drake said as he thumbed the gold retirement badge in his hand. "I will miss the work and I want to thank you for all you did for me."

"Just doing my job," Smythe said and waved a hand. "What a goddamn circus, huh? All hell breaks loose and then God drops the killer in your lap. Yeah, those two bozos that picked him up get some credit, but if it had been business as usual in here, a phone call and a bail bondsman would have had that killing freak back on the street. Who knows when it would have ended?"

"It's true," Thatcher said. "If he had walked, Nancy would probably be dead."

"Yeah, well," Drake said.

"Sounds like you have a promising new career," Smythe said and shook his head. "And to think Nancy and Jerry will make it happen. That is seriously ironic."

With a vigorous handshake and a short, masculine embrace Smythe and Drake said goodbye. Thatcher patted Drake's arm, shook his hand, and said, "Hey, make sure you write about my good side."

"You got it," Drake said and joined Robin at the cage.

"Gonna' miss it?" Serena asked.

"No, but I'm going to miss you guys," he said.

They all gave him broad smiles.

"We got something for you," Serena said. She presented Drake with a beautifully wrapped box. "Better hold it from the bottom, it weighs a lot. Open it when you get home."

"Thank you," he said. Drake put the heavy present under his arm and gave each of the ladies a one-armed hug. "I'll visit."

"You better," Edna said through tears. "We're going to miss you too."

"Well, gotta' go."

Drake waved as he and Robin walked out the doors of the station, turned onto University and slowly made their way home. The afternoon was chilly but the sky clear and blue.

"That was nice," Robin said. "Can I ask you a question?"

"Sure."

"Where are we going to live when the money comes?"

"Well, I was thinking we would get one of those brownstone apartments in Greenwich and spend all our time at the coffee houses and hobnob with our new fancy friends."

"C'mon, I'm serious," she said.

"Oh, we have time to figure that out. We have a wedding to plan and what I really want is to take a trip, maybe a cruise to some place tropical and just relax. Can you handle that?"

"I could. Oh yes I could," Robin said.

They arrived home where the small apartment felt comforting but temporary. Drake took Robin in his arms and she pushed him back.

"Open the present first," she said.

Drake mocked disappointment as he ripped into the paper. The cardboard box was plain and innocuous. He pulled the tape and lifted the lid. Inside were many manila envelopes, each labeled and dated. Drake opened the first and thumbed through the photocopies of documents and memos, files and printouts. He put it aside and examined two more.

"My God," he whispered.

"What honey?" Robin asked. She picked up a sheet and glanced over it.

"Know what this is?" Drake asked and she shook her head. "These are copies of everything, every piece of what was on file on the Hennings case."

"What?"

"*I have access.* That is what Serena said to me the day she gave me the copy of the letter from the old Chief. *I have access.*"

“What can you do with this?” she asked.

“Oh baby,” he said, “I can write another book. Oh my Lord, I can write one for the ages. I can write the truth.”

“Wow,” Robin said.

Drake agreed completely.

LOU DRAKE – NEW YORK CITY 2011 3:35 PM

Chang finished his last note, sat back and tapped his pen on the tabletop. He wore an expression of contented exhaustion as he smiled at Drake.

"Holy shit," he said. "That's how it really went down?"

"Pretty much," Drake said. "I may have forgotten a thing or two or embellished a detail here and there, but, yeah, that's basically it."

"And now I get to tell the world," Chang said.

"That's why I'm here."

"And Hennings?"

"He was arrested," Drake said. "Because he was never tried, double jeopardy was not an issue. The case was deemed federal and with the new testimony and the evidence dug out of the archives, he was convicted and is now doing life. Andrade was also found guilty, as you know, and was killed in prison."

"Oh man," Chang said. "You still have contact with Shakespeare?"

"I visit him once in a while. I send a Christmas card and I send him a copy of my books when they come out." Drake said.

"So you guys are friends?"

"Not friends. We were never friends. More like conspirators in the realm of life's random opportunities. Strange bedfellows at the most. I feel I owe him a lot and he feels the same about me. Neither of us would have accomplished what we have if not for fate bringing us together. I will always be grateful to his role in my success, but friends? No."

"Absolutely wild," Chang said and he turned off the recorder.

"To say the least," Drake said. "Funny thing, after my doctor told me that protein diet would kill me with cholesterol, I went back to my old weight and I don't care. I'm big but healthy. What would the world do with a skinny Lou Drake?"

"It just wouldn't be you, would it?" Chang said.

"Afraid not," Drake said with a laugh.

"I have a pile of work to do here, sorting through all this and getting the story down. Can I call if I need clarification?" Chang asked.

"Please do," Drake said.

Drake stretched his arms above his head. His suit coat was draped over the next chair and his tie was loose. Four empty soda cans were lined up on the wooden table and the light showed it was late afternoon. Drake glanced at his watch.

"Oh, man, I have to go," he said and stood up. His knees complained from the long interview and he rotated his thick neck.

"Have to be somewhere?" Chang asked as he gathered his notes.

"Book signing in the city," Drake said.

"We just need to get some quick head shots," Chang reminded him.

Drake was escorted to the photo room. Drake called downstairs to Josh waiting in the limo.

"We are almost finished here, sorry it took so long."

"No problem. I'll pick you up at the curb."

"Be right down," Drake said.

"Lou, I have to say this has been the absolute highlight of my career. It has been an honor to speak with you. Be assured I will handle this story with utmost integrity. No cheap shots. Thank you for this opportunity."

"Oh, lighten up," Drake said. "But thanks to you as well. It feels good to have said it all out loud. How do I get out of here?"

"I'll walk you down."

Josh opened the limo door and Drake moved carefully into the leather back seat.

"I'll call with any questions and send you the copy before we print," Chang said.

"Perfect," Drake said and Josh closed the door. They pulled away from the curb and entered afternoon traffic.

"How did he interview go?" Josh asked.

"Absolutely great," Drake said. He looked back at the building. "Amazing, Rolling Stone magazine."

"Sorry sir?"

"Nothing. Bookstore, my good man, Times Square."

Drake sat back in the deep seat and dialed Robin.

"We're done."

"That was long. How was it?"

She sounded excited.

"Great, really great," Drake said. "Very cathartic. I said everything I needed to say and now the world will know I am who I am because I made a deal with a serial killer."

"Shakespeare did not make you," she said. "You were destined to be Lewis Drake, successful writer. With or without him."

"Okay. We'll be at the bookstore in a few minutes."

"I'm already here. You have quite a crowd waiting for you," she said.

The pungent odor of the Sharpie filled the small cell as Brian Shakespeare opened a copy of his book REJECTION and scribbled his name across the title page. It was all he was allowed and each book was inspected before it left the prison. The warden did not want any cryptic messages leaving the premises. It had been ten years since the book was published, and people still sent copies to be signed. The guards got a kick out of the steady flow of packages that arrived addressed to him. Even the warden had a signed copy on his desk.

Some readers, mostly women, included photos of themselves and some sent letters telling him how much they enjoyed the book. Some offered prayers and even declarations of love. Three had offered to marry him.

Since its original publication, REJECTION had gone into eight printings and was released through mass-market paperback. He and Drake shared a film option and the movie grossed over two hundred million dollars. Shakespeare was thrilled when his character was cast by a very handsome and popular actor who, he felt, did a wonderful job. A relative unknown played Drake and found himself in great demand after the film's release. He won an Oscar for his role.

Shakespeare signed the last book and placed it with four others in the egg crate to be collected by a guard.

Shakespeare received not a single cent from the book or the film. Federal law prohibits a convicted murderer from profiting from a book written about his actions. Shakespeare was fine with that and made arrangements for much of his money to be paid to the families of his victims, the rest donated to many needy charities. It gave him a sense of redemption and purpose. On his cell wall he taped the magazine covers that his face adorned as a result of his conviction and eventual celebrity. He was content, he was somebody.

Sandy once joked that you knew you had made it when your face appeared on the National Enquirer. Shakespeare's mugshots had been featured there three times.

"Shakespeare," the guard said through the bars.

"Hey," he answered, stood and put his hands on the wall, feet apart.

"Open 234," the guard said into his radio and the cell door slid back.

"How was the vacation?" Shakespeare asked.

The guard collected the box of signed books.

"It was great, the kids had fun. I have one for you."

"Great," Brian said.

The guard handed him a padded envelope already opened on one end. All incoming parcels were scanned, opened and searched to avoid the delivery of weapons or contraband. The door closed and the guard wished him a good night. Shakespeare smiled at the return address. Lou Drake, Greenwich New York. He turned the envelope upside down and a book dropped onto his cot.

"This is great," Shakespeare whispered and stared at the cover.

A skyline was embossed into the dust jacket, a police badge stamped in gold foil and deep red letters were set in bold print across the top of the dark city sky.

CITY BEAT it read. A LOU DRAKE TRUE CRIME NOVEL

Shakespeare flipped the book over and smiled at the photo of Lou, looking distinguished in a herringbone coat and black turtleneck. Shakespeare's eyes were eager as he opened the book and turned to the title page. Drake's awkward scrawl was unmistakable.

Brian, it read, *as always, thanks for everything - Lou Drake.*

"Back at you," Shakespeare said.

His small shelf was crowded with Drake's books and he opened the new one to the first page. By lights out he was at page fifty-three.

Breinigsville, PA USA
18 March 2011
257940BV00001B/9/P

9 781936 593019